WHISPER'S GRAVE

GIANTFUR CAVE

The Coast

THE GATHERING DARKNESS

SURVIVORS

THE FINAL BATTLE

SURVIVORS

THE GATHERING DARKNESS

THE GATHERING DARKNESS

SURVIVORS

THE FINAL BATTLE

ERIN HUNTER

HARPER

An Imprint of HarperCollins Publishers

Special thanks to Gillian Philip

The Final Battle
Copyright © 2019 by Working Partners Limited
Series created by Working Partners Limited
Endpaper art © 2019 by Frank Riccio

Library of Congress Cataloging-in-Publication Data

Names: Hunter, Erin, author.
Title: The final battle / Erin Hunter.
Description: New York, NY : Harper, an imprint of HarperCollinsPublishers, [2019]
   | Series: Survivors: the gathering darkness ; [6] | Summary: "The traitor behind the
   sabotage and divisions within the Wild Pack has been unmasked, and one final
   confrontation will decide whether the Pack survives"-- Provided by publisher.
Identifiers: LCCN 2018025428| ISBN 978-0-06-234353-6 (hardback)
   | ISBN 978-0-06-234354-3 (library)
Subjects: | CYAC: Dogs--Fiction. | Wild dogs--Fiction. | Survival--Fiction. | Animals /
   Dogs. | JUVENILE FICTION / Action & Adventure / General. | JUVENILE
   FICTION / Fantasy & Magic.
Classification: LCC PZ7.H916625 Fhn 2019 | DDC [FIc]--dc23 LC record available at
   https://lccn.loc.gov/2018025428

Typography based on a design by Hilary Zarycky
18 19 20 21 22   CG/LSCH   10 9 8 7 6 5 4 3 2 1
❖
First Edition

For Sarah Sleeper

PACK LIST

WILD PACK (IN ORDER OF RANK)

ALPHA:

female swift-dog with short gray fur (also known as Sweet)

BETA:

gold-and-white thick-furred male (also known as Lucky)

HUNTERS:

SNAP—small female with tan-and-white fur

MICKEY—sleek black-and-white male Farm Dog

PATROL DOGS:

MOON—black-and-white female Farm Dog

TWITCH—tan male chase-dog with black patches and three legs

DAISY—small white-furred female with a brown tail

BREEZE—small brown female with large ears and short fur

CHASE—small ginger-furred female

BEETLE—black-and-white shaggy-furred male

THORN—black shaggy-furred female

<u>OMEGA</u>:

> small female with long white fur (also known as Sunshine)

<u>PUPS</u>:

> **FLUFF**—shaggy brown female
>
> **TUMBLE**—golden-furred male
>
> **NIBBLE**—tan female
>
> **TINY**—pale-eyed golden female

LONE DOGS

> **STORM**—brown-and-tan female Fierce Dog

PROLOGUE

The bed where Lick lay was soft and damp, its moss cool against her ears and paws. It was nothing like the hard-packed mud beneath the house in the Dog-Garden. She hadn't known such comfortable dens existed, and yet she couldn't seem to fall asleep. With a deep, trembling sigh, she wriggled herself deeper into the softness and tried again, shutting her eyes tight.

It was no use. Her small head buzzed with wakefulness. She was grateful to the Wild Pack for taking in her and her litter-brothers, of course she was. But it felt so odd not to smell damp wood above her, not to feel solid cold earth beneath her belly. Even more strange and wonderful were the stars lighting up the black sky. They were beautiful, but a little frightening too. *There's nothing between me and the sky. The world is so . . . big.* Lick blinked up at the sparkling stars, gathered in Packs, her heart thumping with excitement.

At last, reluctantly, she realized sleep wasn't going to come. Lick stretched, hesitantly sniffing the night air, and crept out of the big dog Martha's den.

She peered anxiously around her. She and her litter-brothers had waited so long, hidden and helpless beneath the Dog House. It was exciting to be among other dogs again, but she had to be on her guard—she was sure that was what Mother-Dog would have told her. Some of these new dogs were friendly and kind, like Lucky, Mickey, and Martha, who had welcomed the three tiny pups. Others, though . . . others didn't seem so pleased at the arrival of small Fierce Dogs.

Padding as quietly as she could, Lick looked around this strange, new camp. The smells here were as unfamiliar as every-thing else. In the Dog-Garden, all the older dogs had had a similar, earthy tang. Here the Pack members were all so *different,* and so were their scents. Martha's had a warm saltiness, Lucky's a comforting deep richness. The little white dog called Sunshine smelled sweet and flowery despite her bedraggled fur.

Another scent came to her, drifting heavily above the damp grass. This one, though, was dark and dangerous. As her nostrils flared, Lick's eyes widened with alarm, and she felt her hackles spring up.

She turned her head, her breath catching in her throat when she found herself gazing into the cold yellow eyes of the Pack's Alpha. He was sprawled at the mouth of his den, watching her every move.

It was not the kind and friendly Lucky who was in charge of the Wild Pack; it was this huge and frightening half wolf. And when Lucky and Mickey had led her and her brothers into the camp, the Alpha hadn't seemed pleased *at all* to see them. Now his hostile gaze was filled with distaste, and his lip was twisted back on one side to expose a fang.

I don't think he'll let us stay here long, thought Lick, trembling. *But where would we go, Wiggle and Grunt and I? We'd be all alone.*

Lick stood very still, her hide prickling as she stared at the half wolf. Her breath was coming in small frightened pants. She tried to imagine the Alpha coming around to her brothers and her, growing to be their friend. Dreamily she pictured the great dog playing with them, wrestling carefully and gently, teaching them to fight. If Fierce Dogs came to steal them or harm them, perhaps this big, strong Alpha would protect his new Pack pups, snarling at their enemies, fighting those Fierce Dogs off. *No dog touches the pups of my Pack!* he'd growl.

Lick thought longingly of what it would be like. *I wonder if he'd ever change his mind? If we behave as Mother-Dog taught us, maybe. If we're good dogs and always put the Pack first . . . would we win him over then?*

But when she saw the way his yellow eyes flashed, as his lip curled back to show his fangs, Lick got the feeling that this was not going to happen.

There was a growing twist of nervousness in her belly. The half wolf didn't get up, but his glare was angry and unflinching. Lick knew what he wanted to snarl at her: *Once a Fierce Dog, always a Fierce Dog.*

Always a bad *dog . . .*

Softly, Lick crept backward, trembling. She should go back to Martha's den and curl up with her litter-brothers. She'd be safe there, at least for tonight, protected by the big motherly dog who had taken them in so happily.

But as she turned away, she saw another pair of eyes glowing at her in the darkness. These ones were not pale, cold yellow: they were deep golden-brown.

Her heart turned over in fright, but the dog who was awake was not glaring at her. *It's Lucky's sister,* she realized in relief. *Bella.* She looked so like Lucky, with her golden fur and her soft eyes.

Maybe she was like him in other ways, too.

Bella certainly didn't look angry. She made a movement with her head that might have been an invitation. Nervously Lick edged closer. *Can she really want me to join her? But she doesn't know me, and I'm a strange Fierce Pup.*

All the same, Bella simply watched as the pup crept nearer and nearer. Taking a deep breath, Lick lay down at the big dog's side, not quite letting their flanks touch. Bella did not flinch away, and Lick began to let herself relax.

Her eyes were already drooping with tiredness, and she was so close to Bella she could hear the older dog's steady, rhythmic heartbeat. Slowly, a tingle of drowsy warmth crept through Lick's body. *I'm safe here, just like I am with Martha.* Bella was calm; her breathing was deep and steady, and she didn't seem tense. *She's not scared or angry,* thought Lick with a rush of relief. *She accepts me.*

It felt so good to know that not every dog in this Pack mistrusted her and Grunt and Wiggle. *I think I can sleep now,* Lick thought as drowsiness began to overwhelm her.

Maybe we can make a home in this Pack after all.

CHAPTER ONE

A soft, damp bed, its moss cool against her ears and paws . . .

Distant memory flickered in Storm's head, but it was hard to pin it down; it escaped her like the white tail of a running rabbit. *That was so long ago. I was just a tiny pup. I hadn't even been with the Wild Pack for a day.*

Tormented, Storm jerked up her head and stared around. She was so tired, but she could not fall asleep; she couldn't even relax. She was a prisoner! She may have been in a comfortable den in the Wild Pack's camp, but she was still a captive dog.

Twisting, she let her eyes rove over her surroundings. She had been in this prison all night, and now the Sun-Dog's light was weakly filtering through the branches. This was Sweet and Lucky's den, and because they were Pack Alpha and Beta, it was not the worst place to be confined—but the prowling guard-dogs beyond the entrance were a constant reminder that she was not free to leave. She recognized their scents: scruffy scout dog Chase, and Moon. They had once been Storm's friendly Packmates. Now they refused to speak to her. She could hear their deep breathing, their occasional indistinct murmurs, and when she twitched her ears toward the back of the den, she could hear a dog there, too, rustling the bushes as it shifted position. *Beetle,* she realized. The Wild Pack was taking no chances with their former Packmate, not when they were sure she was the bad dog who had caused so much trouble in the camp.

Storm had gotten wearily used to her former Pack's suspicion that she, as a Fierce Dog, was the bad dog in their midst, but she still held enough affection for them that she'd felt she had no choice but to return—to warn them that the traitor was actually Breeze. The bad dog had already caused so much hurt and grief. She'd killed poor, harmless Whisper, and big Bruno; she'd tried to trick Moon into walking off a cliff—and had kicked rocks down on top of her when that didn't work. She'd sabotaged the prey pile with shards of clear-stone, injuring Twitch badly—and worst of all, she'd tried to drown Lucky and Sweet's pups in the Endless Lake. Storm's stomach clenched at the idea of Breeze hurting the young dogs. She couldn't let that happen, so she'd come back to warn the Pack.

But her old Pack hadn't believed her story. Maybe they never would have; maybe Storm had never had a chance. Had she thrown away everything—her life, her freedom—for nothing?

Perhaps she never should have come back.

No. I had no choice. I had to warn them. Storm couldn't have lived with herself if she hadn't at least tried. But what could she do now?

Breeze had been too sly for her, too cunning. Yesterday, when Storm had finally confronted her in the clearing, the bad dog had even baited her, confessing to everything just to infuriate Storm, so that when the Wild Pack came upon them, what they saw was a snarling Storm standing over a helpless smaller dog. Storm had fallen into Breeze's trap.

After the Pack overwhelmed her, and escorted her back to the camp, it had only gotten worse. Breeze suggested that they could blind Storm, to stop her causing more trouble. Sweet had refused to consider this, but Storm knew the Alpha could still change her mind.

Panic surged in her chest. Could she live as a blind dog with no Pack? Could Sweet live with the knowledge she'd maimed an innocent dog?

I have to convince the Pack. For my own sake now, as well as theirs, I have to make them realize I'm not the danger.

There was a rustle at the mouth of the den, and Storm snapped her head around. Twigs and creepers were pushed aside, and a small pale shape padded through the narrow entrance.

"Sunshine!" Storm's heart filled with warmth at the sight of the fluffy white Omega dog.

Sunshine laid down half a rabbit, then reached behind her to retrieve a lump of moss soaked in cool water. "Hello, Storm," she whispered, her plumed tail wagging.

"Thank you," Storm said gratefully.

Sunshine gave a nervous glance behind her. "I'm not supposed to talk to you too much," she murmured, "but you know I believe you, don't you? The things you said about Breeze? And I've spoken to some of the others. I have faith in you—and I'm not the only one who does. Stay strong, Storm."

Oh, Sunshine. Storm felt a swamping wave of affection and gratitude for the little dog. Suddenly the despair that had tightened her chest felt looser, less painful. A new determination crept into her bones, and some of the grim weariness fell away. *All isn't lost. Not when I have Sunshine on my side!*

"I will." Storm nodded. "I promise I'll stay strong, Sunshine. For you. For *all* the Pack."

The Omega's tail wagged furiously, and Storm felt a warm

tingle of joy to be so close to a friendly dog. But when she looked over Sunshine's head, she felt a sharp twist in her heart when she sensed the others' hostility and suspicion, like angry dogs prowling up and down outside the den.

"They're not all on Breeze's side," Sunshine went on, drawing close, keeping her voice low. "Just hang on a little longer, Storm. Alpha is going to let you out again soon, and you'll be able to tell your story. I know you can convince them. I believe in you!"

If they weren't all taking Breeze's side, thought Storm, that was good. Yet at the same time, it meant that some dogs *were*. Storm's chest ached. The thought was hard to bear: that some of her old Pack, some of her *friends*, had chosen Breeze's word over hers. What must they think of her now? *That I'm a bad dog. That I'm a traitor who'd kill my friends and harm innocent pups. Maybe they think I'm a dog who deserves to be blinded. . . .*

No, she could not think that way. Some of them believed Storm, and trusted her. She had to hang on to that thought, not the terrible one.

Her breathing had become shallow and rapid. "Which dogs, Sunshine? Which of the Pack are on my side? How many?"

Nervously Sunshine glanced back again at the den mouth and gave a quick shake of her head. "I shouldn't say. I'm sorry. Just tell the truth, Storm, and keep calm. Then everything will be fine. I know you can do this!"

"All right, Sunshine." Storm risked a brief lick of her silky ear. "Just be really careful around Breeze, do you understand? She's crazy. Mad as a spring rabbit, and a lot more malicious. If she realizes you're on my side—" Storm hesitated, and took a breath. "She's killed dogs for a lot less."

Sunshine's eyes were wide and dark. "Storm, I'm scared," she whispered.

"Oh, Sunshine. I'm going to do my best to make everything right again." Storm nuzzled her gently. "But I'm so helpless in here. Please be careful."

"Oh, I will be," the little dog told her fervently. "I have to go now. I'm sorry about all of this, Storm."

Storm watched her slip back through the creepers and twigs, her heart sinking with dread. *I couldn't bear it if something happened to Sunshine.* The Omega dog was small, and she wasn't a hunter or a Patrol Dog: She would be so vulnerable to Breeze's murderous malice.

But Sunshine had been right. Storm did not have long to wait until the creepers stirred again, and the faces of Chase and Moon appeared in the dimness of the den.

"Come with us now, Storm," said Chase flatly. "And don't try anything. The whole Pack is here, and we're more than a match for one Fierce Dog."

Storm gazed into their familiar faces, but she couldn't read either Chase's brown eyes or Moon's blue ones. Swallowing hard, she followed her two captors from the den.

For a moment she stood outside the den mouth, blinking as her eyes adjusted to the daylight. Despite the Pack's troubles, this was still a beautiful camp: cool and green and encircled by protective trees. Sunlight speckled the shifting leaves, and a little way away, between pine trunks, Storm could make out the glint of the freshwater pool.

But it did not feel like a welcoming place for her, not today. The Pack was ranged in a solemn circle before her, and she searched their eyes, frantically trying to determine which of them were allies and which were enemies. She couldn't read their expressions. Was Daisy avoiding her gaze because she felt sorry for Storm, or because she hated her? Why did Thorn look so angry? Because she thought this was an injustice done, or because she now thought Storm was a lethal enemy?

It was impossible. She didn't have the energy to interpret their feelings. All the same, and despite the coil of heavy dread in her gut, Storm didn't lower her gaze. *I don't want them to think I feel guilty. I've nothing to feel guilty about. Whereas Breeze—*

She turned her stare to the gentle-eyed brown dog. Lucky and Sweet's four pups still clustered near to her, with only Tiny standing a little apart from her litter-siblings. Storm felt a lurch of dread. Clearly, enough of the Pack still trusted the dog who had so eagerly taken on pup-minding duties. Only Tiny was looking at Storm; the other three pups were evasive and wary, whispering to one another words that Storm couldn't make out.

If the pups still trust Breeze, they're in huge danger.

Her dark thoughts were interrupted as Sweet, the swift-dog Alpha, stepped elegantly forward. Raising her slender head, she gazed around her Pack, and they all turned to her.

"My decision is made," Sweet told them in her clear voice. Her expression was stern. "Blinding Storm is out of the question. This is not who we are as a Pack."

Every muscle in Storm's body sagged with relief. She hadn't realized how fearful she was that Sweet might take Breeze's suggestion.

"As to what we do next," Sweet went on, "we need more information. Therefore, Beta and I will further investigate Storm's allegations, as well as Breeze's defense." She gave a slight nod to her Beta and mate, Lucky. "That is all I can say for now. I'm sorry I can't tell you more at the moment. It hurts me that I can't trust my Pack. But I am your Alpha. It is my job to keep *all* of you safe, and that is what I will do. Keeping matters between Lucky and me is the best way, for now, to do that."

Storm's heart lifted as she watched Sweet's solemn, calm face. *I trust her.* And if Lucky and Sweet consulted Rake and Ruff, two dogs who had once lived with Terror before joining the Wild Pack, they would hear stories that backed up Storm's claims. It was Rake and Ruff who had confirmed all of Storm's fears and suspicions, with their stories of how odd Breeze behaved during the days of Terror's reign. But Rake and Ruff had recently left the Wild Pack to set up a new camp somewhere else, along with Woody and Dart. They would be no help to Storm if Sweet and Lucky couldn't find them, or if they wouldn't talk to the leaders of a Pack who were now their rivals.

But Storm's fur tingled when she remembered: There was nothing Alpha and Beta could find that would restore the faith they'd once had in Breeze. *She has no evidence that she's innocent— because she isn't.*

Her gaze drifted back to the pups—and right at that moment, there was a flash of brown fur behind Nibble. Storm gasped as

Breeze lunged for the pup, her jaws opening, her teeth flashing, malice glittering in her soft dark eyes. Violently, Breeze snapped at Nibble's neck.

Rage and terror surged in Storm's chest. Easily shoving aside her guards, she flew at Breeze, slamming her to the earth.

The camp erupted in a chaos of furious yelps and barks. And as Storm glowered down at the trembling dog beneath her paws, she realized her mistake.

Breeze's eyes were wide, the white rims showing, and she cowered like a trapped and terrified rabbit. "Storm! Storm, what are you doing?" she whimpered hoarsely. "Please don't hurt me!"

Storm jerked up her head to look at Nibble. The pup was completely unharmed. He and his brother and sisters were backing away, and they were gaping at her in shocked disbelief. In their desperation to put distance between themselves and Storm, they stumbled over one another, tucking themselves at last behind the protective bodies of Chase and Mickey.

Breeze wasn't going to bite Nibble. It was a feint, she was only—

Horror and despair clenched Storm's gut. Wildly she stared around the furious Pack. "You didn't see? Sweet, Breeze attacked Nibble! I saw her—"

The Pack's barks drowned her out, until Sweet made herself

heard. "Silence, all of you!" The Alpha glanced questioningly around at the other dogs, then returned her stare to Storm. There was a tinge of pity in it, as well as anger. "No dog saw anything," she said quietly.

"That's it!" cried Breeze desperately, foam flying from her mouth in panicked fear. "Oh, Alpha, don't you see? Poor Storm, she's hallucinating—she's seeing things that aren't there—that would explain everything. That's why she killed Whisper and Bruno—oh, those poor dogs. And poor Storm just doesn't understand—"

"You!" Storm yelped, thrusting toward her. "You devious, cunning—"

"That's enough!" Lucky sprang in front of Storm, his ears back against his head. Mickey and Beetle raced to his side, and together they forced her backward, their teeth bared.

"Don't cause any more trouble," growled Mickey.

"Get back, you! Right now!" Beetle took a leap forward, hunching his shoulders aggressively. Storm could feel his hot, angry breath on her muzzle.

"What did you think you were *doing*?" barked Lucky, his eyes blazing at her.

The other members of the Pack were yapping and howling,

some of them spinning anxiously. Sunshine whined miserably, pacing back and forth. In the middle of it all, Breeze was struggling, trying dramatically to get to her feet, as if she'd been terribly hurt; she was whimpering loudly in feigned distress.

In the confusion and uproar, Storm couldn't even make herself heard to protest. Lucky, Mickey, and Moon were pressing around her now, physically forcing her back toward the den. Toward her prison. As she staggered backward, she caught sight of Breeze's expression, all fear and injured innocence, as the rest of the Pack clustered around to reassure her she was safe.

"You mustn't blame Storm," came her whimper. "Mad—her dreams, the things she sees, they've driven her out of her mind—"

Storm couldn't bear it any longer. "Mickey!" she barked. "Lucky! Don't believe Breeze. *I saw her!* You mustn't leave her alone with the pups, *please*—"

It was no good. Determinedly they half shepherded, half pushed her back to the den. The twigs and branches snapped back into place at the den mouth and she stood in the dimness, shivering and panting, her flanks heaving in distress.

I can't break out and defend myself. I mustn't do that. There was no way she could take on the whole enraged Pack—but more importantly, if she fought back now, one of her former Packmates might really get hurt. Storm didn't want that, and the last thing she wanted was to make Breeze's lies about her come true . . . again.

As the sounds of commotion calmed, she realized the meeting was breaking up. Dogs were padding away from the clearing outside, muttering and growling in conversation, but she could make out only the words of the nearest ones.

"Perhaps blinding her really is the best option." That voice was Chase's.

Moon's sigh was deep and sad. "I hate the thought, but I think Sweet has to reconsider her decision."

Storm couldn't stay on her paws any longer. She sank down onto the soft leaves and moss that covered the floor of the den.

Storm, you fool. How many more times are you going to fall for Breeze's tricks?

Now the bad dog was out there with the Pack, free to make whatever evil mischief she liked. Free to harm Sweet and Lucky's pups . . .

Storm let her head fall onto her paws as misery overwhelmed her. *Why don't I ever think before I act? I didn't bark a warning, I didn't alert the Pack to Nibble's danger—I just leaped right in, like a fool.*

I've lost. And now my Fierce Dog nature might just have destroyed the whole Pack!

CHAPTER TWO

Storm's head felt woozy, her thoughts and vision blurred, and she realized she must have drifted off to sleep after all. The light in the den was unchanging, a mixture of dusty shadow and faint sunbeams, but she thought that perhaps the Sun-Dog's rays had slanted lower. Blinking, she shook herself.

Something was different. Not the light. The air itself . . .

Twisting her head to look behind her, she stared. She was right. The air was fresher and cooler now, because a new hole had been torn in the bush that covered the back of the den. Her nostrils flared as a soft breeze whispered into the darkness, bringing scents of pine and sage.

Storm rose and took a pace toward it, then another. Her heart stirred with excited hope. *I can leave. I can just walk out. I can save myself!*

Some deeper instinct brought her to a halt, her tongue lolling, her mind in turmoil. The ragged gap was her route to freedom, and every muscle in her body yearned to run toward it.

But that was a bad idea—a *terrible* idea. Even though the hole was big enough for her, the Pack would notice in moments that she was gone. They would follow, and without a doubt catch her, and even if by some miracle of the Spirit Dogs she got away, it would only prove to the Wild Pack that she was an untrustworthy, treacherous, bad dog. If Storm *was* caught, Sweet might decide she had no option then but to blind her.

And if she got away, the pups would still be in peril. All her desperate efforts would have been for nothing.

Storm shuddered. It took all the willpower she could summon, but she backed away from the gap, her flanks heaving. Then she turned her rump on it altogether.

The breath of the Wind-Dogs tickled her, nibbling at her, ruffling the fur on her haunches. It was as if they were teasing, coaxing her outside to run at their sides, fast and free. Their cold teeth tugged at her ears and tail. *Race with us, Storm!* She could *feel* them there, so close and enticing. Here in the den, it was cramped and gloomy and perilous. Beyond that gap, there was empty space, and the forest, and long meadows where she could run and run—

No. With a growl, Storm spun back to the ragged hole. As

quickly as she dared, she began to tear at the branches and twigs with her teeth, tugging them back into place. They cracked and rustled, and she forced herself to go slower, to take care, to be *quiet*. Her heart thrashed against her ribs—*don't come in yet, don't find me with a broken gap in the den!* Trembling with frustrated eagerness, she pulled the branches one by one into something like their original position. At last she had closed out the light and the air and that taunting, tempting wind.

Panting harshly, Storm stepped back and tilted her head. The former hole was ragged and patchy, the twigs torn and broken, but it was no longer a gaping mouth to freedom. Just for a moment, she sagged with regret.

Then she stiffened her limbs, and her resolve. *I've done the right thing.* Torn between disappointment and an odd sense of security, Storm sat on her haunches and eyed the mended hole.

The branches at the den mouth crackled, the air stirred, and she heard light pawsteps trot toward her. Storm's throat tightened with fear, and she spun around, prepared to defend herself. Only when she saw the white gleam of fur did she finally recognize Sunshine's scent.

Shaking, she sighed out a breath of relief. *I need to keep calmer. My instincts are fighting with my brain, and if I'm not careful, I'm going to make another mistake. . . . And my next mistake might be my last.*

Sunshine paused in the center of the den, her mouth full of wet moss. She looked questioningly at Storm, her floppy ears pricking as she set the moss down. "Storm?"

Oh, Sky-Dogs, have I lost Sunshine's trust? Has she changed her mind about me because of how crazy I seemed out there?

No, she realized almost at once, Sunshine would always be on her side. After all, the little dog must have dug the hole, had tried to help her just now, even if it was in a very reckless way. Storm waited until her breathing had calmed, then set her jaw and gazed solemnly at the little Omega.

"I appreciate everything you're trying to do for me," said Storm quietly, "but you shouldn't have done *that*."

Sunshine blinked in confusion, her black eyes round and bright. "What? What did I do?"

Storm turned her head toward the patched-up gap behind her. "That. I can't try to escape. That will only make things worse."

On trembling paws, Sunshine stepped over to the mended gap. She sniffed at it and pawed a loose twig. Then she turned to Storm again, her eyes fierce and anxious.

"I didn't do this, Storm!"

Storm pinned back her ears, surprised and wary. "You

didn't? Then was it Daisy, maybe?"

Sunshine shook her head firmly, making her long ears flap. "I don't think any dog would take such a risk right now, even if they truly believe you're innocent."

"I . . ." Storm blinked. "If it wasn't you, or another dog who supports me . . . I don't know. I don't understand."

"You were right not to run away. It wouldn't have done you any good in the end. In fact, it would have done a lot of harm." Sunshine's eyes widened. "Oh, Storm, this must have been a trap!"

Storm padded closer to her, and together they stared at the repaired escape route. Her paws twitched, and her nose yearned toward the fresh air beyond, but she no longer felt that urgent, almost irresistible *need* to push through it and run. She'd been right to listen to her reason instead of her instincts.

As she sniffed at the broken branches, Storm felt a touch of the same faint breeze on her nostrils.

"Breeze," she said suddenly, baring her fangs. "It had to be her. But why would she do it? Just to make me look bad in front of the Pack?"

"Maybe," whispered Sunshine. "Or maybe there was something worse. Sweet would have caught you in no time—you know how fast she is. Maybe Breeze is still hoping she will . . . blind you."

Storm gulped, and flinched at a horrible vision of Sweet's claws lashing at her face. She could almost feel the pain, an agony like nothing she'd ever known before. She blinked, hard and rapidly. *Sharp, tearing claws like a hawk's, ripping at my eyes, taking my sight. There'd only ever be blackness afterward.* A great, cold shudder went through her bones.

Storm clenched her jaws tightly. "I don't know *why* Breeze wants to destroy the Pack, but I'm glad I didn't take my chance to hurt her."

"Me too. Keep being careful, Storm."

"I will," Storm murmured. "Thank you for the water."

Sunshine touched her damp little nose to Storm's, then hurried back out of the den.

As she leaned down to lick water from the moss, Storm could hear the Omega exchanging a few casual words with Daisy and Mickey at the den mouth. She couldn't make out what they were saying and didn't need to; suddenly she was very glad of the guards who were holding her prisoner here. *At least I know Mickey would never harm me, not if he didn't have to.* Their solid presence was beginning to make her feel secure instead of threatened. *And Breeze can't do anything more while they're standing sentry. Not if I avoid being stupid.*

And after all, even if her former Packmates suspected the

wrong dog, they were still standing guard. Their ears and noses would be alert for anything. *And that means the Pack is safe too, for now. Breeze won't dare make a move.*

For a while, Storm tried to get comfortable, turning a circle on the bedding and settling down. But she couldn't sleep. Her ears twitched constantly, alert for any word from the dogs beyond the den mouth.

The Sun-Dog's faint rays were slanting even lower through the screen at the den mouth when the twigs stirred again, and another dog entered. Tensing, she started up, but then recognized his tan coat with pleasure. She'd always liked the Third Dog of the Wild Pack; Twitch was calm, reasonable, and kind. Apart from Sunshine, thought Storm, he was the least likely dog to harm her, or to think badly of her.

Twitch padded in on his three legs. "Hello, Storm."

"Twitch. What's happening?"

He licked his jaws. "Nothing yet. I only wanted to talk to you."

"Good," said Storm eagerly, feeling her hopes rise again. Twitch might be kindhearted and gentle, with a strong sense of fairness—but more than that, he'd been in the mad dog Terror's Pack himself. He'd been a Packmate of Breeze. *He must know something of her relationship with that mad dog.* "I want to talk, Twitch. I have to convince you, make you all understand. Ask me *anything*."

"I will, then." There was a hint of humor in his gruff voice. "I wanted to talk to you before Alpha and Beta and I continue our discussion."

Storm opened her jaws, then closed them again. Did neither Sweet nor Lucky feel enough affection for her to want to hear her story for themselves?

That, Storm thought dully, was not a good sign. If the Pack's leaders truly believed in Storm, they'd surely have come. Had they sent their gentle and sympathetic Third Dog here to break bad news? Had Lucky and Sweet completely turned their backs on her?

Maybe I should have made a break for it after all.

Twitch sat back on his haunches and scratched awkwardly at an ear with a hindpaw. Unbalanced by his stump, he swayed a little, but righted himself immediately. He had coped so well with losing that foreleg, thought Storm, admiring him even through her nerves.

Stay calm, Storm, she told herself, sucking in a deep breath. *Don't panic. You don't know anything yet.*

"Storm," Twitch began, "the first question is the most important one. You left the Pack . . . but when did you start to suspect

Breeze? Was it before you left?"

Storm paused before she answered, gathering her thoughts. *Be honest, and be reasonable.* She trusted Twitch, but convincing him was entirely up to her.

"No. You know how it was, Twitch—I'd been walking in my sleep, having terrible dreams. I . . . I . . ." The words died in her mouth, her jaws feeling suddenly heavy, as though every instinct was trying to stop her from talking. But she knew she had to get the words out. If she lied, or held something back now, and the Wild Pack realized it later, they might never trust her again.

And how might they punish me then?

"I thought for a while it *might* be me who was the bad dog," she told Twitch, a whine creeping into her voice. "I was so afraid it was me, and that I just didn't know it."

"But it wasn't." Twitch's eyes were steady on hers.

"No. I didn't realize till later. I'd thought about it so much since I left—I had time to go over things in my head. I couldn't imagine which of the Pack might be a bad dog—it seemed so unlikely. But Twitch . . . while I was out there . . . I found Arrow and Bella."

His ears pricked up, but he stayed silent.

After watching him nervously for a moment, Storm went on:

"And it was something Arrow said. We were talking about our old friends, and he said he wasn't keen on Breeze. Because she was . . . *cruel*. That took me aback. It wasn't a word I'd ever have used to describe her. But Arrow told me . . . about things she'd done. All the things I tried to tell you later, remember? In the clearing, when you caught me?"

"Remind me," he said patiently.

"Like . . . the times when Breeze wouldn't kill a prey animal— she'd let it suffer. Arrow said it was a far too frequent habit of hers. He'd seen it, and he reckoned she took pleasure from it. Then I started to think . . . I thought about why you'd all distrusted me so much. Why you disliked me, when I hadn't done anything."

For the first time, Twitch's gaze dropped, and he looked uneasy—almost ashamed.

"And I remembered there was one dog who used to stick up for me—except that she didn't. Every time Breeze defended me, she actually ended up making things worse." Storm frowned, remembering. "Twitch, do you remember that awful day we found Bruno? I remember exactly what Breeze said then, up on the cliff top. Moon remarked that his injuries were just like Terror's. And straightaway, Breeze jumped in, saying *that didn't mean anything*."

Twitch cocked his head curiously. "But she was defending you."

"No. Because Moon wasn't suggesting it *did* mean anything. That whole idea came straight from Breeze. And there was something Breeze said after that, too: 'Just because Storm did it to Terror,' she said, 'there's no way she'd do such a thing to Bruno.' And *then* Moon said that '*the killer was as strong as Storm.*'" Storm paused to let her words—and Breeze's—sink in. "Don't you see? Moon hadn't even *mentioned* me at first. Breeze was putting thoughts into every dog's head—thoughts that weren't there in the first place."

Twitch nodded thoughtfully, but he said nothing.

Storm gave him a pleading look. "All of Breeze's words—they were so carefully chosen, I know that now. She was directing you all to think I was the bad dog, and she did it so cleverly."

"That's not proof, Storm," said Twitch softly.

"I know. And I felt that, too—that I was just snatching at birds out of desperation, that I was inventing it all in my head. But there's more. I . . ." Her jaws felt heavy again, her mouth full of dangerous words that might give Twitch reason to suspect her, to be afraid of her. It felt like tough, rotten prey that Storm had to spit out, before it choked her. *You have to be honest.*

"I used to dream of the Fear-Dog, Twitch."

The Third Dog shivered. He must remember very well the Spirit Dog that Terror had invented to intimidate his Pack.

And then Storm shivered, as a realization hit her. Maybe her confession of everything to Twitch had brought her to the answers she had been seeking. "Of course . . . I used to dream of him. And every time I dreamed of him, it was because there was *danger* to my Pack. It happened with Bella and Arrow, when I caught a snake creeping up on their pups—my dream warned me about the danger. And then I remembered that it had happened before—when I took Tumble down to the Endless Lake, that time I walked in my sleep. I wasn't trying to harm him, Twitch, I was trying to *save him* . . . from the Fear-Dog."

"That certainly sounds more like the Storm we knew," mused Twitch.

Storm huffed, her forelegs quivering with excitement. Was she winning him over? "And when the Pack found me and Tumble," she went on, "Breeze played those word games of hers again." Storm clenched her teeth. "Defending me, but somehow managing to make me sound like a terrible bad dog, a dog who had something to hide."

"What else is there, Storm?" asked Twitch quietly. "It's still your word against Breeze's. Tell me as much as you can."

Storm stared at the ground beneath her paws, thinking. "I talked to Bella, too. She told me other things about Breeze, things I'd never known. Bella once overheard Breeze calling me a filthy Longpaw Fang, and a *murderer*. Names I couldn't imagine her calling me—because, at the time, I believed she was a different dog! But I started to realize that the real Breeze wasn't the one I knew, the one we *all* knew . . . or thought we knew."

Twitch scratched his ear, staring at the ceiling.

When he didn't speak, Storm at last took a shaking breath. "And there's another thing, Twitch—Breeze was never afraid of me. She didn't even pretend to be until I accused her. All of you were, at one time or another. But Breeze never feared me. *Because she knew she didn't have to.*"

Twitch looked very thoughtful. His head was tilted, and his narrowed eyes held a light of understanding and realization. *He believes me,* thought Storm with a surge of hope. *He knows it all makes sense!*

Then, suddenly, Twitch's head sagged and he closed his eyes. He gave a great sigh of disappointment, and Storm felt her heart plummet.

"Wait, Storm, wait. Breeze herself was attacked by the

traitor," Twitch reminded her in a gentle murmur. "She was badly wounded. She can't have been her own attacker."

"Forgive me, Twitch," growled Storm, "but you're wrong. She *could* have been the attacker—it turned out she wasn't that badly hurt, remember? And she could so easily have given herself those wounds. The way she bit herself, before you found the two of us in the clearing yesterday!"

"Storm," said Twitch gently. "I can see why you would have suspicions. But look at how Breeze cares for Alpha's pups! She's devoted to them. How can she be a truly bad dog?"

"That's another thing I've thought about, a lot," said Storm eagerly. "I remembered how she used to tell them stories. She told the pups about a secret wonderful world under the Endless Lake, the place where the Sun-Dog had his den. That's what tempted the pups down there—and they nearly drowned looking for it! She encouraged them. She never tried to tell them that world wasn't real!"

"All right." Twitch gave a deep sigh. He looked agonizingly torn. "Later, when you met with Rake, Ruff, Dart, and Woody— what did they tell you about Breeze? About her time in Terror's Pack?"

Storm drew herself up. If she told Twitch, and he went to their former Packmates, they could back her up. Twitch—and Alpha and Beta—would surely *have* to believe her then. "They told me that she was the dog who was most fiercely loyal to Terror. That she genuinely loved him. All the other dogs obeyed him out of fear—but not Breeze. She followed his orders because she *wanted* to. Twitch, you were a Packmate of Breeze's for a time. Do you remember a time when Terror told her to jump into a rushing river, and she actually did it?"

Twitch's head jerked, and his eyes flashed, just briefly. Storm knew he *did* remember.

"She believed in the Fear-Dog as much as Terror did," Storm went on. "Breeze was the dog who meted out punishments for Terror. She was his Fang—and she *enjoyed* it!"

Twitch was silent for a long time. At last he raised his head. "But why, Storm? None of your testimony explains that. *Why* would Breeze do such things?"

"I didn't understand it either, but before you found us she told me everything. It's all about revenge." She raised her eyes to his dark ones. "Breeze was devoted to Terror, and she hates the dogs who killed him. She wants them to suffer like he suffered—worse, even."

"Then why," Twitch continued, his voice level, "would she kill

Bruno and Whisper? Those two had nothing to do with Terror's death."

"Because of me," Storm whispered. "Bruno had just started to believe me. He tried to defend me, so she killed him. And Whisper was completely loyal to me, more than he ever had been to Terror, and that made Breeze furious. I'm the dog whose teeth killed Terror, Twitch. She hates me most of all. And now she's got me right where she wants me." Suddenly a fiery resentment sparked in her chest. She looked back up at Twitch. What exactly was going on? The Third Dog was still doubting her. What was it going to take to convince him? "Is Breeze having to answer these questions too?"

"That's not your concern," he muttered. "Calm down, Storm, and don't worry."

"I have to worry," she growled ferociously. "Do you know what Breeze told Dart? That she'd rejoin their Pack when she was 'finished with the pups.' And I know what that means, even if no other dog believes me!"

"And when we have proof of your accusations, I know Alpha and Beta will act," Twitch told her. "Be patient, Storm."

Proof. What kind of proof could there be? Breeze had made

sure there was none! Storm bristled.

Yet as the moments passed, and the Third Dog stared at her in silence, she found his words strangely reassuring. Her head wasn't drooping as it had before.

If they want evidence, there may be none against Breeze—but there is none against me, either. Perhaps it will *come down to my word against hers.*

At that thought, however, Storm felt her heart sink once more. Breeze was such a convincing victim.

Twitch was turning to leave, lurching on his three legs. "You'll know as soon as there's a development, Storm."

"Twitch, wait!" She took a pace after him. "You can't wait too long for *proof.* Something terrible might happen in the meantime. The pups are in danger—please believe me about that, at least!"

He nodded slowly, his eyes meeting hers. "I understand. And I promise I'll pass all that you've said on to Alpha and Beta. We *will* work this out, Storm, I promise you."

It was the best she could hope for. With a resigned sigh, Storm flopped back onto the ground. Maybe, just maybe, her warnings would make Sweet or Lucky take notice. They might even come to talk to her themselves.

They're keeping me here, fed and comfortable. They haven't killed or maimed me. Was it possible that Sweet and Lucky did believe her, and that they were biding their time until they could figure out a way to confront Breeze safely?

Storm had to hope so. It felt like it was her only chance. The *Pack's* only chance.

The scattered rays of the Sun-Dog vanished entirely as Storm lay there, wakeful and tormented by uncertainty. First a dusty twilight filled the den, and then at last complete darkness. And not long after night fell, a silver glow told her the Moon-Dog had risen.

A little way away she could hear the Wild Pack's voices, joining in a Howl that was tinged with fear and sadness. Pricking her ears, she focused on recognizing each distinctive, mournful cry: *They are all there, all my former Packmates.* They had gathered to honor the Moon-Dog; she must be showing her complete self tonight.

Spirit Dogs, are you near me too? Have you stayed at my side?

For a heartbeat, Storm felt nothing. There was an ache of emptiness in her chest, and a stab of desolate loneliness to hear the echoing, distant voices of the Howl.

Then, slowly, something warm swelled within her rib cage. The bleak despair lifted, and she knew in that moment, with a fierce certainty, that the Spirit Dogs had not abandoned her. She blinked up in gratitude toward the sky she could not see. Of course they had stayed with her. Because whatever mortal dogs might think of her, the great Spirit Dogs must know she was telling the truth.

Opening her throat, she gave a feeble, whimpering howl. *I can't join in with the Pack—I'm not one of them anymore. But I can thank you, Moon-Dog and Sun-Dog, Forest-Dog and River-Dog. Thank you for bringing me this far....*

A shiver went through her spine as she pictured Breeze out there, joining in the Pack-Howl. Perhaps even now the bad dog was secretly howling to her Fear-Dog, drawing him closer and closer. If only Arrow were here, to summon the Fierce Dog spirit he knew, the Watch-Dog, and plead with him to watch over Lucky and Sweet and their pups . . .

At the memory of Arrow, Storm felt a twinge of longing. She missed him and Bella and their pups, so very much—but they'd promised her that they'd come searching if she didn't return. They told her they would wait ten journeys of the Sun-Dog. . . . Had that time passed already? She wasn't sure.

However dangerous her own situation, Storm hoped that it had not, and that she still had time to make it back to them. She didn't like to think of little Nip and Scramble making the long journey to the Endless Lake, only to come within reach of the jaws of the malevolent Breeze.

Her eyelids felt heavy, and as the howls of the Wild Pack faded, she let them close. It was good that the den around her had vanished, and even better that she could stretch her legs at last, racing across the grassland and the meadows.

Ahead of her there was a golden, gleaming streak, always just out of reach, tempting her on. And, Earth-Dog knew, there was nothing this Wild Pack needed more now than the good fortune of catching the Golden Deer! She would hunt it for them, and bring it back. What better way to prove her honesty and good intentions than to capture that elusive spirit-creature for Lucky and Sweet and their pups?

No dog will think me a bad dog when I fulfil the prophecy!

Storm's paws felt light as air, as if they barely touched the ground, and the wind of her own speed blew her ears back against her head. One moment the Golden Deer would be in sight, so close her jaws almost grazed its flank; then it would dart ahead and vanish, only to reappear a few rabbit-chases farther along. She thought for a moment that it paused, turning its great antlered head to gaze back at her. Was the spirit taunting Storm?

Or was it letting her catch up?

She didn't know why such a beautiful, powerful creature would wish to be caught, but the ways of the spirits were not hers to question. Perhaps it was leading her somewhere? If only it would lead her to evidence of the truth . . . On and on she raced, the air around her filled with golden sunlight as bright as the hide of the Deer itself. Where had the creature gone now?

With a sparkling flash of golden pelt, it broke from a copse, coming so close to Storm. Bunching her muscles, opening her jaws, she sprang for it, with a massive bound that was close to a bird's flight. The scent of the Deer filled her nostrils, and every gleaming hair on its hide was suddenly clear and distinct. Storm collided with it and sank her fangs into its elegant neck.

Together, they collapsed to the ground, Storm and her shining, ethereal prey—and as they hit the earth, it was suddenly not the Golden Deer at all. It was Breeze, her dark brown fur streaked with blood, her jaws open in terror, her eyes white and staring. Fury filled Storm and she dug in her teeth, holding Breeze down as her enemy wriggled and writhed in desperation.

And then, with a flash of blinding sunlight, there was nothing in Storm's jaws. They snapped painfully shut on emptiness; the dog beneath her was now no more than a pile of red leaves, dead leaves that whirled and spun and blew away at last on the wind.

CHAPTER THREE

Storm woke befuddled, blinking hard and shaking off the last clinging drowsiness. She must have slept through the whole of the night after the Howl had ended.

The light that pierced the branches at the den mouth wasn't dusky or gray; it was the bright light of late morning. Yet it wasn't the Sun-Dog's rays that had woken her. Just outside her makeshift prison, voices were raised in angry growls and snarls. Sitting up on her haunches, Storm pricked her ears.

Of course the voices were familiar—these dogs had been her Packmates. But one of them seemed so out of place, it took her long moments to recognize it, and when she did, her eyes opened wide with shock. The high, angry snarling was Sunshine's.

I've never heard her sound like that.

"Sunshine, please, calm down and we can talk about this."

That was Daisy, sounding anxious and even a little scared.

"Why should I calm down?" Sunshine yapped furiously. "None of this is fair. We all know what's going on here! Why isn't anyone keeping as close an eye on Breeze?"

"I agree," soothed Daisy. "You *know* I'm on your side, Sunshine. And Storm's."

"And so am I."

The third voice was less familiar, but there was something about it that tugged at her memory. And then Storm realized— it was Tiny. The pup's voice had matured, but still, her nervous determination was unmistakable.

Oh, Tiny, thought Storm, *thank you for trusting me.* Her heart swelled with affection. *But I wish you hadn't had to grow up so fast. I know what that's like. . . .*

"There's no way Breeze should be allowed to roam around freely when Storm is cooped up in our den," Tiny went on, and Storm realized who the three dogs must be talking to.

Sure enough, Sweet spoke at last. "Oh, Tiny. You have to be patient, little one. You must understand that we don't have enough proof to put Breeze in a trap right now. Sunshine, I'm sorry, but Breeze has done nothing that we've witnessed, while we've all seen Storm lose her temper—and the only explanation we have from her is that Breeze is somehow *bad*. It's not enough, not yet."

Not yet? Storm cocked an ear, her hopes rising. *Does that mean Sweet wants to believe me? Will she finally start to ask the right questions, and find the proof that tells her I'm innocent?*

"It's complicated," the Alpha went on. "We have to move with care. Whichever one of them she is, the bad dog is among us, and she's dangerous. We can't provoke her."

Storm was finding it hard to breathe quietly and calmly. She was almost certain now—after all, surely it was *provocative* to imprison her in this den? So . . . Sweet could not be worried about Storm's reaction! The Alpha must *know* Storm wouldn't lash out violently, that she had nothing to fear from a furious Fierce Dog released from captivity. That meant Storm wasn't the dog Sweet was worried about—it *had* to mean that . . .

Her hopeful thoughts stopped in their tracks when a scent drifted to her nostrils—a scent that made her skin crawl with unease. Light, soft paws padded to join the other four dogs, and Storm's breath caught in her throat.

"What a lovely morning," said a new voice. "What's going on?"

It's her. Storm's heart clenched. How much of the conversation had Breeze overheard?

"Where have *you* been?" asked Sunshine.

"I took a little walk." Breeze gave a dramatic sigh. "I needed to clear my head, after all the commotion. I'm so worried about poor Storm's state of mind."

"She's not *poor* Storm," snapped Daisy, before Sunshine could even speak. "And there's nothing wrong with her state of mind!"

Storm couldn't see the group of dogs, but she could feel the atmosphere in the camp. It prickled against her skin, and she could almost imagine the glares Daisy, Sunshine, and Tiny were giving Breeze in the long silence. And there was certainly an edge of surprise in Breeze's voice when she said, "Of course I don't mean to upset any of you. We were all her Packmates, after all."

Sweet interrupted firmly. "Please don't fret, Breeze. I know you're worried about Storm, and of course we trust you. But we need to put *every* dog's mind at rest. That's why I think it's a good idea that for now, you don't look after the pups by yourself."

There was no reply from Breeze. She had fallen very quiet. *She's flustered,* thought Storm, craning her ears forward. *She doesn't know how to handle this. Things aren't going her way, and she wasn't expecting that.*

A surge of triumph in Storm's chest was quickly overcome by trepidation. Breeze must feel threatened by now, and less sure of herself. Storm felt a small shudder go along her spine.

And what does a bad dog do when it's cornered?

It snaps.

It felt good to be patrolling for the Pack. It had been so long. Storm picked up her paws and pricked her ears, determined to sniff out any threats. The Fear-Dog might be close by, but he would not cross this borderline. If the Pack had trusted her to stand sentry once again, and check the boundaries, she was not going to let them down!

The darkness beyond the clearing was total. There was no Moon-Dog, no starlight to outline the edges of the trees or the undulations of the ground. Storm had never known a night so dark, yet she felt no fear. She was guarding her Pack. She would keep them safe. Nothing would emerge from those shadows to attack her friends, not while Storm stood in its way.

She felt no fear . . . until an eerie, echoing howl splintered the silence.

Her hackles sprang erect, and all her muscles tensed. The howl had faded abruptly, and cold flooded Storm's body from nose-tip to tail. The darkness had not been total after all. It couldn't have been, because something even darker was walking past her—something huge and menacing. It wasn't so much a shadow as an absence of light—against it, the night seemed merely gray.

And it had not walked out of the forest, but from the camp behind her.

As the Fear-Dog stalked past, close enough to send shudders of horror through Storm's bones, it turned hideous, glowing red eyes on her. But it did not touch her; it walked on, seeping into the shadows of the forest and vanishing.

The horror was gone, yet Storm could sense it everywhere, flooding the whole forest. The air itself was rank with that awful presence. The silence was the silence of death.

Hot panic filled Storm. Spinning around, she hurtled back into the clearing.

There was light now: a pallid, ghostly glow that was enough to show her the carnage. Every member of the Wild Pack lay dead, their corpses strewn around the glade.

Lucky's broken body had been flung across a low branch. Sweet lay crumpled, her slender legs shattered and twisted. Sunshine's white fur was clotted with blood. Daisy's dead eyes stared into Storm's, accusing. Snap, Chase, Mickey: they were tumbled in a pile, their throats ripped out. Moon, too, lay dead, her belly ripped open; beneath her lay the bodies of her grown pups, Thorn and Beetle.

She'd tried to protect them to the end. She had failed.

Storm twisted and spun, struck by horror and despair and grief. Where were the pups? Were they dead too? Where were Nibble and Fluff, and Tumble and Tiny?

And where was Breeze—?

They weren't here. The pups were gone, and so was the bad dog. Storm felt a fresh wave of terror. Were they gone forever? Powerless, hopeless, she threw back her head and gave a stricken howl to the Moon-Dog.

Her voice seemed to vanish into the forest, soaked up by that terrible presence of horror. She could not howl loud enough to shatter its suffocating evil. Her heart crashed in helpless terror, and her legs began to tremble violently.

Then, even the ground beneath her was gone. She was standing on nothing; she was falling, falling through space and blackness—

She woke, still howling. Her legs were flailing at the den floor, kicking up twigs and leaves, and cold shudders still rippled through her body. She was not the only dog howling.

But I'm awake!

She sprang unsteadily to her paws. No! She hadn't been scrabbling at the den floor. She was *outside the den mouth*. It was the middle of the day, the Sun Dog's rays shone straight down on her through the gaps between the trees. She must have nodded off briefly after overhearing that conversation—but why was she outside? The forest litter was kicked up around her, and there was no sign of her guards.

They let me walk straight out. Why—?

And then she saw. The guards had abandoned her to join the rest of the Wild Pack. Dogs were darting and bounding all over the clearing, barking and howling, almost crashing into one another in their frenzy.

"Daisy!" barked Storm, running to the nearest dog. "Daisy, what's going on?"

The little dog spun around, eyes wide with fear, and suddenly Storm *knew*. She knew before Daisy said a word what had happened: that her dream, yet again, had been no dream at all.

"Storm! *Help us!* Breeze has vanished—and so have the pups!"

CHAPTER FOUR

"*Nibble!*"

"Fluff! *Where are you?*"

"Come back, Tumble! Come back!"

"There's no *scent!* Nothing I can follow!"

Storm heard the Pack Dogs calling out for the pups and felt a tingle of hope that there would be only three names called. That Tiny, the suspicious pup, would not have allowed herself to be lured away by Breeze and would be around to confirm to the rest of the Pack exactly what Breeze had been up to.

"Tiny! Tiny! Can you hear us?"

Storm's head drooped. She should have known better than to hope—of course Tiny would not leave her littermates, no matter how dangerous the situation.

Outside the den mouth, Storm saw a frantic Mickey collide

with Moon, knocking both dogs off their paws. Daisy was bolting around the boundary, her muzzle to the ground. Chase flung her head this way and that, her eyes wide and white-rimmed with panic. Thorn tripped and stumbled, and Beetle rushed to stand over her, his ears pricked high and his nostrils flared as if he was afraid the bad dog would come for his litter-sister next. Dogs dug and scraped beneath trees and bushes; they raced in circles and bounded out beyond the clearing to howl hopelessly into the trees.

It's madness, thought Storm, horrified. *They don't realize how vulnerable they are in this chaos!*

Sweet stood facing the forest, her quivering nose held high, her tail low and stiff. When she turned to face the Pack, her huge eyes were fearful, but her bark was commanding.

"Quiet! All of you, calm down!"

One by one, the dogs turned to her, panting, their barks and cries falling. When she had their attention, she spoke again, her voice trembling only a little.

"I will take Mickey and Moon to look for them," she said, and nodded to Lucky. "Beta will stay behind to organize more search parties, but right now there's no time to be lost—we have to start hunting."

Poor Sweet, thought Storm with a stab of sympathy. As the

pups' Mother-Dog, she must be in an agony of worry, but she had to stay calm and in control as the Pack's Alpha. *It must be the hardest thing Sweet's ever done, but she's managing it.*

"Breeze might be a fully grown dog," Sweet went on grimly, "but she has four pups with her, so she'll have a tough time keeping them going at a fast pace. They can't have gotten far."

The Alpha turned, briefly, to her mate, and Storm saw her eyes lock with Lucky's. Their shared look spoke of determination—but there was doubt there, too, and a terrible fear. The next moment, the swift-dog spun and raced into the trees, Mickey and Moon at her heels.

Storm watched them vanish, her heart pounding. Breeze had gotten her dreadful way. She'd achieved all her vicious and vengeful desires now, and had flung the Wild Pack into despair.

She had outwitted them all.

How dare she? Storm thought as her muzzle curled with fury. *How dare she do this to Alpha and Beta—dogs I love and respect!*

An agonizing thought struck her. *This is my fault too. My warning came too late. I didn't manage to protect the pups.*

But she wasn't the one who had undermined the Pack at every turn, and she wasn't the bad dog who had stolen away the pups. Breeze had done this—all of it! Storm's guilt turned to a ferocious determination, and she bounded forward into the center of the clearing.

"This is what I feared," she barked. "You were closing in on her, so Breeze has made her move. Nibble, Fluff, Tumble, and Tiny are now in terrible danger."

Lucky stared at her. His jaws opened as if he wanted to speak, but then he closed them again. His tail twitched, and his face was tormented.

He's realizing now, thought Storm, though with no satisfaction. *He's realizing I was right all along, that he should have listened to me.*

Snap the hunt-dog stepped forward, with a sidelong glance at Storm. "Lucky, don't worry. Breeze has probably just taken the pups somewhere to play."

Storm curled her lip and growled. Just how stupid could these dogs go on being?

No, she realized, calming herself. *That's not fair, Storm. Snap's just trying to convince herself. She doesn't want to believe the pups are in danger, or that the Pack could have harbored such a bad dog—and who can blame her?*

Beetle bounded forward abruptly, and Storm jumped, turning. He glared at her, though his expression was edgy and uncertain. "It could be that Storm's done something to Breeze and the pups. We don't *know* she's innocent, do we?"

Before Storm could retort, a bolt of white fur dashed forward from the edge of the clearing. Sunshine skidded to a halt right in front of Beetle, her small teeth bared at him in fury.

"Storm has been right all along, you big idiot, and you were too stubborn to see it!" The little Omega looked tiny against the startled Beetle. "And you're *still* not listening to her! Why, because you just don't want to be proved wrong? The *pups* are in danger!"

"Sunshine is right." Lucky had found his voice at last, and Storm twisted to face him, surprised and relieved. "I stood guard on Storm last night. Moon and I were both outside the whole time. She didn't come out. She didn't *move*. We heard her whimpering in her sleep, for the Earth-Dog's sake!" He bared his teeth furiously. "It's time to stop pretending we were right, Beetle!"

The glade exploded into noise again, with barks and growls and whines of distress. Daisy's clear voice rose above the others'.

"This was all Breeze!" she yelped. "It's Breeze who was the bad dog, and you all need to accept it." She turned to Storm, her stubby tail waving in agitation. "I'm sorry, Storm. So sorry. I should have had faith in you—we *all* should have!"

"Oh, Daisy," murmured Storm, lowering her muzzle to touch the little dog's. "Don't apologize, you don't have to. All that matters is getting the pups back, and—"

"Wild Pack!" A sharp bark interrupted her; it was familiar, but the voice wasn't one of this Pack. Storm spun, surprised to see dogs emerging from the forest at the edge of the clearing. All the Wild Pack were turning, too, their voices hushed in surprise.

"Lucky, we demand to see Storm." The thin chase-dog Dart came padding from the trees, her muzzle peeled back in fury. "The brute has killed again. And this time it's one of *our* Pack."

Storm was too flabbergasted to reply, and she could only watch as Dart led the small Pack into the clearing. First came their Alpha, big, scruffy Rake, and behind him walked Woody, his kind eyes sadder than ever. In his jaws, Woody gently carried a limp, bedraggled black corpse.

"Ruff," breathed Storm, horrified.

"Don't pretend you're surprised," Dart barked, her eyes hard and bright. "You murdered her, Fierce Dog."

"Dart, wait," growled Rake softly. "We don't know for sure—"

"Who else would do such a thing?" snapped Dart, as the Wild Pack crept forward, staring. "Last night, some savage tore her throat out, even as the Moon-Dog watched! It must have been another dog—and it can't be a coincidence that Storm has only just returned!"

Solemnly Lucky paced forward to stand before Dart. "I'm

sorry," he told her quietly. "Ruff was a good dog. Her murder is a terrible crime. But Storm did not commit it."

"You would say that, Lucky," snarled Dart. "She's your foster-pup."

"We had our own suspicions about Storm," he said, meeting Dart's eyes steadily. "And so we kept her prisoner. Moon and I stood guard, all last night. You can ask her too, when she returns, but she'll tell you the same thing—Storm didn't leave this camp. She can't have killed Ruff, Dart. I know it for a fact. Snap?"

Snap trotted forward, her ears anxiously pricked. "Yes, Beta?"

"Go and sniff around the den where Storm has been held captive." He jerked his head in its direction. "Check that Storm's scent is there and there alone. That she didn't sneak out in the night." He cocked an ear at Dart. "Will you trust Snap's word?"

Dart said nothing, but she gave a curt nod.

Every dog in the clearing seemed to hold their breath while the tan-and-white dog padded dutifully toward the den and disappeared into its mouth. Storm could feel her muscles quivering with tension, and her legs were so stiff they ached, but she couldn't make herself relax. *I know I never left the den that night . . . but I did wake up outside it just now, which means I did sleepwalk again. . . oh, Sky-Dogs.* She swallowed hard, her throat as tight as if the Fear-Dog had it in his jaws. *Fury and fear are running through every dog! If they turn on me now, two Packs at once, I don't have a chance.*

I'll be dead.

Snap seemed to take an age at her task, while Storm's heartbeat thundered ever louder in her own ears. In the heavy silence, she heard the light crunch of leaf litter and glanced down to see that Sunshine had positioned herself directly in front of Storm's paws.

The Omega's hackles were still raised, her head slowly turning as she glowered at every dog, her delicate fangs bared. "Storm's innocent," she snarled. "And if I have to fight every one of you to prove it, I will."

Staring down at that fluffy white rump and the trembling plume of Sunshine's tail, Storm felt her heart swell with love for the little dog.

After what felt like a full journey of the Sun-Dog, Snap reemerged from the den and trotted to Lucky's side. She nodded at him, then turned to Dart, her expression firm.

"Storm's scent has not left that den," she declared. "Not until just now."

Lucky sat back on his haunches. "Are you satisfied, Dart?"

Storm was afraid she might collapse with relief. Thank the

Sky-Dogs, Snap had not mentioned the roughly patched hole in the back of the den, though doubtless she'd checked the scent there too. *I'm so glad I didn't give in to temptation and try to escape,* she thought, closing her eyes. That agonizing decision might have saved her life.

If I had made the wrong choice, she realized suddenly, *I would have had no alibi. I'd have been blamed for Ruff's murder. And by now I'd be blinded, or dead.*

Breeze had torn that hole in the den so that Storm would try to escape, and then killed Ruff. *She wanted yet another murder blamed on me.*

Storm felt sick to think that another dog had died for Breeze's terrible obsession. Then a cold fury swept through her bones. *This is not what I should be thinking about. . . .*

"We're wasting time," she yelped. "Breeze might be slow because she has four pups, but she is still getting farther and farther away from camp."

The dogs stared at one another. It was as if all movement in the glade had ceased; even the Wind-Dogs had stopped running. But at last it seemed that both Packs knew two truths: that Storm was innocent, and that the pups were in dreadful peril. Around her, a low growling rose as the dogs exchanged glances of horrified realization.

"Dart. Rake. Woody." Lucky's voice was cold and determined. "Will you help us? We have to find my pups before Breeze can hurt them. She killed your Packmate, that's clear now. I want her to face justice as much as you do."

"Of course we'll help," growled Rake. "Breeze has made more than enough mischief already."

"We'll form separate search parties so we can cover more ground," said Lucky, trotting briskly around the Packs. "Snap and Chase, you go with Dart. Rake and Woody, come with me. Daisy, Thorn, and Beetle will make up the third group, and—" He turned slowly toward Storm, his eyes filled with guilt and remorse. "Storm. Please, will you go with Daisy's group? We need you."

Something hot and fierce surged in her chest. *That's all I wanted you to say, Lucky. That you believe me, and you want my help.* "Of course I will," she told him.

She twisted to meet Beetle's gaze. He was watching her, but there was no hostility on his face now. His head dipped submissively, and he lowered his eyes.

He's finally had to admit it: I'm not the bad dog. Storm was glad, but she felt a twinge of resentment that he hadn't trusted her until now. It made her appreciate the loyalty of Sunshine and Daisy all the more.

Despite the circumstances, Storm felt real joy as she bounded out of the clearing, with Daisy, Thorn, and Beetle running hard behind her. It had been days since she had been able to run free, to stretch her legs across open ground. The forest was a blur around her. At first her legs felt stiff and awkward, and her underused muscles protested, but it didn't take long to loosen them up. Her ears blew back in the wind of her own speed as she leaped and raced across branches, hollows, and fallen logs. The day was cool, the breeze keen and scented with pine; it would have been fun if not for her terrible, nagging fear for the pups.

In spite of her flying pace, Storm kept her ears alert and her nostrils open. There was no telling where Breeze might have taken the pups, and they couldn't afford to miss the faintest clue. Storm found she was clenching her jaws as anger bubbled up inside her. *I'm not going to let Breeze win. I'm not going to let her harm those pups.*

A little way behind and to her left flank, she heard Daisy give a sudden, breathless yap. "I smell them! The pups!"

Storm skidded to a halt, the others drawing up behind her.

They stood in silence for a moment, panting.

"Is it a fresh trail?" asked Beetle, raising his muzzle to snuff at the air.

"It is," Thorn confirmed. "Well done, Daisy."

"I·can smell all four of them," gasped Daisy. "They seem worried. I don't think they trust Breeze so much now—can you sense that?"

"That has to be good," said Storm darkly. She lowered her muzzle to the ground beside Daisy and breathed in. *Yes.* There was Tumble, earthy and boisterous, and there were the lighter, muskier scents of Nibble and Fluff. *And Tiny,* she realized with an ache of anxiety. *She smells like new leaves and berries.*

There was one scent missing, though. "Do you think Breeze is still with them?" Storm asked.

"I can't tell." Daisy's black eyes glimmered with worry as she shook her head.

"Don't worry," growled Storm. "I expected this. She's a cunning dog. It's not surprising she might have found a way to mask her scent."

Daisy nodded. "But the trail leads farther and farther away from camp. Come on!"

This time it was Daisy who took the lead, bounding confidently on her short legs as Storm, Thorn, and Beetle followed. She picked up remarkable speed for such a small dog, Storm thought—Daisy was clearly resolute, and she seemed very sure of the scent trail. Hope rose in Storm's chest as she loped after the little dog.

Hang on, Tumble and Tiny. Be strong, Nibble and Fluff. We're coming for you!

When Daisy stopped without warning, the other three almost cannoned into her. They all skidded to a halt, sending up showers of leaves and broken twigs, and one by one they sucked in stunned breaths as they followed Daisy's horrified gaze.

"What . . . what happened here?" whispered Beetle.

The ridge they crested had once overlooked a sweeping meadow of long yellow grass, rabbit holes, and wild, choking weeds. Now it was unrecognizable.

The sunlight that spilled over the scene was murky and yellow-gray, and a low cloud of kicked-up dust hung over what had once been wilderness. Beyond this plain, Storm knew, lay the longpaw town, but even its harsh lines were indistinct in the haze. No rabbits browsed here now, or bolted at the dogs' approach: the meadow itself was a torn gash of mud and loudcage-tracks, the only sign of its lush grass a few straggling blades that were upturned or flattened in the earth. Storm's jaw slackened as she stared at the changes.

Huge yellow loudcages slumbered in the mire, their blunt-toothed jaws hanging wide and still; others were awake and hunting, churning up the ground at the bidding of their longpaw riders. The echoing clamor of their roars made Storm flinch back, and as she bumped into Beetle's flank, he didn't jerk away. He pressed close to her, and on her other side, Thorn did the same, as if the two dogs were huddling against her for safety. Glancing down, Storm saw that Daisy had backed up, trembling, to stand between her forelegs.

The field was heaving with longpaws, looking like ants on a disturbed mound, and every single one wore a strange, shiny, yellow head covering. Some didn't have loudcages to ride, and they milled busily in the sunken tracks, pointing and barking, or staring intently at great white leaves in their hands. The odors of metal and torn earth were almost overwhelming.

"Are they digging for the Earth-Dog?" whined Daisy.

"But . . . But . . ." Thorn's eyes were wide and white-rimmed. "They'll hurt her!"

Would they? Storm had no idea if they could harm the great

Spirit Dog, but if they kept on digging? The longpaws were barking at one another, though she couldn't hear them over the roar of their loudcages as they ripped mercilessly at the ground. They didn't look angry, but rather intent, and determined—and so very *busy*.

"So many longpaws," Storm murmured, her forelegs beginning to shake. *So many.*

CHAPTER FIVE

"I hate this," whined Thorn. *"*I hate that they're so close to the camp. This is dangerous for the Pack!"

"But when did it happen?" asked Storm, pricking her quivering ears at the commotion below.

Daisy shook her head slowly. "I came here two days ago, on patrol, and it wasn't like this. It was the rabbit-meadow! How could they have done this so *fast?*"

Storm felt her skin begin to crawl. It was true: Longpaws could do so much damage so quickly. And this meadow had been well beyond the longpaw camp. They had sent these loudcages and their yellow-capped riders far beyond their usual territory— so close to the Pack's camp, it was astonishing that the dogs hadn't realized until now. *The Wind-Dogs hid it from us,* she thought. *Why would they do that? Perhaps it's not a danger after all?*

But the cold shivers in her spine told her otherwise. *This is bad.* She didn't know *why* it was bad; the feeling in her bones was a creeping dread of something unknown. The longpaws had a purpose, that was clear; not knowing what it was made it seem even more mysteriously evil to Storm.

Daisy cleared her throat and gave a hoarse yap. "Remember, I used to be a Leashed Dog?"

The other three nodded, still stunned.

"I used to travel in a loudcage with my longpaws. It wasn't as big as these ones, but it went so far, so fast. When the longpaws let me out, I sometimes didn't recognize the place they'd taken me. I couldn't even *smell* home. I don't know how my longpaws ever found their way home again, but they always did." She drew a shaking breath. "These loudcages here are such big ones. I can't imagine how far they can travel. And how very quick they must be . . ."

"They don't look so speedy," said Beetle doubtfully. "But they do look big and strong. And they clearly don't mean well. Look at them!"

He hardly needed to say that, thought Storm. None of them could tear their eyes away from the devastation.

"I can't imagine being inside a loudcage at all." Storm

shuddered. It was incomprehensible that a dog would ever consent to ride in one—and at the command of longpaws?

"I wouldn't do it now," said Daisy quietly, "but it wasn't so bad. All the same, I never understood how they traveled so far. Farther and faster than deer."

Storm shook herself. The stench of the loudcages was pungent. "It doesn't make sense to me."

"You know, there used to be longpaws *everywhere*," Daisy breathed. "Back before the Big Growl, you couldn't walk anywhere without seeing them. It didn't matter how far a dog ran, there would be longpaws around you. And that's just how this looks now—the ground covered in longpaws like grass. As if the longpaws are everywhere again, and now they always will be."

Thorn shuddered. "The Earth-Dog got tired after the Big Growl and calmed down. And now that she's off her guard . . . what if they're trying to stop her growling ever again?"

"If they conquer the Earth-Dog herself," muttered Beetle, "nowhere will ever be safe from them."

There was an edge of angry terror to his voice and his sister's, and Storm glanced at him. Both his and Thorn's eyes were wide and staring, and their paws trembled, but Storm didn't know if that was with fear or rage.

Of course, she remembered, both these litter-siblings had a gut-deep hatred of longpaws. It was evil longpaws who had killed their Father-Dog, Fiery, trapping him and torturing him with bad water and thin metal sticks that they drove deep into his body. Thorn and Beetle had never forgiven the longpaws for that—indeed, they had once tried to sabotage another longpaw site in revenge, an impulsive act that had brought the whole Pack into danger.

"Thorn! Beetle!" Storm urged them nervously. "Don't do anything crazy, will you? Don't even *think* about attacking these longpaws."

Beetle's claws raked the earth as viciously as one of the big loudcages, and his muzzle was curled. "I want to, Storm. I can't help it."

"Me too." Thorn's eyes were red with repressed fury. Both of them quivered with rage, and Storm felt a jolt of alarm.

"Please don't. Calm down." Desperately Storm licked their necks and jaws. "If you want revenge on longpaws, you can have it another day." *Though I hope for their own sakes that we never see them again.* "Right here and now, though, there's only one thing that matters—finding Lucky and Sweet's pups!"

Beetle was staring hard at his paws, and Storm couldn't see his expression. Anxiety swelled inside her. *Is he sulking? Gathering himself to attack the longpaws?*

Her heart in her throat, Storm glanced from Beetle to his sister. Thorn was taking deep, shaky breaths, and her lips were wrinkled back from her teeth. But as Storm eyed them, afraid of what both the dogs might do, Thorn consciously relaxed her muzzle, so that it once more covered her long fangs. Gradually, Beetle's paws stopped trembling.

They were calming themselves down, Storm thought with relief. *Getting themselves under control. I should have realized. I know that feeling myself. . . .*

"Don't worry, Storm," said Thorn. "We'll avenge our Father-Dog another day. Beetle?"

"I'm fine," he growled. "You're right, Storm, I know you are." His eyes raised to hers, remorseful and guilt-stricken. "And I guess I owe you some trust."

She licked his muzzle again. "Don't worry about that right now. Do you think we can make it across this . . . this plain?" It didn't seem right to call it a meadow anymore.

"If we're careful, I'm sure we can," said Daisy, her lip drawing back, showing a single disdainful fang. "The longpaws look very distracted with what they're doing to the Earth-Dog. And there are plenty of mud heaps for us to sneak behind."

Storm lowered her snout to the ground and crept tentatively forward. A quick dash, and she was crouched behind a torn-up pile of earth. There were pawsteps behind her, and she heard the close, panting breaths of the other three dogs. Her heart pounded in her rib cage, and her throat felt tight. *We can't afford to be captured by longpaws. Not now!*

"It's so hard to catch scents here," whispered Daisy, snuffling at the mud. "Everything's so confused."

"Soil, loudcages, longpaws," growled Beetle. "It's impossible."

The ground beneath their paws trembled, and the dogs jumped back as a loudcage rumbled into life nearby. Wide-eyed, they watched as it lifted its vast metal jaws and sank them into the earth. With a roar it lumbered forward, scouring a deep gash in the land.

"Poor Earth-Dog," whimpered Daisy, cowering.

"Breeze did this deliberately," snarled Storm. Her sensitive nostrils were smothered in odors of longpaw-sweat, metal, and that acrid drink that fueled the loudcages. "She took the pups here because she thought we would lose their scent."

"Yes," growled Thorn, "and she didn't care about the danger."

Daisy stopped snuffling at the ground, lifting up her head and looking at them with wide, panicked eyes. "We still have the scent," she yelped, "but it's fading. And if Breeze took them through this mess, their scent might be mixed with who knows what?"

"We might lose them for good," Storm whined. "No! We will catch up to them. Come on!"

"Can't we go around it?" asked Beetle, narrowing his eyes.

"It'll take too long," said Storm. "By the time we make our way around this place, the trail could have faded." *I'll give Breeze this,* she thought bitterly, *she's clever.* How could they possibly outwit her? Cunning *and* crazy: There was no way of predicting the actions of a dog like that. And if she wanted to hurt the pups, there would be nothing they could do about it.

Storm swallowed the growl that wanted to rumble in her throat. *If the Pack had just listened to me earlier . . .*

But she wouldn't say any of that to the others; they were anxious enough. Desolate, Storm stared across the ruined meadow and the longpaw chaos that filled it. Never mind Breeze: There was no way of knowing what the longpaws were up to, either.

None of their movements or barks made any sense to her at all. Bewildered, she pinned her ears back against her head. *Longpaws are such a mystery to me.*

Wait. They weren't. Not completely . . . *The last time I had a run-in with longpaws, they weren't hostile. At least, not when I stopped being aggressive.*

"We'll just walk straight through," she told the others.

"*What?*" chorused Beetle and Thorn.

"That's mad dog behavior," added Beetle in a growl.

"No, listen." She spoke slowly, thinking hard. "I met other longpaws, while I was on my own."

Beetle drew in a horrified breath.

"Don't look so shocked, Beetle. They weren't like these longpaws, or the ones who harmed your father. I don't think all longpaws are the same at all. They all behave so differently, and I've seen some of them being kind. Maybe these ones aren't so dangerous either."

"She's right, they aren't all the same," Daisy said.

"All longpaws are lethal," growled Thorn.

"No, they're not. Believe me. Remember Whine, the old Omega?" Storm cocked an ear, and they nodded. "Well, I found him. He'd been taken in by longpaws."

"That figures," said Daisy darkly.

"I think it was what suited him best." Storm nodded. "He was happy, Daisy. And the longpaws weren't so bad. They had other Leashed Dogs—Coco and Rex, and they were happy too. Like you were once, Daisy, and some of the others. I guess they'd never known anything different." Her muzzle twisted ruefully. "You can imagine that Whine wasn't completely happy to see me. He didn't want me joining his longpaw Pack, any more than I wanted to be part of it."

Daisy snorted with amusement.

"But he did teach me to make friends with them," Storm went on, ignoring Beetle's and Thorn's scandalized stares. "He taught me—how to manipulate them, I guess. That's why I think we can walk right through here, if we're careful. If we're friendly, and confident—and not hostile—we can get through without a confrontation at all. At least it's worth a try, isn't it?"

Daisy looked thoughtful. "When I was a Leashed Dog, longpaws were sometimes very tolerant of me." Her face turned mischievous. "Quite gullible, actually."

Storm snorted. "That certainly seems to be what Whine

found out. Seriously, Beetle and Thorn—I spent a night in a long-paw cage, and they never tried to harm me."

Beetle gasped. "Apart from putting you in a *cage*."

"Yes, but they weren't malicious. It was easy enough to escape, with the Leashed Dogs' help. And that's not what's going to happen here, I promise." Storm set her teeth. "If they come for us, we run. We can outpace them."

"Storm's right," said Daisy. "We have to give this a try. We don't have a choice."

"I'll do it," said Thorn after a pause. Her eyes were narrowed as she surveyed the longpaws, seeming strangely sure of herself, which Storm found odd. *Even I'm nervous about this, and I'm a Fierce Dog. Thorn should be quivering.*

The black-and-white dog turned to her littermate. "For the pups' sake, Beetle."

Beetle nodded firmly. "All right. But I won't go into any cage."

"You won't have to." Storm knew she couldn't think longer about this, or she'd lose her nerve. Placing one paw determinedly after another, she padded forward into the open.

She didn't dare look back, but she didn't have to. She could hear the others close at her rump, their breathing shaky, their paws squelching in the soft mud.

For a rabbit-chase or two, none of the longpaws even noticed them, they were so engrossed in their discussions or their big white leaves and boards. Her shoulders low, Storm slunk on, her eyes on the terrain in front of them.

Suddenly her paws trembled. It seemed such a long way to the far side of the meadow: had the longpaws somehow made it even bigger? It was hard to tell where the old boundaries had been, and the loudcages seemed to take no notice of gullies or tree lines or natural borders. They ate up everything in their path, tossing the crumpled earth aside.

One of the great yellow brutes was standing right in their path, and Storm felt cold to her bones with fear. But it was completely still, its great jaws resting on the earth. Asleep.

It'll be like hunting a deer. She took a nervous breath. *Except that I'm never scared that a deer will attack me . . . But I just have to be silent, and not alarm it.* Cautiously, she lowered her belly and crept around the loudcage's rump, feeling the cold touch of its shadow falling across her.

Then, with an abrupt, rumbling growl, it woke up.

Storm froze, terrified. Behind her she heard Thorn give a strangled yelp.

It didn't move. A longpaw emerged from its flank and jumped down, landing in the soft earth with a squelching thud. He took a step away from the loudcage, then stopped dead, staring at Storm and her companions.

He gave a great bellow of surprise, his eyes popping wide. To Storm's astonishment, something like a smile curled his mouth.

Then, with a single, drawn-out bark, he summoned his Pack.

CHAPTER SIX

For an instant they all gaped at one another. The longpaw's yellow-capped Packmates were ambling toward them now, unhurried, their fascinated gazes aimed at the dogs.

Then, from behind her, Storm heard Thorn's howl of fury.

"Get out of our way!"

Storm spun around to stop her. "Thorn, no—"

Thorn wasn't listening. Her forepaws were jammed into the earth, her shoulders hunched in threat, and her ears were back tight against her head. Her muzzle was peeled back in rage, baring slavering fangs, and her eyes were white-rimmed and frenzied.

"Thorn, calm down!" urged Storm desperately.

The longpaw was not intimidated. He walked slowly forward, peeling off the hide that covered one of his long forepaws. He made a soothing, rumbling growl as he approached them.

Storm looked from Thorn to the longpaw and backed protectively closer to the black-and-white dog. "It's not going to hurt us. There's no need to attack it!"

But when she looked at Thorn, and saw her lips twitching, instinctively curling back over her fangs, Storm realized why she and her littermate had been so calm. Thorn and Beetle had *wanted* a confrontation with the longpaws.

"They *all* hurt us!" howled Thorn, and sprang.

Aghast, Storm watched her hurtle at the longpaw. Thorn's dripping jaws sank into his leg. Even in her horror Storm realized that the bite wasn't deep—the hide covering his legs was thick and tough, and Thorn's teeth couldn't have given him more than a fierce nip—but all the same he gave a scream of shock that alarmed the other watching longpaws and made them run faster.

"Thorn." But there was no time to remonstrate. Storm twisted and spun, searching for an escape route, but longpaws were approaching from all directions. Daisy whimpered in panic. Beetle leaped to Thorn's side, snarling at the longpaw, who clutched his injured leg. Another longpaw whipped off his hard yellow head covering and flung it at the dogs; Beetle jumped, but stayed firmly where he stood, barking in angry unison with his littermate.

"Thorn, *go!*" Infuriated, Storm bolted toward them,

head-butting Thorn's flank. That seemed to jolt Thorn out of her frenzy, and she stumbled, then ran. Beetle followed, with Daisy panting after them, but Thorn seemed maddened with fear and rage. She scrabbled to a halt again, spinning to run in the other direction, almost tumbling over Beetle. Storm darted after her, but there were more longpaws ahead; once again, Thorn doubled back, colliding with her friends. They were all confused for a moment, barking, frantic.

It didn't help that all the longpaws were now barking and hollering, too. They were not rushing in, but they were not backing off, either—slowly, they were encircling the four dogs, their postures now hostile and angry.

"Storm, which way should we run?" barked Beetle.

"Help, Storm!" whined Daisy.

"I told you! I told you!" Thorn's howl rose. "They hurt us! They hate us!"

Storm spun again, and a movement by one of the longpaws caught her eye. The hazy sunlight glinted on a stumpy silver stick that he drew from his side.

"No!" she barked.

"Run!" howled Daisy, as the longpaw raised the thing to point it.

Another longpaw was snapping angrily at the one with the stick, reaching out to slap it away, but he was too late. A crack like a lightning-struck tree echoed across the air, making Storm's ears ring and bringing her to a frozen halt.

In the sudden silence, the air smelled acrid. Storm's ears rang with the deafening *crack*, like thunder on the ground. For long moments, her hearing was muffled to nothing. Panic stirred inside her, and she gave a whimper she couldn't hear. *It's all right. It's all right.* Nothing had happened—the only thing bothering them was the noise, and the stench.

Storm turned slowly, staggering, a little off-balance with the ringing in her ears. Thorn was standing right in front of her now, staring at Storm, her eyes wide and bewildered.

Then Thorn lurched sideways, stumbled, and crashed to the ground.

Storm bolted to her side and stood over her, panting in confusion. There was a stink of blood and smoke in the hot air. Thorn gazed up at her, uncomprehending, the fury in her eyes replaced with white terror.

Her foreleg had been smashed at the knee. Storm stared at the mess of blood and broken bone.

At least she's alive, Storm thought with sudden understanding. *For now. Until they kill us all.*

Spinning on her hindquarters, Storm peeled back her muzzle and snarled at the longpaws. They backed off, but they no longer seemed so interested in the dogs. They were hollering at the one with the loudstick, and they sounded enraged. One of them waved his forepaws, howling at his Packmate.

The longpaws were quarreling, yelling: That was all Storm needed to know. *A Pack in confusion can't act fast. They're not aware of what's happening around them.*

"If we don't run now," Storm growled, "it's all over. Get her up! Go!"

Between them, she, Daisy, and a violently trembling Beetle shoved Thorn onto her three last working legs. She gave a long, drawn-out whine, more of shock than of pain, Storm thought. They huddled around her, half pushing, half dragging her back toward the forest's edge. Thorn's injured leg dragged and bumped horribly, but she made no sound except for the odd gasp. She was in shock, Storm realized.

Storm shot a glance toward the longpaws. They were still barking angrily at one another, and their circle had broken:

There was space for dogs to escape.

"Go!" Storm clenched her teeth and shouldered Thorn through the gap.

The black-and-white dog seemed too stunned to resist—or even, thought Storm, to feel real pain yet. Lurching, Thorn staggered for safety, supported by Beetle at one flank and Storm at the other. Daisy, helpless, spun and fussed, urging them on with frantic barks.

A huge broken log lay just within the tree line, where a loudcage had dumped it. Storm gently took Thorn's scruff between her teeth and hauled her over to the other side, with Beetle pulling at one of his sister's good legs. When she heard Thorn land with a thud, Storm scrambled over the log herself, and the two dogs dragged her farther into the undergrowth, panting and desperate.

At last they scrabbled into a grassy hollow and crouched low over her limp body. The three uninjured dogs peered out over the hollow's edge, gaping at the confused longpaws in the field.

"They're still arguing," Daisy panted. "Some of them are looking for us now, but I don't think they'll find our trail. We're safe."

"Not for long," growled Storm. "We have to get farther away. Thorn, are you all right?" *Silly question,* she thought at once, staring at her former Packmate's shattered leg.

"Thorn!" howled Beetle softly. "Thorn, speak to me!"

Clearly, Thorn couldn't. Her snout was twisted with agony, and her limbs were sprawled uselessly on the earth. A low, rasping panting came from her throat.

The pain has finally hit her, Storm realized with a gulp of dread. *And if we don't do something to help, she might bleed to death. But what can we do?*

The answer came to her almost instantly. But when she tried to speak, Storm could not get the words out—she felt like she had swallowed a mouthful of dirt.

"We have to get Thorn back to camp," she growled at last. "Right now."

Daisy backed up a few steps, yelping. "The pups . . . Storm, we were on their trail . . . we might not find it again if we turn back!"

Storm's head drooped. A whine was building in her chest, an anguished howl in her throat—but she was unable to make either sound. The trail had been right there beneath their noses and would surely disappear no matter how quickly the dogs were able to get back here. Not to mention, Breeze and the pups were only getting farther and farther away.

"We have to help Thorn, Daisy," Beetle howled. "If we don't, she'll die."

"Yes." Daisy gritted her teeth. "Of course we must. But—oh, rot those longpaws! We were so close! Or at least, we were on the right track."

Storm clambered to her paws, staring down at Thorn, then looking out at the dead meadow, which they had not managed to get past. Once again, her efforts to save the pups had been thwarted—this time because Thorn and Beetle just couldn't stay calm—and she was beginning to wonder if, somehow, the Spirit Dogs didn't *want* her to succeed.

She should never have told them to walk across the field. *I should have known Thorn and Beetle wouldn't be able to control themselves around longpaws.* A whining growl of remorse and fury rose in Storm's throat.

"Let's get Thorn back where it's safe." Lifting her head, she gazed darkly out at the longpaws on the churned field.

How will Thorn survive a wound like that? Storm wondered, as the search party staggered away.

Can *she even survive a wound like that?*

CHAPTER SEVEN

The way back to the camp was long and arduous. Thorn could barely walk on her injured foreleg, and Storm and Beetle had to press close to her flanks to keep her upright at all. Daisy padded ahead, finding ground that was as level and uncluttered as possible, guiding them around fallen logs and tangled undergrowth, occasionally darting ahead to clear the way of rocks and twigs that might cause Thorn to lose her already precarious balance.

By the time the familiar scents of the clearing came to their nostrils, the Sun Dog was on his descent toward his den and the black-and-white dog was barely conscious. She felt very heavy against Storm's flank now, like a dead deer; her eyes were almost closed, and only the force of will kept her lurching forward. Beetle's eyes were stark with terror as he urged his litter-sister on.

"Storm!" A white blur bounded over a small ridge, her small

pink tongue lolling. Then her eyes clouded with sadness. "You didn't find the pups?"

"No, Sunshine." Storm hated to disappoint the little Omega, but she was at the limit of her strength and could only pant the bad news curtly.

Sunshine scrabbled to a halt in front of them, her expression horrified. "What's happened to Thorn?"

"She was attacked by a longpaw." Storm took a gasping breath.

"*No!* Oh, poor Thorn! Bring her quickly. I'll fetch moss." Sunshine spun and raced back to the clearing, and they followed far more slowly. By now they were almost carrying Thorn.

At last they let her collapse onto a hastily gathered bed of leaves just outside her den. Sunshine stood back and watched, her eyes wide. In the little dog's jaws was a big clump of fresh moss, soaked with water from the pond. She edged forward and pressed it gently to Thorn's gaping wound. Thorn winced and whimpered.

Beetle stood over his litter-sister, panting. He began to pace, four or five steps one way and then the other. It was clear he could barely contain his fear.

Sunshine fussed over Thorn, licking delicately at the wound, and Daisy helped as best she could—but really, thought Storm, there was not much they could do. As the mess was gradually cleaned away, she could see the wound was clotting—but trickles of dark blood still leaked down poor Thorn's foreleg. And the damage itself was so dreadful, it made unseen claws clutch at Storm's gut.

How could one stubby little stick have caused so much harm? Storm could hear again that sharp crack, could smell the acrid stink in her nostrils.

Thorn's leg wasn't just broken; the bone had been smashed altogether. The lower half of it hung loose, attached only by a flap of raw skin, and splintered bone jutted horribly from the flesh. Storm swallowed hard as she stared at the wound. *That leg will never heal.*

As Thorn gave another agonized yelp, Sunshine skittered back. "I'm so sorry, Thorn. I know it hurts, but I have to clean it."

"She's right." Twitch was loping toward them from the trees, looking appalled. Behind him padded Snap, her head hanging down.

Storm turned, anxious. "You didn't find any sign of the pups?"

Twitch shook his head as he halted beside Thorn's prone body. "No. And I see why you had to give up your hunt, too."

"It was longpaws," snarled Beetle. "They hurt her like this without even *touching* her."

Twitch lowered his muzzle to sniff carefully at Thorn's leg. "All of you, move," he said sternly. "Give her space and air."

As they all shuffled back, Storm couldn't help but stare at the stump of Third Dog's missing leg. Of course—he too had lost a limb.

And why had I forgotten that? Because it barely holds him back at all. He hobbles a little, and he can't turn fast, but Twitch is fit and strong, a good hunter.

In fact, Storm thought suddenly, Twitch had fared better on three limbs than he had when he was encumbered by his fourth, lame leg. He'd chewed off the limb himself for that very reason, after he'd been exiled from the Pack by its old half-wolf Alpha. By the time the rest of the Pack had met him again, he'd been a nimble, quick dog once more. *One with three legs.*

For the first time since Thorn's dreadful injury, Storm felt a stirring of hope. If Twitch could manage on three legs, surely the young and strong Thorn could, too.

Twitch leaned over the black-and-white dog, murmuring to her. "Wake up, Thorn."

She did not stir. There was only a strangled, distant groan, deep in her throat.

"Thorn!" he barked, much more sharply, and he nudged her hard with his nose. "Thorn, *wake up.* You mustn't drift off to sleep.

There's a fever in you, and you have to stay awake."

Thorn's eyes blinked open into slits; they looked wild and glazed as she tried to lift her head from the bedding. It fell back with a thump, and she groaned.

"Easy, Thorn." Twitch licked her ear. "Listen to me. You're going to lose this leg. The wound is terrible, and it's no wonder you're in such pain. But be strong."

She gave a choked whimper.

"You're going to be all right, I promise." He nuzzled her. "But you must keep licking that wound. Sunshine's done a good job, but you have to keep it clean. That's important, do you understand?"

Thorn gave him a feeble nod of agreement.

"Focus on doing it now. It will help you to stay awake—and you *must* stay awake, Thorn."

Sucking in a gasp of air, Thorn managed to jerk up her head. She blinked a couple of times, then shuddered when she focused on her wound. But she craned over and began to lick it listlessly.

"That's good." Twitch nodded. "Keep at it. We'll all help you."

Thorn flinched in a sudden twinge of pain but clenched her fangs, and her eyes narrowed with determination. Hesitantly she licked at her leg again, and Sunshine crept closer to help once more.

Watching Thorn suffer, guilt clenched inside Storm. *I should have known Thorn needed to be kept away from the longpaws. I should have led them another way.*

Branches rustled at the edge of the clearing, and Storm realized more dogs were returning from their search: Sweet, Moon, and Mickey. Sweet was swaying on her slender legs, and her head drooped almost to the ground; Moon and Mickey limped and stumbled. Only moments after they appeared, Lucky, Rake, and Woody pushed through the undergrowth on the opposite side of the glade and shook themselves. Rake flopped onto the ground, his eyes closing, and Woody, after only a moment, slumped at his side. Lucky lurched forward toward Sweet.

The Alpha stared at the dogs who'd been with him, and at Storm, and Thorn's bloodied leg, and then turned her gaze on Lucky and whined an exhausted "What is going on here?" Her Beta hurried over and began to explain in a low rumble all that had happened after her search party had left.

"Thorn?" As if a bolt of new energy had shot through her, Moon bounded to her pup's side and crouched beside her, murmuring in grief and licking at Thorn's ears.

All the returning dogs had realized something was wrong, and every one of them was alert once more. Woody and Rake scrambled back to their paws and trotted after Lucky into the center of the clearing.

"What happened?" Sweet sprang forward, followed by Mickey.

"Longpaws—" Beetle began to howl again, but Storm stopped him.

"Thorn needs quiet," she reminded him gently.

"My pups," said Sweet urgently. "Storm, did you find any trace of them?"

Storm's head drooped. "I'm sorry, Sweet. We found a trail—but then we ran into the longpaws. We had no choice but to come back. I'm sorry."

Sweet gave a choked whimper of distress. "But you did find some kind of scent?"

"Yes. I'll explain." She told the Alpha how they'd come to the churned-up meadow, how they'd tried to cross but then the long-paws had spotted them.

"And one of them had something that hurt Thorn," she finished, her head sagging with tiredness. "It was some kind of loudstick, but a very small one. We barely managed to get Thorn away."

"And did the longpaws track you back here?" asked Sweet in alarm.

Storm shook her head. "No, I'm sure they didn't."

"But you did *scent* the pups?" Sweet's tail lashed in agitation. "You found the direction Breeze took them, at least?"

Daisy sat down on her haunches at Storm's side. "Yes. The trail was a little confused, but they definitely went that way."

Sweet and Lucky exchanged a glance of tormented, desperate hope. "That's some good news, at least," said Sweet. "Now we can focus on that direction. We know where they went!"

"Do you think you can pick up the trail again?" asked Lucky urgently. "It won't be lost in—in whatever the longpaws are doing to the dirt?"

"I'm sure we can," Daisy told him, with a glance at Storm for reassurance.

Storm nodded.

"We should get going!" exclaimed Rake. "The Sun Dog's light is fading fast."

They had all clustered near to Sweet's den now, except for Moon and Sunshine, who were still tending to Thorn; and Beetle, who seemed unable to stop pacing.

"Now, before the trail goes cold," said Mickey firmly.

"Let's choose the fastest dogs, and go!" chimed in Chase.

Growls and barks of agreement rose around Storm, and she felt a surge of excitement.

"We will find my pups," said Sweet, and took a step toward the forest.

Storm stared at her. Sweet's eyes were brilliant and eager, but her legs shook almost uncontrollably, and her flanks heaved. Storm shot an alarmed look at Lucky.

The golden Beta had already noticed. "No, Sweet," he said gruffly, padding to her side. He licked her ear. "You're in no shape to go, however much you want to."

"I don't *want* to," she growled feebly. "I *have* to."

"You can't help the pups when you're exhausted," Lucky told her. "Please, Sweet. Let me go. I'm not nearly as tired."

She hesitated, yearning toward the trees. Then her whole body sagged, and she nodded.

"All right. Oh, my Lucky. Please find our pups. . . ."

She slumped to the ground. Lucky gave her neck a last caress with his tongue, then turned to the others. "I have to keep going," he told them, his voice hard but hoarse.

"I'll come, Lucky," volunteered Storm. "I know exactly where we turned back, and where the trail leads. I'm not too tired either,

Sweet, and I can't stop now. This is all my fault."

Sweet's head jerked up in a sudden burst of energy, her eyes glittering. "No, Storm!" she barked. "I won't let you say that. It's *not true*. Only one dog is responsible for our troubles, and that's *Breeze*. And if we'd listened to you earlier, this would not have happened at all. Never forget that!"

Storm's throat was so tight, she couldn't reply. Her heart swelled with love and sympathy for her former Alpha. Sweet was worn out, and desperately frightened for her pups, but she still had it in her to reassure Storm—to own up to the Pack's guilt, too. Storm swallowed hard and raised her head to gaze at them all.

Her heart turned over inside her. Every dog was looking at her with the same expression as Sweet: guilty, remorseful, apologetic. And *trusting*. They knew they'd failed, they knew they'd gotten it wrong, and they trusted her to put it right. They trusted her to *want* to put it right, even after what they'd done to her.

A wave of love rose inside her chest as she looked over the dogs in her former Pack. "I will find your pups, Sweet, I *promise*." She bared her fangs in renewed determination. "Breeze will *not win*."

"And I'll come with you," said Rake, taking a pace forward. "I won't let you lose your pups, Alpha—and if I'm fortunate, maybe I will have a chance to avenge Ruff."

"I'll come too," piped up a higher voice. Daisy trotted into the center of the group, and Storm looked down at her in surprise. "I may not be fast, but my nose is good. And I wasn't one of the dogs who dragged Thorn back to camp, so I still have plenty of energy for the hunt."

Storm bent to lick the little dog's head, overwhelmed by affection.

Lucky said nothing to welcome the other hunters; he was already gazing out fiercely at the darkening forest. "Then let's go. Now!"

Dusky twilight blurred the trees, and a slight evening mist was rising from the earth as the four dogs loped steadily through the forest. None of them spoke; the only sound was the thump and crunch of their paws, and their steady, panting breaths. Ahead of Storm, Lucky was a racing blur of gold, but as they passed the spot behind the dead log, where they'd first dragged the injured Thorn, Storm put on a burst of speed and caught up with him.

"We're close to the old meadow," she growled. "Be careful."

Slowing to a walk, Storm led Lucky up the small ridge that overlooked the meadow. When they reached its crest, they both stopped, and Rake and Daisy trotted up behind them.

"It *has* changed," said Lucky in a low growl. Rake's ears were pinned back with shock.

The longpaws were gone, but the evidence of their work was obvious. The rising Moon-Dog glowed at the eastern edge of the devastated meadow, but her gleam was nothing compared to the white light that spilled from tall posts at regular intervals around the former meadow. Their cold glare edged the mounds of soil with silver, and spilled across the flat earth with a light as bright as day.

"They must have known we'd come back," said Storm grimly, and nodded at the boundary. All around the excavated land, a high metal fence had been built.

"That wasn't here before?" Lucky stared in shock.

Storm shook her head, and shuddered. "They work so fast, the longpaws."

"Scarily fast," growled Rake. "Imagine what they could do in a few days. In a moon or two . . ."

The four dogs crept down the slope on silent paws, and then along the edge of the fence, sniffing for gaps. There were none. Lucky stopped, stretching his forelegs.

"Can you dig under it, like you did at the Dog-Garden?" asked Daisy hopefully.

"There's no point," he growled. "I'd rather go around, anyway. I don't trust this place at all."

"It's bad to have longpaws so close to your camp," observed Rake.

Lucky whined in agreement. "It is."

Storm glanced at him, worried. She couldn't read his expression, and she couldn't imagine what he was thinking, or the emotions that must be racing through him at this moment. It was probably sensible to take the long way around, but was Lucky thinking clearly? It was unlike him to be so taciturn and abrupt. He must be beside himself with fear for his pups. Anxiously she followed him along the fence.

"Here!" Daisy called back to them, when they'd followed the fence almost the whole length of the field. "I've got the pups' scent again!"

The other three loped to her side. She gazed up at them, her eyes excited.

"That's good," said Storm. She sniffed at the ground, and then again, her eyes narrowing. Yes, four pup-scents were intertwined here: faint, but distinct. It was as if they'd gone out of their way to brush against rocks and roots and low-hanging branches. *There's something odd about this. . . .*

"Let's get going," rumbled Lucky, and took a pace forward.

"Wait." Storm stayed still, and he turned to give her an impatient glance.

She pricked an ear and sniffed the air. "It's too obvious," she growled at last as they all stared at her. "Breeze doesn't leave a trail this clear. Not unless she wants to."

"You're making too much of it," said Lucky sharply. "She was in a hurry. She's afraid of us." A dark heat glinted in his eyes. "And so she should be."

"No, think about it." Storm eyed the boundary, frowning. "The longpaws didn't raise that fence till late. There was plenty of chaos in the meadow to confuse the trail—mud, loudcages, longpaws. Breeze went through earlier, and she did it deliberately because she knew it would be hard for us. So what's this new trail?"

Rake sniffed doubtfully. "It does seem odd. . . ."

"It's been a long time since we were here," Storm murmured, "and Breeze has had plenty of time to get farther away. Why is this scent so fresh and strong?"

"It doesn't matter why," snapped Lucky after a pause. "This is my pups' scent. We have to follow it, no matter where it leads."

He was right, but all of Storm's senses were on edge as they followed the trail away from the longpaw meadow and through a belt of trees. It grew faint on a bare and rocky outcrop, but Daisy picked it up easily once again in a patch of grass on the far side; so easily, the little dog stopped and wrinkled her muzzle.

"The scents on this spot are so very strong," she murmured. "It's like Breeze *wanted* to make sure we didn't lose her."

"I told you, it doesn't matter," said Lucky, forging on impatiently.

Storm, Daisy, and Rake exchanged looks of trepidation, but they followed the golden-furred Beta as he set off through long, dry grass.

Daisy sighed and scampered ahead to seek out the trail, but Lucky seemed not to notice her. His own snout was low to the ground, and he moved fast, not even acknowledging Daisy's presence. He stopped at the exact same moment she did, and Storm and Rake hurried to catch up.

Daisy's tail drooped. "That's the end of the trail," she yelped.

A cold breeze rose to ruffle their fur; Storm lifted her muzzle and breathed in the dark air, then peered out with creased eyes. Her hide prickled. She sensed nothing ahead but a massive emptiness.

While Lucky remained still and silent, Storm took another tentative pace. There was something strange about the nothingness out there. She paused, waiting patiently for her vision to adapt.

Oh. She blinked and took an instinctive pace back. It wasn't *nothing*. Far, far below her, there was sea and shoreline. There was indeed a vast emptiness—but it lay between her and the foot of the sheer, plummeting cliff.

So this was why the scent trail had ended. The ground fell away sharply, the wind-cropped grasses at its edge whispering in the breeze. Far below, picked out of the darkness by the light of the Moon Dog, Storm could just make out tumbled rocks among stunted trees.

She tipped back her head and gave a howl of frustration. "I knew it! Breeze misled us." *Of course* that trail had been too clear and good to be true.

Still, Lucky said nothing. He seemed to be waiting and watching, his hackles raised, his tail trembling slightly. And then, from below them on the cliff, came a high, wailing howl in response to Storm's.

Storm froze, peering over the edge as Lucky bounded recklessly to her side. A low growl came from his throat.

As Storm stared, her eyes adjusting to the darkness, she saw that the cliff was not completely smooth and straight; there were jagged outcrops and hanging rocks. And on one flat blade of sandstone that jutted clear of the cliff face, a small, pale form was huddled.

"Tiny!" barked Lucky.

For a moment, Storm thought he was going to bound forward and fall straight over the edge. His legs were stiff, his muscles coiled tight.

She nudged him gently, murmuring to him, "We'll get her, Lucky . . . I promise!"

The little pup was cowering against the wall, her shoulders hunched and her tail wrapped tightly around her haunches as she peered up at them in terror. Behind her there was a smeared trail of dark blood, clear against the pale rock. The little dog lifted her jaws again, and her wail was feeble, high, and desperate in the emptiness.

"Father-Dog! Storm! *Help me!*"

As Lucky gave an answering howl—"We're coming for you, my pup!"—Storm's fur tingled with dread as a horrible thought raced through her mind. They had found Tiny, but why was she alone?

Where were the other three pups?

CHAPTER EIGHT

"Tiny, are you all right?" barked Storm.

For a horrible moment, there was silence. Then a feeble whimper rose on the cold wind.

"I . . . I've got blood on me. It hurts. Father-Dog?"

Whose blood? Storm wondered, trying to ignore the images of Breeze's jaws clamping down on the necks of Fluff, Nibble, or Tumble, their blood spattering their litter-sister.

"I'm here, Tiny." Lucky's voice was strangled and hoarse. "I'm coming to get you!"

"Stay still!" barked Storm.

Beside her, Lucky was breathing hard, his flanks rising and falling swiftly. He seemed barely able to speak, and Storm could understand why. To see one of his pups down there, pinned against a cliff, with the heaving waves beneath her and the cold blackness all around . . . She looked so precarious, so fragile and vulnerable. All it would take was a rockfall, or a single misstep, and . . .

No. We mustn't think that way.

Lucky gave a low, tormented growl, and lunged his forepaws down over the edge. They caught against an almost imperceptible ridge of stone, but fragments of it crumbled away, and pebbles rolled and bounced down the cliff. Far below, Tiny cowered as grit rained down on her.

"Lucky, no! We can't." Storm gripped his shoulder fur with her teeth, trying to drag him back gently.

With huge reluctance, Lucky let himself be pulled away from the cliff. "How will we get to her?" He whipped around to face Storm. "I'm not leaving my pup!"

"None of us are," said Daisy firmly.

"Keep calm, Lucky," added Rake, though he shuddered as he glanced down over the edge. "We'll think of something. But none of us will make it down the cliff, not right here."

"Which is why Breeze led us to this point," said Storm grimly. "But look." She nodded along the cliff. "The slope is not so steep there—see, where the Moon-Dog catches that big tower of rock? It juts out into the water, and it looks as if it's protected the cliff from the Endless Lake."

"I see it," murmured Rake. "The Lake always seems to eat at the land, but it hasn't been able to take such a big bite there. Because of that rock."

"You're right. I'm sure that we can find a way down that part of the slope," said Daisy.

"Father-Dog?" The small voice was almost lost in the crash of breakers and the whistle of the wind.

"Don't worry, my pup. We're coming for you. Everything will be fine!" Lucky's whole body quivered as he peered desperately over the edge.

Storm trotted along the cliff top, eyeing the rocks below, but in moments she heard running pawsteps and Lucky overtook her, his head turning left and right as he searched the darkness frantically for a way down. When the jutting tower of rock loomed before him, he paused, and sniffed, and peered closer.

"Yes," he barked sharply. "There's a split in the rock, and it's made a thin ledge where the two slabs separate. It runs all the way along." He peered back toward the point where they'd seen Tiny. "Tiny, don't panic! Stay still. This won't take long!"

Storm hoped that was true—but it did not look like it would be an easy descent. Standing beside Lucky, she examined the cliff as best she could. It wasn't a path or a track, exactly, but Lucky was right: The crack where the stone had shifted had formed a narrow, flat ridge. It might just be possible for a dog to jump down onto it, without falling farther.

"Let's think about this," she said. "We should—"

But Lucky didn't wait. He took a single breath, and then he jumped.

Storm's heart froze. His paws had found the ridge. For a few horrible moments she saw him wobble on the impossibly narrow ledge, his tail quivering. Then he found his balance, adjusted his paws, and began to creep along the ridge, his flank scraping the cliff wall.

Storm didn't give herself time to think; if she did, she knew she would never take the leap. Clenching her jaws, she bounded down after Lucky.

Her paws landed hard on the rough stone, sending dust and pebbles rolling into the darkness, and she gave a grunt of shock. She lost control, and her body swayed wildly, but like Lucky, she held her nerve, until at last she had her balance back and her paws felt secure on the thin ledge. Then, cautiously, she paced on after him.

She didn't dare look back at Rake and Daisy, though she heard the thump and yelp as they landed; Rake's squeak of panic was barely distinguishable from Daisy's. But there was no howl of a falling dog, so Storm assumed they were safely behind her. Trembling a little, she let her paws find the way along the ledge and down the face of the cliff.

Lucky's haunches glowed pale gold ahead of her, his tail stiff and quivering as he balanced himself. Storm kept her eyes fixed on that; *I mustn't look down.* The ledge was beginning to curve in, following the cliff in a landward sweep, and when Storm dared to peek, she could see past Lucky to the faint shape that was Tiny. The pup was a quivering, pale dot against the black cliff. *We're closer now, but not close enough.*

"We'll get to her, Lucky," she growled. "Don't worry." Storm didn't know if he could hear her, and she wasn't sure she was even right. Tiny looked so precarious there, huddled between the black sky and the crashing waves.

Lucky turned his head, slowly and cautiously, and barked back to Storm. "The ridge gets wider here—"

With a rattle of dislodged rocks, one forepaw slipped from under him.

The Beta dog staggered sideways, and with a lurch of horror, Storm saw his hindquarters go over the edge. He lashed out his forepaws, managing to break his fall. But only his claws and shoulders were still hooked onto the track, and he couldn't even yelp: His jaws were too tightly clenched from the effort of holding on.

There was no time to be careful. Storm bounded forward, trusting desperately to her paws to find the ridge, and lunged down to grab at him. Rake landed just behind her, panting, and he, too, reached his long neck around her flank to sink his jaws into Lucky's scruff.

Storm's eyes were squeezed shut with effort, but she could hear the scratch and scrabble of Lucky's hindclaws against the cliff, and the rattle of falling stones. Squatting, stiffening her forelegs, she hauled as hard as she could. Rake backed away in unsteady, effortful steps, grunting through his mouthful of golden fur.

For long moments, there was no sound but the three dogs' high-pitched, panicked breathing; then, with a final yank from Storm and Rake, Lucky tumbled back onto the ledge. As she released him, a bolt of pain went through Storm's knee, and she staggered, yelping.

In the silence, they heard the *click-clack* of Daisy's claws as she trotted frantically to catch up with them; then there was a terrified whimper from up ahead.

"Father-Dog?"

"It's all right, Tiny," panted Lucky. "I'm fine. We're coming. Hold on, little one."

He wasn't even shivering as he forged on; clearly, Storm realized, he was focused on one thing only. She, on the other hand, could feel her muscles trembling with delayed terror, and pain shot up into her shoulder with every step. *I've damaged my leg . . . and what a time to do it!*

The injury was unnerving, but the memory that came abruptly into her head was worse. *That dream!*

Storm swallowed hard. Like all her dreams, it had been so vivid; and what was more, she'd dreamed it *twice*. It had been so long ago—Bruno had still been alive—but she still saw the moving image unfold like a true memory in her mind's eye. *The Wild Pack, trapped on the cliff and harried by white birds.* The dream-dogs had crouched, backing up and milling, trying to dodge the stabbing beaks. *And then one dog slipped and fell over the edge, twisting and turning in the air, plummeting toward the pounding waves at the foot of the cliff.*

The dog in my dream had golden fur. . . .

Had that dream been a warning . . . a prophecy? She'd had prophetic dreams before; had this been another? And if so . . . had the danger just been thwarted? *Did we defy the dream and save Lucky?*

Or is the real vision still to come? Is Lucky's fatal fall still going to happen?

Storm shuddered. *No. I won't* let *it happen.* She limped on along the ledge.

It felt like a very long time before Lucky came to a halt ahead of her. Storm, Rake, and Daisy cautiously approached him. *He was right,* thought Storm: the track had widened quite a bit as they made progress down it. It was broad enough now for three of them to stand abreast—but Tiny, crouched shivering only a deer-length away, was just out of reach.

And they'd run out of track. The ledge ended at Lucky's paws, and a narrow chasm yawned between him and his pup. From above, it had looked barely as thin as a dog's tail; now that they had reached it, it seemed terrifyingly wide.

Tiny whimpered, a pale and shivering form in the darkness.

Lucky strained over the gap, his shoulders shaking. His breath had to be touching Tiny, but his muzzle and his teeth couldn't. His expression twisted with despair, and Storm saw his jaws open and close, helplessly. His pup whined in desperation.

"Tiny," Storm growled gently into the awful silence. "Are you all right?"

The pup made a squeaking sound that could have been a yes or a no. She looked exhausted and terrified, and her fur was streaked with blood.

"Tiny." Daisy pushed her way carefully between Lucky and Storm. "We'll get you, don't worry. Stay calm!" She licked her jaws, frowning, and eyed the gap. "Lucky, can you lean out over the drop, do you think? Let your forepaws hang over, and put your shoulders over the edge?"

"*What?*" began Rake.

"Yes," growled Lucky, without hesitation. "I can do it."

Storm took a deep breath. *Lucky's only just escaped death, but he'll risk his life again. He'll do anything to save Tiny.*

And so will I.

Daisy turned her face to Storm. "If you hold me steady," she said, her little voice shaking, "I'll be able to balance on Lucky's shoulders. I think I can stretch for Tiny."

Storm exchanged a glance with Rake, whose eyes widened. He trod carefully forward.

"There's room on Lucky's other side, Daisy, if you're going to be climbing on to him," he said. "I'll stand there, and I'll help Storm keep you steady."

Storm nodded. "Tiny," she called gently, and with as much confidence as she could summon. "Get as close to us as you can. Daisy will grab you."

The four adult dogs watched, hearts beating hard, as Tiny

shivered, her eyes tight shut. But at last the pup stretched out a paw and pulled herself forward to the edge of the rock she lay on. Another heave brought her even closer. And another . . .

"All right, Tiny!" called Daisy nervously. "That's far enough." The little pup was right on the edge of the chasm. Down beneath them, waves rolled and crashed.

Lucky lay down on his belly, edging out over the drop. Just as Daisy had suggested, he let his forepaws dangle in the emptiness and squirmed a little farther. His shoulders jutted out over the chasm now, and Storm laid a paw briefly on his haunches to hold him steady.

"Right." Daisy took a deep breath, and scrambled up onto Lucky's back. Shivering, she crawled over his shoulders, paused to gather her courage, then squirmed farther, onto the top of his head.

Storm and Rake pressed close on either side of Lucky, taking the little dog's hind legs in their jaws as she wriggled forward. Storm was terrified that she would bite Daisy too hard, or not hard enough—that she would misjudge the weight, and that they would all end up hurtling down to their deaths.

Her heart felt like a fluttering moth in her chest. Lucky was blind now, Storm realized. Daisy had crawled so far forward that her body covered his head, and her shaking forepaws were clamped over his eyes. The sight would have been ridiculous if the situation hadn't been so desperate.

Storm heard Daisy take a gasping breath, before she gave a sudden lunge forward, with an involuntary yelp, and snapped her jaws. Her teeth clamped together over Tiny's scruff, the pup giving a yap of surprise and fear. Daisy whimpered through her mouthful of fur.

Storm pressed her body into Lucky's, to signal: *Daisy's got her!* The Pack's Beta shoved himself awkwardly backward, pushing and grunting, his shoulders straining so hard that Daisy swayed. His foreclaws scrabbled, slipping and sliding against the rock. He gave a last mighty heave, his forepaws almost touching safe ground.

With another yelp, Daisy slipped forward over his face. Rake bit so hard into her leg she gave a muffled squeal. Tiny dangled in midair, helpless and rigid.

Storm let go of Daisy's other hind leg, lunging to grab her by the neck. *Don't let go,* she told herself. *Do not let go . . .* Daisy was strong, but Tiny had grown bigger now—their combined weight made Storm feel like all her teeth were going to be ripped from her jaws.

Together, she and Rake hauled Daisy up, while Lucky tilted his head back and tried frantically to balance her. For long, horrible moments, Storm thought they would all fall forward together.

Then Daisy tumbled abruptly backward onto the level ridge. The little dog lay there, belly heaving, her eyes squeezed shut. Her jaws were still locked tightly on Tiny's scruff.

The five dogs lay as still as corpses, aside from the rise and fall of their flanks as they panted. Storm's heart felt as if it would burst out of her rib cage.

But we got her. We saved Tiny!

Slowly, shaking, Storm got to her paws, nudging the others. Lucky crouched with his forepaws around Tiny, hugging her close as if he never wanted to move again.

Storm followed close behind Lucky, who held Tiny in his jaws. Despite the pain in her leg, her muscles were coiled tight in readiness—she was terrified that her thwarted dream would come true again, only this time, its ending might be far worse.

When they finally hauled themselves up onto the cliff top, three of the adult dogs collapsed, limp, onto the salty grass. Lucky, though, crouched over Tiny, nudging her gently with his nose, licking her all over and checking for wounds.

"Is she all right?" panted Storm.

Lucky didn't answer at first; he was too busy rolling Tiny over gently and nuzzling her belly. He licked her again.

"Yes," he said at last, his voice thick with anger and pity. "Nothing's broken, I don't think. But she has a nasty cut on her flank, and she's badly bruised."

"I'm all right, Father-Dog," whispered Tiny faintly. "Now that you're here."

Lucky pulled her close to his belly and lay down, sheltering her protectively against the fierce, cold wind. All five dogs lay there for a long time, their fur buffeted by the gale; now that she knew Tiny was physically fine, although hurt and scared, Storm could let herself enjoy the rise and fall of her chest, the way the air filled her rib cage. *We're all still breathing, including Tiny. No thanks to Breeze.*

That thought brought her to her paws, her muzzle curling. "We need to get Tiny back to Sweet."

Crouched once more with Tiny between his forepaws, Lucky nodded. He licked his pup's nose and gazed intently into her scared eyes. "Where are your brother and sisters, Tiny? Where did Breeze take them?"

She whimpered, covering her nose with her paws. "I don't

know. I didn't see." Her voice grew fainter with exhaustion. "I'm sorry."

"It's all right," he assured her, nuzzling her again. "It's not your fault."

Daisy was already sniffing thoroughly at the stiff grasses and the moonlit clumps of sea pinks. "There's no trace of Breeze," she growled. "That sly, wicked, vicious—"

"Never mind that just now." Lucky rose and turned to face back the way they'd come, and Storm caught sight of his eyes: There was a glint of cold, deadly fury in them.

"We'll get Tiny to safety," he told them. "And then we'll hunt down Breeze."

"We'll find her," growled Rake.

"Yes. We will." Lucky leaned down to reach for Tiny but paused to meet all their eyes again. "Because I'm going to have a reckoning with that evil dog."

Tiny was weary, barely conscious, and trembling with delayed terror; now that her ordeal was over, she seemed utterly drained and helpless. She was too big now for Lucky to carry her all the way in his jaws. When he stumbled to a halt, worn out, Storm stepped forward.

"Can I—" But one look at Lucky's face told her he did not want any help. He looked as if he never wanted to let go of his pup again.

Storm closed her jaws and nodded in understanding. Together she, Daisy, and Rake nosed and coaxed Tiny onto Lucky's back. The exhausted pup clung on there, one paw hanging on either side of her Father-Dog's shoulders.

That was how they arrived back at camp, emerging from the darkness between the trees into the faint glow of the Moon Dog. Storm was limping badly, and Daisy and Rake hobbled as if their paw pads ached; but Lucky, despite his close calls with the Earth-Dog and the long trek back with the burden of his pup, now looked barely tired at all. That spark of lethal intent glowed in his eyes as he crouched to let Tiny slide down to the grass.

Sweet raced to meet them, howling with joy. "Tiny! My own Tiny!"

Behind Sweet bounded the other dogs of the Wild Pack, as well as the rest of Rake's Pack, their tails wagging furiously. Sunshine collided with Daisy, barking her happiness, as Mickey and Chase and the others spun and leaped and yapped.

"You found Tiny!" yelped Moon.

Sweet skidded to a halt. "But the others," she murmured. "Tumble and Nibble and Fluff . . . Where are they?"

The Pack grew instantly subdued as Tiny shivered against her Mother-Dog's legs. "There was no sign of them?" asked Mickey sadly.

"There was no trail at all," growled Daisy. "Or if there was, it was cunningly covered. Breeze is a clever one, all right."

"Too clever for her own good," snarled Lucky. "But we *will* find them, Sweet, I promise."

Sweet's head drooped for a moment, her grief and fear seeming like fangs biting into the joy she felt at seeing Tiny again. Then she shook herself and began licking the little pup till her fur was damp. Beetle and Chase joined in. Tiny swayed dizzily beneath their eager tongues.

"Come, little one," urged Sweet. "You need rest." She gazed at Lucky, her eyes tormented by a combination of happiness and despair. "You brought one of our pups home, my beloved Beta. And Storm, Daisy, Rake—I'll never be able to thank you enough." She closed her eyes in agony. "We will get the others back from Breeze, too."

"And Breeze will be sorry for what she's done." Sunshine was nuzzling Tiny, running her pink tongue over the pup's head to soothe her. The Pack stood in a circle, watching as the pup relaxed into drowsiness.

"That's right. And soon, she will face justice." Lucky's jaws were clenched. "I'm going back out there to find the others."

"Lucky," said Storm, alarmed, "you can't. You're too tired!"

"It doesn't matter. There's no rest for me while my pups are missing."

"I understand that," said Mickey softly. "I think Storm, Rake, and Daisy should rest, but I'm coming too, Lucky."

"So will Chase and I." Beetle nodded to the scout dog as they both stepped forward together.

Sweet dipped her head, clearly touched. "Thank you, all of you," she murmured. "I'm grateful. But for now, I have to stay with Tiny. She's still scared, and hurt, and I can't leave her."

"Of course you must stay," said Storm, "but I'll go with Lucky too."

"Absolutely not!" barked Lucky sharply. "Not only are you exhausted, you've injured your leg. You have to rest, Storm—we need you to be fit and strong."

"I agree." Sweet nodded. "You've done more than enough tonight, Storm."

"But—"

"I am no longer your Alpha," Sweet told her gently, "but I would be grateful if you would stay here to guard the camp—and Tiny."

Storm gazed at the Wild Pack Alpha, her heart swelling. How good a sentry she would be with her wounded leg, she did not know—but she knew that she would lay down her life for the little pup, and Sweet knew it, too. *She's telling me she has faith in me. And that she needs me.* It felt so good, to be trusted once more to protect the Pack.

"Then of course I will stay," she told Sweet softly.

"The rest of us will prepare to continue the search tomorrow," said Moon, stepping forward. "We will take turns, sending out search parties as often as we send out patrols."

Lucky nodded to Mickey, Chase, and Beetle. "The five of us should go now."

Without another word he bounded from the clearing, and Storm's heart turned over as she watched the other four follow him. Lucky was so tired, only his fear and anger were keeping him going. *Please be safe, Lucky.*

Woody, Rake, and Dart exchanged glances as quiet fell over the glade. Woody cleared his throat and turned to Sweet, but it was Rake who spoke.

"We have a proposal," he said hesitantly. "The pups are every dog's priority, and our Pack would like to stay, until Breeze and the pups are found, or for as long as we can be useful to you."

Sweet looked up from Tiny and dipped her head in recognition. "We would be grateful for it," she said. "It's very generous of you."

Rake nodded. "But tonight, we rest. And my Pack and I— we'd like to take some time to hold a ceremony for Ruff."

"We need to say a proper farewell to her," added Dart, dipping her muzzle. "We buried her just before we left with our search parties, but it was too quick. She needs to be properly sent on her journey to the Earth-Dog."

"And if you'd like to," murmured Woody, "you are all welcome to join in. She once belonged here, and you were her Packmates."

"Of course we will," said Sweet, nodding at all three of them. "She was one of us. And Lucky and I owe your Pack so much."

"We'd be happy to honor Ruff," said Twitch, and other Wild Pack dogs rumbled their agreement. "And even though we live in separate Packs now, I think we share a bond that crosses borders."

"Then I will speak of Ruff," said Rake formally, sitting back on his haunches as the circle of dogs drew tighter. Storm settled onto her belly beside Sweet and pricked her ears to listen. "I was her Alpha, and she showed me loyalty and trust. There was a time when she lived her life cowed by the threat of the Fear-Dog. It took courage to turn from him, and even more to defy the poisonous hate of the mad dog Terror who ruled us."

"She fought battles with honor," said Mickey quietly, tapping his tail. "She was small, but fierce."

"I remember once when I was sick," spoke up Woody, "Ruff brought me cool water and licked the wound that had given me fever. She was kind."

"There was a time," Twitch declared, "when I lived with Terror's Pack—I injured one of my remaining legs, badly. Terror would have left me to look after myself, to live or die as the Fear-Dog saw fit. But Ruff secretly tended me, and she brought me food against his command. She fought against her own fears to do it, and that is true bravery."

As dog after dog spoke of their memories of Ruff, and the Moon-Dog rose above the trees, Storm remained silent. She didn't trust herself to speak calmly; a coil of bitterness was tightening in her gut. *Ruff was afraid to talk to me about Terror's Pack, even after Terror was dead. That was how much he scared her! But Twitch is right: She had the courage to walk away from Terror's insane Pack and make a new life.*

She endured all that. She fought for a new future, a new Pack, free from fear and tyranny.

And Breeze killed her anyway.

The voices around her were growing quieter now, the dogs falling silent as they finished their stories of Ruff. When the last Pack member had spoken, and the dogs sat quiet and thoughtful, Storm still hadn't spoken. And she wouldn't. She would pay tribute to Ruff in her own way.

Breeze was a poison, thought Storm. That soft-eyed, wicked dog had infected the Wild Pack with Terror's hatred, causing chaos and horror and death in the name of her former Alpha.

We will find Breeze, and she'll pay for what she's done. That's how I will honor Ruff.

I vow it to the Sky-Dogs and the Forest-Dog.

None of the dogs left in the camp slept soundly; Storm knew this because she spent a fitful, restless night herself. She would wake to the hoot of an owl, and hear murmurs, whines, the crunch and rustle of bedding beneath bodies that just could not relax. It was strange for her to be sleeping freely with the Pack once more—rather than as a prisoner—but she knew that was the least cause of her wakefulness; like the others, she suspected, it was stinging, buzzing anxiety that kept her wriggling and squirming in the hunters' den beneath the Moon-Dog's light.

Dawn did not bring any reassurance. Lucky's search party had not returned, and the Pack's fear for the pups had swelled to a palpable, constant tension. Even the Sun-Dog's morning rays felt too bright and hard through the branches.

Wriggling out of the den, blinking away her weariness, Storm tested her foreleg, pressing it to the ground. It felt weaker than usual, but the pain had faded a little. *There's nothing broken, thank the Sky-Dogs; I only wrenched it badly.* She had hoped she would be well enough recovered to join one of the search parties today. *I have to!*

Snap was rolling in a pile of leaves, her legs waving in the air, but as she saw Storm approach, she jumped to her paws. "Your leg looks better."

"It is," growled Storm. "I'll be back out to join the search very soon."

"Me too. I can't wait to go after Breeze," Snap went on as Daisy and Moon padded up to them. "I wonder what she's done with the other pups? Trapped them somewhere, like she did with Tiny? It would be terrifying if they were lost in some dark forest.

I just hope Breeze hasn't found another cliff—or drowned them in the river, or—"

"Hush!" snapped Storm, pricking her ears and twisting her head to scan the glade. "Sweet might hear you."

"Yes, Snap," agreed Daisy, scratching her ear. "Don't say those things. Please?"

"We mustn't think the worst," said Moon grimly. She stretched, clawing the grass. "Oh, I can only hope they're all right. Worry for your pups is the worst fear of all."

"How's Thorn?" asked Storm, grateful for a change of subject.

Moon's ears drooped. "She's in less pain, I think. She was able to eat the food I brought her this morning. But that leg . . . it's terrible, Storm."

"Just make sure you keep the wound clean," warned Sunshine, sitting down beside them. The little Omega looked tired, and Storm licked her floppy ears.

"Did Tiny sleep, do you know?" she asked.

"Sweet says she had a bad night," sighed Sunshine, "which isn't surprising. The poor little thing, she must have been petrified." She exposed her tiny fangs and snarled. "Why, if I get my claws into Breeze—"

"Wait," said Storm quickly. "Here they come now."

Sweet was emerging from her den, shepherding Tiny, who could barely detach herself from her mother's side. Both pup and Mother-Dog looked exhausted, and Tiny's eyes were still haunted with terror. Sweet bent to lick her comfortingly.

Squirming from his den and stretching his single foreleg, Twitch limped to the center of the clearing and raised his head. "Pack," he called. "Sweet has asked me to organize more search parties. It's time to continue the hunt."

Eagerly Storm and her companions trotted toward him, as the rest of the Pack gathered. They sat down around him, heads tilted and ears pricked expectantly.

"Sweet must stay here, to take care of Tiny," said Third Dog, gazing around at them all.

All the dogs nodded. "Of course," yapped Sunshine. "And I'll look after them both, don't worry."

"I know you will, Sunshine." Twitch gave her a grateful wag of his tail. "But I also want a separate hunting patrol to go out and bring back prey."

"I can do that," said Rake. "I've had my rest. Woody, will you come?"

"Gladly," growled Woody.

"Thank you." Twitch dipped his head in thanks. "Both our

Packs will need to be well fed. It's important we're strong for the search—and to face the bad dog when we find her."

When we find her. Storm liked that. There was no *if.*

Rake and Woody had barely vanished into the forest when the undergrowth rustled and cracked again. Every dog turned, tails thumping the earth.

The dogs that slouched into the glade looked weary, their fur matted and tangled with scraps of leaf and twig. But their leader trotted forward briskly as if he still had enough energy for all of them, his golden tail held high, his dark eyes sunken but bright with undying determination.

"Lucky!" Twitch greeted him as every dog rose to their paws and barked a welcome. "Did you find anything?"

Sweet hadn't left Tiny's side, but she was staring at her mate, her ears pricked high with fearful hope.

"We searched all night," growled Lucky, "but we didn't find a single trace of their scent. That's why we'll be going back out there. Soon."

Sweet's ears drooped, and she moved protectively closer to Tiny.

Storm's heart plummeted. Lucky's fierce certainty, she knew, must cover an awful fear—but how long could he keep it up?

He had barely eaten; he must be running on nothing but defiant anger. His patrol looked exhausted, hobbling into camp on unsteady paws that, Storm could tell, had to be aching terribly.

Lucky can't keep this up forever. It isn't possible. And what if we never find the pups—what then? She couldn't bear to imagine the grief of Lucky and Sweet.

No, she couldn't even think that. *We will find Nibble, Fluff, and Tumble, we* will.

The trouble was, Storm thought as her heart ached, that it was getting harder to believe. And the Sun-Dog ran a shorter course with every passing day; soon, the chill of late Red Leaf would blast the landscape, harden the earth and freeze its scents.

For a moment there was silence in the glade, as the returning patrol stood with their heads hanging. Twitch blinked sadly at Lucky; Sunshine lay down with her paws covering her nose. Moon closed her blue eyes and edged closer to Beetle. Lucky simply stood there, his jaw clenched, and Storm thought she saw his legs shaking.

Then a high, scratchy whimper broke the silence, one that no dog had expected. Tiny crawled out from between her Mother-Dog's paws, her tail tucked against her rump, and crept forward. Her small face looked miserable, but she sat down before her

Father-Dog and gazed up mournfully into his eyes.

"Tiny?" asked Lucky gently. "Don't you want to rest more?"

"No, Father-Dog. I want to tell you," she said, her voice small and trembling in the dawn quietness. "I want to tell you what happened."

CHAPTER NINE

"*Breeze said we were going on* an adventure," Tiny began, her eyes downcast. "I didn't believe her, but Nibble, Fluff, and Tumble were so excited. I tried to tell them not to go, but . . . but Breeze would have heard me."

Twitch growled. "That sneaky, conniving . . ." He let out a huff, as if he couldn't find the words. Then he barked, "Bad dog!" His voice was so loud, the gathered Packmates flinched as one. Then Twitch dipped his head to give Tiny a reassuring lick. "None of this is your fault, little one."

"I tried to tell them without speaking," whimpered Tiny. "But they just thought I was playing at being scared of the dark. I *knew* something was wrong. I wanted to bark at my littermates and tell them we needed to run. But Breeze is a big grown dog, so . . ."

"You didn't think you could outrun her," Storm said softly.

"That's completely understandable." She felt her heart turn over with pity for the little pup. Tiny looked so lonely and frightened without her litter-siblings; her shoulders sagged and her tail was tucked so tightly against her rump, it quivered. She must still be sore and exhausted, but she had the courage to come out and tell all these adult dogs what she knew.

"I'd been getting a little nervous around Breeze lately," Tiny went on. "She always wanted to be with us, taking us away from Mother-Dog. And she said horrible things about you, Storm. What she said—it didn't feel right, it felt like lies." She licked her jaws anxiously. "Nibble and Fluff and Tumble . . . they always said I was imagining it. But I knew I wasn't. I couldn't let them go without me. So I went along too."

Sunshine shook her head. "Breeze took advantage of your littermates' youth," she growled.

Storm nodded, her jaws clenched. The other dogs rumbled their angry agreement.

"Tell us what happened when she took you away, little one," said Twitch gently. He was so good at coaxing the story from the pup, thought Storm: gentle and encouraging.

"She led us through the forest," Tiny went on, her ears drooping. "We walked such a long way, and we all got very tired, but

Breeze didn't let us stop, not till we were far from camp. I don't know how far. I'm sorry, Mother-Dog."

Sweet lay down against Tiny and caressed her head with her tongue. "Listen to all these grown dogs," she told her pup softly. "You're not to blame, and neither are Fluff or Nibble or Tumble. You were doing what you were told, and trying to be good dogs. What happened next?"

Tiny swallowed hard. "Breeze let us rest, in a hollow under a tree. But I couldn't sleep very well, and she woke me up anyway. She told me to come away from the others, and to follow her. I knew it was wrong, I knew she was doing something bad, and I . . . Mother-Dog, I was scared. So after a little while, I ran away from her."

"You have good instincts, young one," said Mickey.

"But she was so fast!" Tiny blinked at him. "I didn't know Breeze could run like that. And she was so different now, too— like she wasn't Breeze at *all*. She always acted so nice before, but she growled and chased me and caught me."

Dart exchanged a grim look with Chase. "Breeze is good at pretending she's something she isn't."

Tiny's body trembled as she retold the story of her terrify-ing day. "She picked me up in her mouth and she carried me to that cliff. I didn't know she was so strong, I thought she was a *gentle* dog."

"I think Breeze is stronger than she looks," murmured Storm. "She hid a lot about herself, Tiny. You're not the only Packmate who didn't see it."

Tiny gave her a grateful wag of her tail. "She wasn't gentle *at all* anymore. She was bumping me against trees and rocks. And sometimes she'd drag me along the grass."

"The scent trail!" growled Daisy, her tail lashing with agitation. "Breeze did that deliberately. Storm was right—it was too obvious."

"And when she got to the cliff," mumbled Tiny, "she dropped me on the grass and she started barking at me. She talked about a big monster called the Fear-Dog that was going to come and get us all, and she said Storm and my Father-Dog would pay for what they'd done. And she said the Pack would soon find my body, right there, and then you'd know it was time for the Fear-Dog to punish all of us." Tiny's voice faded to a high, fearful whimper.

Sweet pulled her between her paws and licked her feverishly. "You're safe, Tiny. You're safe."

Storm stared at the little dog, her gut clenching. How could Breeze have done this to a small, helpless pup? She bit back her rage, forcing stillness into her shaking muscles.

At last Tiny's breathing calmed again. "I thought maybe she didn't mean it, Mother-Dog, but then she suddenly barked that she was going to . . . to . . ."

"It's all right, Tiny," Sweet murmured. "You're safe. You can tell us."

"She said, 'I'll tear out your throat!' And she jumped at me *really fast*." Tiny crouched back, her eyes shut tight with the horror of the memory. "I jumped away from her and I thought I was going to fall, but I couldn't let her t-tear my throat out so I just—I just—I let myself fall . . . over the cliff."

"You poor little thing!" Sunshine whimpered. Storm gave a snarl of angry distress.

"And I hit that ledge and stopped, and it hurt—a lot—but I knew I couldn't cry. I just lay very still and quiet and shut my eyes. I listened for ages, and didn't hear anything. Then I heard Breeze make a noise and walk away, so she must have thought I was dead."

"My clever, clever pup," said Sweet, nuzzling her.

"That was wise, Tiny," growled Moon.

Tiny blinked gratefully at her Mother-Dog and the black-and-white dog. "I told myself not to move, in case she came back—but she didn't." She swallowed hard. "I looked around and I tried to get down, but it was so high. And when I tried to stand up, it really hurt, and the Wind-Dogs nearly blew me over. . . . I was *so scared*."

"The Wind-Dogs didn't mean to scare you, Tiny, I know it." Sweet nuzzled her.

"They're just boisterous," Storm soothed, her ears flicking in agitation at the thought of the poor terrified pup, alone on the cliff. "They didn't know how frightened you were."

"I *was* scared, Storm, so scared, but I was cold and tired too and I fell asleep." Tiny laid her head on her paws. "And after that, I kept on falling asleep and waking up again. I don't remember much, but I had funny dreams. Sometimes I thought there was another pup next to me, and I thought it was Tumble, and I was so scared Breeze had dropped him over too." She gazed up at the alarmed Sweet with wide eyes. "But it wasn't Tumble, Mother-Dog, I'm sure it wasn't."

Lucky had risen to his paws. "Are you sure, Tiny? Are you *sure*?"

She shook her head quickly. "The pup was too little, Father-Dog. And it wasn't a litter-brother at all. I think it was just a pile of sand, but it made me feel better. Sometimes I squeezed my eyes a bit and it really did look like a real pup. I would cuddle up with her and I felt warm and safe. Like I had a sister-pup with me."

Her. Storm stared at Tiny, her throat tightening. *A sister-pup.* Neither of Tiny's litter-sisters had pale gold fur like Tumble's. A rippling chill raced through her hide.

This was like hearing Bella's pups, Nip and Scramble, talk about the litter-sister they'd never known. Tufty had died just before she'd been born, but Nip and Scramble had never forgotten their tiny litter-sister. They would actually *talk* to her. They wouldn't hear of any suggestion that Tufty might not have been there—and Storm had found them unnervingly convincing.

Tiny is kin to Nip and Scramble. And to Tufty . . .

It made the fur on Storm's neck stand up, but at the same time it gave her a strange sense of hope. She'd almost opened her jaws to say so when Lucky's urgent voice broke into her thoughts.

"So when she took you away, Breeze still had Fluff, Nibble, and Tumble," growled Lucky. "But she left them asleep, Tiny?"

"I think so." Tiny's eyelids were drooping with exhaustion.

"Then they might have escaped," Lucky said, his voice breaking with desperate hope. Storm's heart ached for him. "But if so, they haven't found their way home yet. They're still in terrible danger."

"I think they still trust Breeze," whimpered Tiny. "They weren't suspicious, like me."

"That cunning coward," growled Lucky, but quietly enough that Tiny wouldn't hear him. "Tiny, I think you need to get some rest again. You've done so well. I'm proud of you."

Shuddering tremors jolted through Storm's body. Tiny's story had brought back a memory she'd longed to bury like an old bone: the time Blade had taken her and her two brothers away from the Wild Pack. Blade had turned on little Wiggle, killing him with a single snap and shake of her jaws, and then she'd tried to kill Storm too. Storm could remember the helpless terror of those moments, and she hated Breeze with all her heart for putting Tiny through it, too.

Sunshine padded over to Tiny and nuzzled her flank. The pup, her eyes closed now, gave a feeble whine.

"Her sides seem very sensitive. I'm worried she might have broken some bones in her rib cage," Sunshine told Sweet softly. "They'll get better, but she'll be so sore. She'll need lots of sleep and care."

"And she'll get all of that," murmured Sweet.

Daisy was staring at the pup. "It's obvious just how malicious Breeze was," she growled quietly. "That business with leaving a trail—she *wanted* us to find Tiny's body. She wanted us to feel that grief! There's such a depth of hatred in her." Daisy gritted her teeth. "We have to find those other pups, and soon."

"You're right. There's not a moment to lose." Lucky's muzzle curled.

But before they could gather the next search party, there was a rustle in the depths of the forest, and the sound of careful paw-steps. And then, as every dog turned with ears pricked high, there came the high yap of a pup.

Sweet and Lucky bolted for the edge of the clearing, barking with excitement—but Storm's heart twisted. The rest of the Pack were on their paws too, standing quite still, and they clearly knew what Storm knew—that the yelp didn't come from one of Alpha and Beta's pups. Every member of the Wild Pack knew the pups' voices, just as their parents did.

Poor Sweet and Lucky, thought Storm with a pang of pity. The two parent-dogs were so desperate, they must have hoped against hope.

Sure enough, Alpha and her Beta stopped at the border of the forest, their tails drooping a little. Lucky's tail had stilled, but it began to wag again, slowly, as two dogs and two pups appeared from the shadows.

"Bella?" he barked.

His litter-sister's golden shape emerged from the trees,

followed by the slender, darker form of her mate, Arrow. They trotted into the glade, their pups Nip and Scramble running between them.

"Storm!" Bella yelped, her tail wagging wildly with relief. "You're all right!"

The Wild Pack loped forward as Bella and Arrow greeted Storm with licks and fond yaps. Lucky was gazing at his sister in delight, and when she turned to him, he licked her face and jaw in enthusiastic welcome.

"Bella, I can't believe it's you," he barked. "And these are your pups?"

Sweet crouched to nuzzle the two little dogs, her expression a combination of affection, sadness, and longing. "They're very beautiful. Congratulations, Bella and Arrow."

"This is Nip, and this is Scramble," Arrow introduced the pups, his eyes guarded.

"They're fine, strong dogs." Lucky nodded to him respectfully.

The whole Pack was fussing over the pups now, with Daisy and Sunshine especially giving them excited nudges and licks. Storm was so happy to see the little ones, she had to swallow down her urge to put herself between the older dogs and the pups, saving all the affection for herself. She had missed them so much!

But her eagerness to fuss over Nip and Scramble was tempered when she saw Tiny limping over to meet her new kin. The two half-Fierce pups stood still, their heads tilting to one side, as if confused by a dog almost as small as them. *Of course,* Storm thought, a lump forming in her throat. *It must be strange for them, seeing a pup when they've only known grown dogs up until now. The only pups they've known are each other . . . and their litter-sister, Tufty, but she was just in their imagination. Wasn't she?*

Now the three pups bumped their noses together, pink tongues exploring one another's faces with curiosity and excitement.

Nip made an experimental leap, yapping as he butted Tiny's shoulder, and Storm hurried to press her body between them. "Careful, Nip. Tiny's been injured. You can play with her, but be gentle."

Nip and Scramble both gazed up at her solemnly. "We understand," they chorused. But it didn't stop them nuzzling Tiny—more cautiously this time—and squeaking with excitement.

Storm glanced at Lucky and Sweet. They were watching the pups in silence, their eyes dark with emotion. It wasn't just the reminder of their own missing pups, Storm knew: *They're thinking the same thing I am. These three pups don't have to be told that they share blood, that they're family—they already sense it.*

Tiny drew back suddenly from Nip and Scramble, glancing to either side. She tilted her head, and one ear flicked back, as if she was listening to another dog. Her little face creased with confusion as she peered around to search for it. Then she yipped softly and licked something that wasn't there.

Storm felt her fur prickle. *Was she . . . ?*

"Bella, Arrow." Lucky's voice broke into Storm's thoughts. She saw the golden-furred Beta gazing from his litter-sister to her mate. "It's so good to see you both, and we're thrilled to meet your pups." He took a breath. "But why have you come?"

Bella nodded toward Storm, her eyes soft. "We wanted to make sure Storm was all right. We promised to come and look for her if she wasn't back within ten journeys of the Sun-Dog."

Storm touched her muzzle affectionately. "You did say that, Bella. And you kept your promise. Thank you."

"We were worried," Arrow told Lucky, fixing him with his gaze. "We were afraid she had run into trouble—or that she'd been mistreated by the Wild Pack."

A guilty silence fell at his words. Moon sat back and scratched at her ear. Mickey coughed, and Daisy shot a look at Sweet. Sunshine simply tilted her head contentedly and stared up at the sky, her tail plumed high, as if she had no need for words.

Lucky cleared his throat. "Arrow. Bella. The bad news is, we did treat Storm badly." He turned to Storm, his tail drooping, and nodded in silent apology. "We found her confronting Breeze, and Breeze convinced us Storm had attacked her. I think you can guess that Breeze was lying. But, unfortunately, we were foolish enough to believe her."

"And because of that misjudgment," said Sweet quietly, "Lucky and I have lost our pups. Breeze has stolen them away—which is exactly what Storm was trying to warn us about."

Bella gave a yelp of horror, and Arrow stiffened, pricking his ears. "She took your *pups?*" he gasped.

"We found Tiny," said Sweet. "Lucky, Storm, Rake, and Daisy rescued her. But the other three—" She gulped. "Fluff, Nibble, and Tumble are still missing."

"How could she—how could *any* dog do something so wicked?" cried Bella. "Oh, poor things. We'll help you search for them, Lucky."

"Just think," said Arrow, his voice level and hard. "If you'd listened to Storm, it would never have happened."

Bella gazed from Lucky to Sweet, then back at her brother. "Storm was never anything but loyal to this Pack," she told him quietly. "How could you believe Breeze's word over hers?"

"I know how," said Arrow, before a stricken Lucky could respond. "It's because Storm's a Fierce Dog like me. Because she was born a type that you believe is not to be trusted."

"Yet Fierce Dogs," added Bella, "are some of the most faithful dogs you'll ever meet."

There was silence. Lucky stared at the ground, and Sweet closed her eyes as if she was in pain.

A defensive growl came from the fidgeting ranks of the Wild Pack. "Maybe Storm didn't do the things we accused her of," mumbled Chase, "but we still don't know for sure about Arrow."

"Exactly," put in Dart, tipping up her muzzle. "You were one of Blade's Pack, Arrow, and it looks now as if you've been lurking near our territory, so you might have had something to do—"

"What?" Storm gasped.

But she didn't have time to tell them what she thought. Lucky sprang forward, as if to physically defend Storm and Arrow, and stretched his jaws wide in a snarl at Chase and Dart.

"You fools!" he barked. "After all that's happened, you're still trying to pin the blame on Fierce Dogs?"

Sweet strode to his side, facing the two smaller dogs down. "Have you learned *nothing*?" she growled. "Breeze looked like the kindest, gentlest dog who ever walked above the Earth-Dog's den.

Didn't she? Why do you think I let her care for my pups? And yet look what she did! How *dare* you blame Arrow!"

"Dart, you should be ashamed of what you just said!" howled Rake furiously.

In the stunned stillness, Chase sank her shoulders low to the ground, and Dart shrank back and sat down hard on her haunches. They both peered up at Lucky and Sweet, eyes wide and scared, tails pinned close to their rumps.

"I . . . I'm sorry," Dart whimpered.

"So am I," whined Chase. "It was a stupid thing to say, Alpha. We should have thought."

They both cowered so low, they looked as if they wanted to sink into the grass and meet the Earth-Dog—*and even the grimmest Spirit Dog couldn't be more scary than Sweet and Lucky right now,* thought Storm.

"Storm. Arrow." Lucky turned to face them both, and Sweet joined him.

Storm shot an uncertain glance at Arrow. He tilted his head quizzically.

"This Pack has something to say to you both, in the sight of the Forest-Dog and the Sky-Dogs," said Lucky. His voice was clear and loud, and not a single member of the Wild Pack stirred;

they barely seemed to dare to breathe.

"What my Beta says is true," said Sweet. "We all need to say it. This Pack has not behaved as it should toward good Packmates. We have mistrusted you both, Storm and Arrow, and misjudged you; even when you proved your loyalty, we did not return it. Faithfulness goes two ways, my friends. You gave it to the Wild Pack. But when we were tested, we failed you both."

Storm couldn't speak. Her throat felt constricted, her heart full of emotions: relief, joy, pure vindication. With a glance at Arrow, she saw that he looked equally stunned and gratified.

"As a Pack," declared Lucky, nodding to the dogs behind him, "we will offer you our full and formal apology. And we ask for your forgiveness."

Storm's heart missed a beat. She expected hesitation, or even argument, but every dog of the Wild Pack, its Alpha and Beta included, lowered their heads at once. Tails wagged slowly, beseechingly, and voices rose from every dog.

"We're sorry," barked Daisy first, clear and strong.

"Forgive us," growled Mickey. "We should have known you better."

"I should have trusted you," said Moon. "We all should."

"Yes," mumbled Beetle, his eyes lowered. "And I speak for my litter-sister too. We both apologize."

"I'm sorry," whined Snap. "For all the vicious things I said about Fierce Dogs."

Sunshine padded forward, gazing up at Storm with her bright black eyes. "And I," she whined, "knew you were right all along. I should have fought harder for you."

"Oh, Sunshine." Storm's voice was choked. "You never lost faith in me. *Thank you.*"

The stillness that followed might have been awkward, had not Woody and Rake padded out of the trees at just that moment. Woody bore two rabbits in his jaws, Rake a jumbled mouthful of rats. Eyeing Bella and Arrow and their pups with surprise, the two dogs trotted forward and laid the prey down in the center of the clearing.

Woody gave himself a vigorous shake, and Rake extended his forepaws, stretching.

"Well done," said Twitch. "You've both had a long night."

"That's because we had to go farther than we intended," growled Woody.

"We did." Rake nodded. "The bad news is, that new longpaw settlement has grown even bigger. Their loudcages are eating into the forest itself."

The Wild Pack pricked their ears, horrified, and wagging tails went still.

Woody hunched his shoulders. "All the large prey is being scared off. The rabbits are still around their warren—the one that hasn't been dug up, anyway—but deer, squirrels, even weasels: they're all gone, or leaving."

Mickey swallowed hard and stared down at the prey haul. Lucky paced around it, his brow creased in thought.

"This is not good," said Sweet. "But let's worry about it when we have the pups back."

It wasn't good? That was an understatement: It was unnervingly bad news. Storm licked her chops anxiously, but she remained silent.

Even if we can find the pups and bring them home, the Wild Pack may not be able to keep this territory for much longer. Where would they go?

But, as Sweet had said, that was a problem that could wait for another day. First the Pack had to bring back the pups from Breeze's malevolent clutches.

If they failed in that attempt, only then would it be time to lose hope.

CHAPTER TEN

"Sit down, Storm!" Sweet's horrified cry made her jump. "You still need to rest that leg!"

The movement sent a sharp and alarming twinge from Storm's knee to her shoulder, but it subsided quickly to a dull throb. She breathed out in relief. It had been a full night and day since Tiny had told her story and the next search party had set off, without Storm; the last thing she wanted was to aggravate her injury and be out of action for even longer. Storm rolled her eyes and turned to the concerned swift-dog.

"It's fine, Sweet. Truly. I can put more weight on it than I could yesterday."

"And *you,* Sweet, need to treat Storm with more respect," growled Bella. She padded across the clearing, the dying rays of the Sun-Dog glowing golden on her coat. "Remember—Storm and Arrow and I aren't part of your Pack anymore, and you're not our Alpha. We're not helping out of duty or loyalty—we're doing it because we *want* to."

Pinning her ears back, Sweet swallowed and took an awkward step away. "I'm—sorry, Bella. I didn't mean to be rude." Defensively she tilted up her head. "But I just wanted to make sure Storm doesn't hurt herself. She might try to do too much too soon. . . ."

"Honestly, it's fine," Storm interjected quickly. "Really, I feel much better. I'll go out with the search parties tomorrow."

"Thank you, Storm," said Bella, with a rather pointed glance at Sweet. Then she sighed. "We've searched every tree and field and burrow in the territory, but we couldn't find a trace of those pups."

Sweet's ears drooped. "I know. Lucky told me. Uh . . . thank you for trying, Bella. I know you didn't have to do this."

Bella gave a brief nod. Both she and Sweet looked very awkward, thought Storm. Sweet looked quite taken aback at Bella's scolding, almost as if she'd forgotten she wasn't Storm's Alpha anymore. And Bella herself suddenly looked unsure, as if being back in Sweet's territory made Storm's status and allegiances a little unclear.

Lying down with her head on her forepaws, Storm considered

the odd situation. It *was* strange to imagine being out of the Wild Pack for good. These dogs had raised her from a tiny pup; they'd given her a home and a future when she had none. After her Mother-Dog's death, she and her brothers might have died too in that cold, dark space under the doghouse, had Lucky and Mickey not found them. The Wild Pack had been her home for as long as she could remember.

Yet after her exile, when she'd found Arrow and Bella and become part of their little family, she'd felt completely at home. She'd felt secure, and best of all, happy—there was no dog to glance at her with suspicion, no dog to mutter behind her back or jump up in alarm when she unexpectedly appeared at their side. With Bella and Arrow, she was welcome and trusted, and Storm felt more a true member of their Pack than she ever had of this one.

Bella is my Alpha now.

Still, it was hard to think of three adult dogs and two tiny pups as a Pack! They'd been lucky so far—they had come across no enemy or hostile Pack that they couldn't deal with—but their luck surely could not continue forever.

Another search party was straggling back into the clearing, their tails low and their heads hanging in disappointment.

"Nothing," said Dart, nodding to Sweet. "I'm sorry."

But she and Woody, though respectful to the Wild Pack's Alpha, trudged on past her to join Rake. Storm couldn't hear what they said to their own Alpha, but they muttered deferentially, and Rake cocked his head to listen solemnly to their report.

They're a separate Pack, too, thought Storm. *How can this last?* Three Alphas in one place, even with a shared goal, was bound to end in conflict. It was only the hunt for the pups that was keeping the peace—for now.

Even the slanting, dark gold rays of evening had faded now, and a dusky twilight was settling over the forest. Sweet padded to the center of the glade, and Storm noticed that her paws were trembling. The swift-dog's eyes looked as if they had sunk into her skull, and her ribs were even more prominent than usual beneath her dull coat. *How long can she endure this much fear and stress?* Storm wondered, pity tightening her throat.

The Sun-Dog might be lingering, reluctant to end the long summer, but his journeys would soon be shorter, Storm knew. The remaining leaves would redden and fall, and what if they hadn't found the pups by then? *Poor Sweet. Poor Lucky.*

"Wild Pack, Rake's Pack, Bella's Pack," Sweet called carefully. "We should eat now. The hunting party has brought more prey while the rest of you searched for my pups, but what Woody and

Rake told us last night is true: The creatures of the forests and meadows are being driven away by the longpaws and their loud-cages. I know how hungry you must be after your long search, but I'm afraid we should all eat sparingly tonight." Her head droop-ing, Sweet stepped back as the dogs gathered tiredly around her. "Bella and Rake will eat after me, and before my Beta. Woody and Arrow, the Betas of their Packs, will eat directly after Lucky."

Storm managed not to gasp. What an extraordinary conces-sion for Sweet to make—and proof that despite her agonizing anxiety, she was trying to treat the three Packs gathered in this glade with equal respect. Bella looked at Sweet with wide, grateful eyes. It must have been strange for her to see Rake now the Alpha of his own Pack, too, but she bowed her head in a nod to him now, and he returned it politely.

All the same, Storm thought, it wasn't entirely certain that Sweet's Pack appreciated their Alpha's kind gesture. Chase exchanged a resentful glance with Beetle, Snap frowned, and even Mickey raised his brow in surprise. But for now, no dog barked an objection.

Sweet approached the prey pile cautiously, examining it as if she was judging exactly how much food was available for each dog. At last she stretched out her slender head and withdrew a single small rat; she carried it back to her position and nodded to Bella. *Sweet must be starving,* thought Storm. *But she's ignoring her own hunger to make sure the searchers get enough to eat.* A renewed respect for her former Alpha warmed her blood.

As soon as Bella had picked up a small rabbit and returned to her place in the circle, Nip and Scramble dashed over to her, yapping in excitement. Nip almost tripped over Arrow's paws in his eagerness, and Scramble bumped into Daisy's rump and fell over. But the pup sprang instantly back to his feet.

"Oops!" he yapped, and bounded away to collide with his litter-brother in a tumble of fur.

Daisy was laughing, and Storm saw that all the dogs, of every Pack, were watching the pups with fond amusement. *All the grown dogs like these pups, despite them having a Fierce Dog father! Maybe there's hope for an end to their prejudices,* thought Storm with amusement. Even peevish Dart was grinning at the pair's clumsy antics, her tongue lolling.

Storm had to wait a little while for her turn at the prey pile, but after Sweet's humble and generous gesture, she didn't mind. When she finally made her way to the food, she nosed around what was left to find a thin squirrel; as she carried it back to her place in the circle, Nip and Scramble bounced over to join her, panting with enthusiasm. Scramble crawled up onto her shoulders and peered down at the squirrel, as if he wanted to study every bite Storm took.

"That looks nice," he yapped. "It's small but it looks nice. I think I like squirrels the best of all the prey."

Storm coughed a laugh through a mouthful of flesh. "Well, I hate to say it, but squirrels won't think much of *you*."

"But we'll be nice to them!" declared Nip, his nose and whiskers held high. "We'll *explain*. I'll say, 'I'm sorry, squirrel, but I'm going to eat you.'"

"And we'll be so polite, the squirrel won't mind *at all*," giggled Scramble.

"You know, I almost believe you," growled Storm.

"Will you play with us after you've eaten?" begged Nip.

"Please, Storm." Scramble hung down over her ear and peered into her left eye.

"You both need to sleep!" yelped Storm. "Honestly, pups, I'm tired, and I have to join the search tomorrow." She hesitated, then said tentatively, "Do you still play with Tufty? Is she . . . around at the moment?"

She'd been afraid the question would upset them—had they already grown up enough to know that Tufty was really gone forever?—but she needn't have worried. Nip shook his head firmly.

"Oh, no, Tufty isn't here just now. She's too busy." He gave Storm a very serious look. "But we don't mind. We know she has an important job. She's helping the little lost pups."

That's a little creepy, thought Storm. *But it also seems kind of . . . sweet.* Whichever it was, that familiar chill rippled through her hide. Storm glanced nervously around the glade, but no other dog seemed to have heard the exchange. *I don't want the Wild Pack to think these pups are a little bit delusional. . . .*

Her instincts prickled. Storm hoped Nip and Scramble *were* just imagining their lost sister.

But if Tufty really was watching over her brothers and her other small kin . . . ?

Deep down, Storm found that thought eerily reassuring.

Her dreams that night were vague, misty, elusive; as soon as Storm found herself in a solid landscape it would wobble, fray, and dissolve before her eyes. Figures bounded at the very edge of her vision, just out of sight or clear recognition. If she turned to bark a greeting to a familiar, sturdy dog, she would see only a tree stump, or a branch, or a yellow rock by the Endless Lake. Nervous tremors ran constantly through her paws, and the ground beneath them seemed shifty and translucent. She hovered and veered between dreams and wakefulness, like a bird caught on a capricious wind.

Then, abruptly, there was a clear face before her, slender and gray and full of concern. At once the dream enveloped her properly, and the half-awake world of her den vanished.

"Whisper!" she cried joyfully.

He reached for her with his trembling nose, straining and just failing to touch hers. His jaws opened, but Storm couldn't hear the words he spoke. His voice was drowned out by the yelping, desperate cries of pups.

The pups! Where were they? Tensing, Storm strained her head forward and cocked her ears. She turned abruptly, twisting to home in on the source of those wails. But whenever she thought she'd located them at last, they would drift away, fading; then the eerie voices would start up again from another direction. It was impossible! And Whisper was still speaking to her. . . .

"Whisper, I can't hear you! What are you trying to tell me?" Desperately she craned her ears toward him, and Whisper seemed to summon his energy to bark louder, but still Storm could hear nothing. The elusive wailing of the pups was just too loud, blotting out every other sound.

Jumping back, Storm glanced right and left. She was sure she'd seen a shadow—there, at the very edge of her vision! But it was gone like mist.

"Whisper, did you see that?" But he didn't seem to hear her, any more than

she could make out his words; the gray dog went on speaking, straining forward, his eyes full of urgency.

"Is it the Fear-Dog?" whispered Storm, half to herself and half to Whisper. "Is it him, skulking there?"

Horror gripped her gut. That shadow was there! Again, the dark shape prowled in the corner of her eye, and when she spun to face it, it was gone.

The cries of the pups swelled around her, making it impossible to focus. She couldn't hear Whisper, couldn't properly see that circling shadow. Her ears ached with those ringing howls of lonely fear. She didn't know what to do—

And the dark shape was suddenly right in front of her. It strode out of nothingness: the vast dark form of a dog, with high-pricked ears and slender, powerful shoulders, and blazing, ice-blue eyes.

Relief and joy rolled over her like a river in flood. Not the Fear-Dog.

The Watch-Dog!

Arrow, it's the Watch-Dog, everything is fine—

In an instant, Storm woke. The morning air was still and peaceful around her, the first birdsong trilling in the forest. The Sun-Dog's early rays pierced the branches of her den, and a ghostly mist shimmered on the grass beyond its mouth.

And the cries of the pups were real.

CHAPTER ELEVEN

It wasn't a dream. Faintly, the pups yelped and cried and whimpered. Their words were muffled and distorted, but Storm thought she could make out two or three: "Help us!"

"Lost!"

"Mother-Dog!"

Storm leaped to her paws, every muscle quivering with tension. Lifting her head, she began to bark: loud, commanding cries of alert.

"The pups! I hear them! The pups!"

The effect was instantaneous. Dogs came squirming and crawling from their dens, shaking themselves, stiffening as their ears pricked. Daisy and Chase raced to the pond, yelping. Mickey began to bound around the perimeter, stopping every few paces to cock his ears. Sweet and Lucky stood outside their den, their legs rigid, their flanks heaving.

"Where is it coming from?" cried Sunshine, hopping up and down. "I can't tell!"

The little Omega was right, thought Storm: Just as in her dream, those cries seemed to come from everywhere and nowhere. Woody and Rake were sniffing through the undergrowth, growling in frustration, shaking their heads.

"Quiet, everyone!" barked Mickey, and a tense silence fell over the Packs.

The dogs stayed still for long, aching moments, as the feeble whines and howls drifted and lingered through the branches all around them. At last Daisy shook herself, frustrated.

"It's impossible," she barked. "They could be anywhere."

"Are they even the right pups?" Dart cocked her head, listening intently.

"Yes." Sweet was trembling as she paced forward. "Yes, that's Fluff and Tumble. I'd know their voices anywhere."

"We did mistake Nip and Scramble . . . ," Dart reminded her hesitantly.

"Yes, but only for an instant." Sweet's limbs tensed as she

listened. "Those voices—they are *my pups*."

"I don't hear Nibble," Lucky said, his voice cracking. "Where is Nibble? Why isn't she with them?"

"Wherever Fluff and Tumble are, they must be close," said Mickey grimly. "Come on!"

Her leg aching only slightly, Storm bounded after Mickey, Daisy, and Rake into the woodland shadows. She could hear the other search parties forging into the forest, their pawsteps urgent as branches snapped and bushes crackled around them. Every leaf and twig seemed so brittle and sharp, and in the shaded hollows there were white streaks of frost left over from the dawn. *The pups will freeze if we don't find them soon,* she thought with a lurch of fear. Yet despite the closeness of those heartrending cries, there was no sign of the little dogs.

Ahead of Storm, Mickey hesitated, turned, and ran off at an angle. Then, as distant pup-howls rose, he stopped again, his ears twitching. Daisy was running in almost constant circles, her frustration making her hackles bristle.

Storm knew how the little dog felt. There were those cries *again*, yet now they seemed to come from behind her. Twisting, Storm ran a short way back toward the clearing, but again the sounds faded. From beyond the trees, she could hear Chase and Woody barking to each other, and they sounded as confused as she was.

The others were all running, circling, darting back and forth in bewilderment. Storm halted, sniffing the air, her heart pounding; once again the whimpering cries rose. *Where are they?*

There! Under that thorn scrub! The cries seemed so very loud now, and she yelped in excitement. She raked and scraped frantically through the tangle of branches, pulling them apart, sniffing at every gap and hollow and cracked root.

No! Her heart plummeted with disappointment.

Her blood thrumming, she halted and pawed at the ground, throwing up gouts of earth. *No, that's a ridiculous waste of energy. The pups aren't buried with the Earth-Dog!*

Yet . . . growled a small and dreadful voice inside her head. Storm shuddered, and shook herself to chase it away.

The Sun-Dog rose steadily beyond the trees as the dogs continued their search; his rays were bright and surprisingly warm for the Red Leaf season. As the day wore on, the whimpering cries would fade to nothing, then start up again; still no bark of joy and triumph came from any of the searchers.

Storm's coat felt sticky, and her tongue lolled from her jaws;

there was a twinge of constant hunger in her belly, and she knew it must be the same for her companions. *No dog ate well last night. How many more days can we do this, if we can't find prey to sustain us?*

The Sun-Dog was on his homeward run when Storm and her three companions plodded miserably out beyond the tree line. They had heard the pups' calls in the forest; now it seemed to Storm that the sounds were still faintly audible, here in the broad sweep of an open meadow.

"How could this be happening? Maybe they're out here. Maybe we misheard," she said, her tail and ears drooping. It was hard to feel any hope.

"Maybe," grunted Mickey.

Exchanging exhausted nods, the four dogs spread out to begin a methodical search of the meadow. Its grass was yellowing, and fallen leaves were caught in the blades; no summer flowers bloomed in the whole expanse. Already, evening frost was forming on the tips of the grass.

They'd set out this morning with such high hopes; now, Storm was imagining the lost pups freezing, alone, still undiscovered. A cold horror gripped her, as if Ice Wind were already sinking its claws into her gut.

They reached the far end of the meadow, where rocky ground

sloped down toward another stretch of woodland. Storm halted, waiting for her fellow hunters to emerge from the straggly grass. Glancing up at the sky, she saw that the Sun-Dog was already yawning, stretching, circling low toward his den beyond the Endless Lake. A breath of cold wind drifted from the same direction, and she shivered.

They had hunted all day and found nothing. Even the pups' cries, still wafting occasionally on the wind, seemed to mock their efforts. The chill in Storm's hide as the evening darkened was echoed by a cold claw of nerves in her heart. There had been something so unnatural about those yelping cries: the way they seemed to come from nowhere. It was as if the pups now existed only as a desolate sound on the wind.

Mickey limped to her side; Rake crept from the grass, looking worn out, with Daisy right behind him. "It'll be dark soon," growled Mickey. "That's going to make it harder than ever!"

Storm nodded. The Sun-Dog had flicked his glowing tail and vanished, and now the sky was darkening rapidly. Stars began to glimmer above them, and the night breeze held an edge of ice.

"We have to rest," murmured Rake.

"No!" exclaimed Mickey. "We have to keep going!"

"The pups are close, I *feel* it," whined Daisy.

"They've been close the whole time," said Storm, lashing her tail in frustration. "Yet we haven't found a hair of them!"

Rake shook his head. "I'm as disappointed as you are, but we can't help the pups if we collapse from exhaustion. And Mickey, you look like you're about to do just that."

"I'm not going back to camp before we've found those pups!" barked Mickey.

"I agree with that," said Storm. "But Rake's right, Mickey—we *do* need to rest. If we curl up together, we can keep warm."

"Fine." Mickey's head sagged. "But I can still hear those pups right now! *Listen!* Hear them? It almost sounds like they're back the way we came, but that can't be true . . ." He twitched an ear toward the elusive wailing, now distant again. "We begin the search again from this spot—first thing in the morning. Agreed?"

"Agreed." Rake nodded. "We'll hunt better when we're rested, Mickey, honestly."

Daisy sounded half-dead from weariness. "Come away from those rocks, Storm. There's a clump of bushes on the edge of the meadow, see? We can sleep there."

Under a sky that was now black with night, the four dogs collapsed in a tangled heap at the roots of the bushes, nose to tail and flank to flank, their warmth seeping into one another. Storm was afraid she wouldn't sleep, but even her anxiety was no match for her exhaustion; she felt her eyelids droop almost immediately.

"I need to sleep, Whisper. Leave me alone."

The little gray dog nudged her with his nose; it felt wet and real. Only a little irritated, Storm rolled over and scrambled to her paws. Whisper was right: She wasn't tired at all. She didn't mind going with him.

He trotted off, then paused and glanced back. Storm turned to look down at her companions; they were still cuddled up snugly together, and not one of them had stirred. Mickey was snoring. It was best that they slept on, she decided. She would follow Whisper alone.

It had to be nearly dawn already: mist drifted eerily through the hollows, the same color as Whisper's coat, and just as translucent and ethereal. That must be why it was hard to see him. Because however fast Storm ran, Whisper was quicker; he kept disappearing into those tendrils of mist, and each time he reappeared, his fur sparkled with dewdrops.

Whisper beckoned her again with an urgent jerk of his head, and she gritted her jaws and ran after him.

But the mist was thickening, coalescing into a silvery gray fog. In one instant Whisper's shape was visible, as if carved out of the air; in the next, he was gone.

Storm halted. She raised her head.

"Whisper?"

She jolted awake. The fog was not thick at all; though the

Sun-Dog hadn't risen, the sky was lightening with the first of his rays, and the mist was soft and pearly, making dewdrops sparkle just as they had on Whisper's coat. Storm staggered to her feet, blinking.

Mickey's gentle snores rumbled on the peaceful morning air. He, Daisy, and Rake were still fast asleep. Perhaps she should wake her companions soon, but they still looked so exhausted, and for now they were free from their worries.

As she debated inwardly, Storm's eye caught a gleam of gold on the far side of the meadow. She stiffened, slowly turning to look.

There it stood, its great antlered head turned to observe her: the Golden Deer. The tips of its horns sparkled with what might have been sunshine or morning dew, and its eyes shone dark gold, alight with a challenge.

Storm's heart leaped. *If ever we needed good luck . . .*

Without another thought, she sprang into the chase, her legs eating up the ground. She barely felt tired anymore, and the ache in her foreleg had faded to a faint, meaningless throb. The grass rustled and bent before her as Storm bolted through it, her paws light and fast.

The Golden Deer had not moved yet. It stood very still,

watching her approach; Storm felt like it was taunting her. Only when it was within a long bound-and-spring of being caught did the Deer spin and race away, its golden pelt flashing in the dawn.

The chase felt almost joyful. This time, Storm knew, the Deer would fall to her; she would catch it in her jaws and bring its good fortune back to the Packs. The creature was only just ahead, its cloven hooves glinting with every swift pace of its flight.

Storm didn't even know where it was leading her; she focused only on the speed of her paws and the Deer itself. But she became aware when the ground beneath her was no longer grassy and soft, when it became gritty stone and tufts of stiff vegetation. She suddenly recognized where she was: this was a hunting ground, quite close to the Pack's camp. She was coming to the top of a low, craggy cliff that overlooked a grassy slope down to the shore of the Endless Lake.

The Deer twisted, gave a high bound, and halted at the edge of the crag.

It stood facing her, its antlers held low. Those dark bronze eyes gleamed into hers.

Storm skidded to a halt, momentarily confused. Then she clenched her jaws and bunched her muscles to spring—

And the Golden Deer turned, and leaped from the edge.

Gasping, Storm bolted forward. At the last moment, her claws scrabbled to a halt at the rim of the drop. Peering over, she could make out the steep slope of rock that leveled out at its lower point toward the grassland below. It was peaceful, and utterly empty.

There was nowhere the Deer could have crawled, fatally injured; there was nowhere it could have hidden in those brief instants since it had sprung from the cliff.

Yet it had vanished.

Breathing hard, shivers rippling through her skin, Storm began to back away. *The Deer is a creature of the Spirit Dogs,* she told herself. *It's not meant to be caught by mortal dogs. How else could it have survived that leap? How else could it have disappeared?*

Distantly a golden gleam flashed, and her head jerked up. It wasn't the Sun-Dog, because that was rising behind her.

Storm narrowed her eyes. There, near the horizon, a swift glowing shape ran freely between earth and sky, fleet and elusive as a bird. Its hooves seemed not to touch the ground.

Am I seeing that? Or is it only an illusion that the Deer runs on the wind? Storm swallowed, feeling her fur rise. *Oh, Sky-Dogs and Wind-Dogs. I am really never meant to catch it.*

But that meant, she realized as a sickening heaviness swamped her, that she was not meant to find luck for the Packs. Perhaps they were not meant to find the pups. . . .

Perhaps the Deer simply came to show me that all Wild Dogs are doomed.

It was as if the spirits of all fallen dogs heard her thoughts at that moment and howled in sympathy. Storm thought she could hear their wails: a rising, desolate lament that filled the air around her, a cry of lonely mourning that rang and echoed in her ears. For a moment, all the sadness and bleak despair of every dog that had died since the Big Growl seemed to flow through her blood.

No. Wait.

Those howls were real, and louder than they had ever been.

"Father-Dog! Mother-Dog! Help us. We're *lost.*"

A surge of excitement went through Storm. Her ears craned, her tail quivered as she yearned toward the sound of crying pups. *Their voices are loud . . . which means they're close!*

Lowering her head, she flared her nostrils and sniffed at the dry ground. A great crack ran along the edge of the cliff; a wound in the rock like the one that had formed their precarious path to Tiny. Here, too, rock had shifted against rock, leaving a deep scar; gazing along it, Storm could see where that scar widened, where the crack became a broad dark shadow in the pale stone.

She sprang toward that deep dent in the stone, skidding to a halt and panting. Only it wasn't a *dent*: it was a deep, black hole in the rock, and the howling high cries rose directly from its depths. A memory flashed into Storm's mind: *The time we climbed up through the cliff, escaping the anger of the Endless Lake. Lucky found a tunnel that led to freedom. There's a tunnel here, too. A cavern in the rock.*

Her whole body shook with waves of happiness and excitement. The Golden Deer *had* brought the Pack some good fortune. With a sudden, strange impulse, she shut her eyes. *Thank you, Deer of the Spirit Dogs. Thank you for bringing me to the pups.*

Raising her head, she half crouched, opening her throat and giving a wild, urgent howl of summons.

"The pups! *The pups!* I know where they are!"

CHAPTER TWELVE

Mickey, Rake and Daisy sprinted toward her, panting with desperate eagerness, but they weren't the only dogs who had heard Storm's ringing barks and howls. Borne on the stiff breeze, her summons must have reached the other search parties and the camp itself, because the rest of the dogs began bursting in small groups from the forest and racing across the meadow.

"My pups!" Lucky barked. "We're coming!"

"Hold on, Nibble!" howled Beetle. "It won't be long now, Fluff and Tumble!"

As all three Packs gathered around the chasm in the cliff top, scratching and digging frantically, only Sweet was absent; the swift-dog Alpha must have stayed with little Tiny and poor injured Thorn. But Lucky's furious energy was enough for both the parent-dogs. He and Mickey had the edge of a slab in their teeth, tearing at it; as they gave a last violent heave, it creaked and scraped loose, and clattered aside. Earwigs and woodlice skittered in search of shelter. Dart, Beetle, and Moon raced forward to claw at the loose earth beneath the slab, widening the hole.

Even Nip and Scramble had joined the rescue party, though Storm reckoned their parent-dogs must have carried them part of the way; apparently, they'd refused to be left behind. They too were raking with their small claws, biting at the soil and then spitting it from their jaws; their paws and muzzles were black with damp earth.

Below, a little farther down the sloping cliff, Chase, Woody, Snap, and Daisy began to hunt methodically along the rocks, searching every cranny and nook for a way through to the pups.

"Can you find a way in?" Storm barked down to them.

"I don't know!" yelped Daisy. "But we'll do our best."

"Storm! Lucky!" barked Beetle from the excavated hole. "I think we've found the start of a tunnel."

Bounding back to him, Storm clawed violently at the exposed soil, showering the cliff top in spatters of dry earth. Other dogs were digging too. Mickey's claw scratched Storm's paw in his haste, but she barely felt it. Sunshine yapped uncontrollably as she scrabbled with her tiny paws; most of her white fur was splattered with earth, but she didn't seem to mind at all. Excitement rose in every dog as the hole was effortfully, gradually scraped deeper.

Then, horribly, Storm's claws screeched against stone. She halted, panting. Bit by bit, more slowly this time, the dogs excavated more soil, but by now it was clear that only a thin layer was left. There was nothing underneath it but more slabs and shelves of rock.

Storm stepped back, flanks heaving with exhaustion and disappointment. "This is crazy. We *know* they're in there, we can hear them! How did Breeze get them in under these slabs?"

As Moon opened her mouth to reply, sudden thunder rumbled across the hill, and every dog froze, cowering. Moon tilted an ear, glancing at the sky, but it was cold blue from horizon to horizon.

"Longpaws," snarled Mickey, nodding to the sparse woodland below the cliff.

He was right, Storm realized: That had been no thunder of the Sky-Dogs, and Lightning did not spring joyfully between the clouds. The grating roar came from the far end of the woods, where they met the foot of the cliff; Storm could make out yellow loudcages there, lurching across the earth. Distantly she heard the barks of their longpaw owners.

"They're making the whole cliff shake," whispered Nip, his

eyes wide and afraid. Arrow licked his head.

"What if they bring it all down on the p—" began Snap, but shut her jaws at a warning glare from Mickey.

It was true that the cliff was shaking; tremors rose up from the ground beneath Storm's paws, up through her bones. The longpaws were closing in, eating up more and more of the land, and a horrible thought flitted across her mind: *Soon there will be no territory left for wild dogs.*

"We have no time to waste," Storm growled. As the noise faded and stopped, and the cliff seemed to steady, she returned to scrabbling at the edges of the hole the dogs had dug. "There has to be a way through. There *has* to be!"

Crouching low on her belly, she pushed her nose up against the stone. Her nose filled with the tang of disturbed soil, insects, and roots. Ignoring those, Storm inhaled deeply, and her nostrils found a faint puff of cool, damp, slightly stale air.

"There is a tunnel down there." Wriggling back, she rose to her paws. "I'm sure of it. That must be why we could hear the pups all over the place, these tunnels must run right through the cliff! But there's a stone wedged across the top of the entrance, and it's a big one."

"Mickey and I can deal with that." Lucky's eyes were narrowed with fierce determination.

"Wait. Listen!" Storm cocked her ears.

An eerie, high barking echoed from deep beneath their paws.

"Tumble!" Lucky's bark was agonized. "Fluff!"

Storm licked his neck fervently. "We'll get them, Lucky. I promise!"

Daisy appeared at that moment, hauling herself over the lip of the cliff and trotting toward the excavated hole. Chase, Woody, and Snap scrambled up behind her and shook themselves.

"There's no way into the cliff face from down there," Daisy told them all. "No hidden entrance."

"We've looked everywhere," added Chase. "I'm sorry."

"Don't worry," said Sunshine. "We think the entrance really is this one, up here. But it's blocked. I don't see how Breeze could have shifted it by herself. It doesn't make sense."

Daisy padded closer, tilting her head to stare down into the hollow. "I see it, the rock that's blocking the tunnel. It's big but it's flat, and it's tilted."

"I don't think it'll be too *heavy*," said Mickey. "The trouble is, it's jammed tight."

"I don't know," mused Daisy, frowning. "If a dog could crawl through that little crack, down to the underside of it . . . you could shove it from below. Look at the way it's angled. It'll unbalance that way, and it can come loose."

Snap panted eagerly and sniffed at the crevice. "Could you get through there, Daisy?"

"I wish I could, but I think I'm too big." Daisy jumped down into the hollow and nosed experimentally at the black gash at the end of the slab. "I definitely won't fit. Sunshine, what about you?"

Unhesitating, the little Omega leaped down. The stone rocked beneath her as she landed. Clawing impotently at its edge, she pushed her snout down into the narrow crack between it and the solid rock, but though she strained hard enough to make her give a pained whine, she could not even get her whole head through, let alone her shoulders.

"It's no use," whimpered Sunshine. Her ears flattened in distress as the voices of the pups rose again from the depths.

Fluff's howl drifted up to them. *"Mother-Dog, help! Please come!"*

Lucky's legs stiffened. "I am here, my pups! Not much longer!"

"Mother-Dog!" That was Tumble, his whine short and sharp. *"It's so cold!"*

"They can't hear me!" Lucky turned to Storm, his eyes agonized. Storm wanted to reassure him, but her mind was attacked by a terrible thought. That was the second time she had heard the calls of Fluff and Tumble. *Why isn't Nibble howling along with them?*

"We'll work this out, Lucky," Mickey growled in frustration. "But even if Sunshine *could* get through this gap, your pups are bigger and stouter than she is now. Even they wouldn't be able to wriggle up through it from below."

"We can't let them die down there!" howled Sunshine.

Storm saw Lucky flinch in pain, but his eyes hardened. "We won't, Sunshine. There's *something* we can do, I'm sure. We just have to figure out what it is."

Desperately, Storm cast her eyes around the Pack, and suddenly she went still, her eyes widening. "There are two dogs here who *could* fit through that gap," she growled softly.

Every dog stared at her, and then, as realization dawned, they turned to Nip and Scramble. The two pups exchanged a bewildered glance, then gasped. Scramble gave a high yip of excitement.

"No, we can't." Storm found herself backtracking immediately. "It's so dangerous. They won't be strong enough."

"*Yes, we are!*" barked Nip, offended.

A whine escaped Storm's throat as horrible images of Nip and Scramble falling down into the darkness filled her mind. *I wish I'd never suggested it.* "Nip, it's too risky—"

Nip and Scramble looked positively enraged. "We want to

help the pups!" they chorused.

Bella was staring at Lucky, her eyes dark and gentle and full of sympathy. "Arrow," she told her mate quietly. "I think we should let them try."

"Please, Father-Dog. Please!"

Arrow swallowed. He sat back on his haunches and licked his jaws. Bella said nothing more, but waited.

At last Arrow nodded. His voice sounded hoarse. "It'll be difficult, little ones, and it's dark down there. But I think you might be able to help move that stone."

"We'll be very careful," said Scramble, "but we want to *help*."

Lucky did not speak. He just stared at Bella and Arrow, his flanks heaving like his gratitude was going to burst out of his body.

Determinedly the two pups trotted to the hollow and jumped down. Scramble cocked his head and peered through the narrow crevice into the darkness. "I'm smaller," he announced with determination. "I'll go first."

"I'll be right behind you," Nip assured him.

Storm wondered if every dog had the same lump in their throat as she did. She could hardly breathe as she watched first Scramble, then Nip, squirm and wriggle through the crack. With a last twitch of his stubby tail, Nip vanished.

A silence fell over the dogs of the Packs. Only a tiny, anxious whimper from Sunshine broke the tension.

"We're fine," came Nip's oddly booming voice. "And we can see where to push the stone!"

The collective sigh that ran through the grown dogs was audible.

"Come on, Storm," said Lucky, stretching his head and shoulders down into the hollow. "Well done, Nip and Scramble. Now wait for my word, and then push as hard as you can!"

Storm dropped her forepaws down and grabbed the edge of the slab in her teeth just as Lucky did.

"Now," growled Lucky though the stone in his jaws. "*Go!*"

Below them, Storm could hear the grunts and pants of the two pups as they shoved and pushed. Her heart thrashed in her chest—what if the slab came loose badly and fell onto the pups?—but with painful slowness, it started shifting sideways.

The stone vibrated against her fangs, and it made a hideous grinding noise as she and Lucky pushed, but the pups had gotten exactly the right angle. They'd dislodged the jammed end of the slab. It gave very suddenly, tipping up and sideways, and Storm let go, finding herself staring down into the excited, mud-covered faces of Nip and Scramble.

"Did we do it right?" yapped Nip.

"You did it right." Storm let her tongue loll, laughing.

"You are good dogs," howled Lucky, his voice choking with emotion. "You are *such good dogs.*"

The two pups looked delighted. Storm reached down to grab Scramble's scruff, and Lucky Nip's, and together they hauled them up and set them on solid ground at the edge of the hole. Arrow and Bella fell on their pups, licking them clean and nuzzling their faces.

"Well done, little ones. Well done!"

There was no time to be lost. Lucky nodded once at Arrow, then turned and squeezed through the gap the pups had helped to make. Storm waited till his plume of a golden tail had vanished, then followed him.

The two dogs stood for a moment in the darkness, nostrils flared and quivering. Sunlight filtered in from above now, and as their eyes adjusted, they could make out the tunnel clearly before them. The air smelled musty, and a little salty, but there was a distinct tang of pups. What lay before them looked like a long, steep drop into blackness, but there was no question of turning back.

Storm dug her claws into the thin, loose earth, feeling hard rock beneath it. "Let's go."

But there was no need to say it. Lucky had already bounded forward into the tunnel.

Storm took a deep breath, and a leap—and suddenly she was plunging forward with no effort at all. The feeble light vanished rapidly as she hurtled forward and down, her legs bounding out of control. Instinctively, she stuck out her forepaws and leaned back on her hindquarters, trying hopelessly to slow herself.

Ahead of her, Storm could hear the slithering sound of Lucky's haunches against the slope, and his gasping pants. He must be sliding as fast as she was; it gave her a horrible twist in the pit of her stomach to feel the ground skidding by underneath her, not knowing when or if the long fall would ever end. Her claws scraped painfully against the rock; she couldn't help digging them in, though she couldn't stop even if she wanted to. Her forelegs still jammed out in front of her, Storm felt the earth scrape painfully against her rump.

The slip and slide ended abruptly when she felt herself collide with something warmer, softer than the rock she was expecting . . . *Lucky's haunches.* For a moment the two of them lay tangled, panting, their hearts thudding. Then, shaking, Lucky got to his paws.

The darkness was complete down here, but Storm could hear him sniffing at the air. "There are a few tunnels," he growled softly. "We could get lost if we're not careful."

"We can't get back up that drop, anyway," Storm reminded him with a shrug of her shoulders that he couldn't see. "We'll just have to keep going. Follow the pups' scent."

"We can certainly do that," said Lucky. "The scent is clear. But we could use some extra guidance." Raising his voice, he gave a bark that echoed shockingly and unnervingly through the blackness. "Pups! Tumble, Fluff—we're on our way!"

"Father-Dog!" The eerie, eager voices drifted through the darkness, their direction hard to pinpoint. Storm creased her brow and stiffened. It still sounded like only two voices. . . .

When her eyes met the Beta dog's, she knew he was thinking the same as her. His nostrils flared and his flanks heaved, just for a moment, before he clenched his jaw. Lucky was not going to let his fear or worry get the better of him, Storm could tell.

"This way," he growled, and set off before her.

It was so dark, Storm could follow him only by his scent and the urgent click of his claws. He seemed confident, though, twisting and turning ahead of her, ignoring some branching tunnels and forging determinedly down others.

He knows what he's doing, Storm thought—and at that exact moment, she collided with his hindquarters.

His body was shaking, she could feel it. It seemed to take him a long moment to speak.

"Dead end," he said at last, gruffly.

Backing up the tunnel was much harder than running down it, and it felt much more unsettling. No dog, Storm thought, should walk backward into unseen danger. Forcing herself to do so sent ripples of instinctive fear along her spine and chilled her blood.

Finally her haunches emerged into what felt like a bigger space. Relieved, Storm took another couple of awkward paces back, and heard Lucky reverse out in front of her, panting with panic.

"We'll try again," he said, and growled, "Sorry."

"You're doing great," Storm assured him. She twitched an ear. "Listen. The pups again. To the left, I think."

"And they're getting louder," agreed Lucky, his tail lifting and wagging so suddenly, it slapped her nose.

Storm's heart beat a little faster with excitement. Surely they were getting closer to the pups, however long it took.

And at that moment, the tunnel shuddered around them, so suddenly, Storm almost lost her balance. From far away—quieter, yet much more frightening than the pup's cries—came that grinding, shuddering thunder.

"The loudcages," Storm whispered. She could feel loose grit

and stones showering onto her hide. "They've started again."

What if the tunnel collapses, and Lucky and the pups and I are still inside? She didn't dare say it aloud, and besides, Lucky was surely thinking the same thing. *It doesn't matter what's going on outside. We can only control what we do. We have to keep going.*

They set off yet again, the slight vibration of the rock enough to keep them bounding along so fast it felt like their paws were barely touching down. Storm had grown almost accustomed to the terrified pounding of her heart, the expectation that at any moment, the whole gigantic cliff would collapse and bury them both.

"How far do you think we've come?" she panted at last. Of course Lucky wouldn't know any better than she did, but Storm longed to hear the sound of a normal voice. "I think we've traveled a long way sideways." *Closer to where the forest ends, right below the cliff. Where the loudcages are feeding on the earth . . .*

No! I mustn't think about that. She tried again for a response from Lucky. "We've come along the side of the cliff face and—"

"Hush." Lucky halted ahead of her. "Listen."

Storm tilted her head, trying to angle her ears and focus; to blot out the muffled grumble of the loudcages. The yapping of the trapped pups was still audible, but there was something else there, a more familiar and natural sound . . . a sound of something that lay in the same direction.

"Water," she breathed. "Dripping water. Or maybe, running . . ."

"The tunnel goes sharply down here," Lucky grunted. "But the pups are at the bottom of it. Listen, Storm—can you hear?"

She cocked her ears, straining to catch every sound.

"Father-Dog! Father-Dog, we're here!"

"Yes," Storm barked with fierce delight. "Come on."

"Be careful." But Lucky himself was already plunging down the slope.

The tunnel's black descent wasn't as steep as the first drop, and this time Storm was able to slow her headlong trot. As it leveled even more, she found she could feel her way, claw by claw, in the pitch darkness. What was that gurgling ripple—a spring? A river beyond the rocks?

Just ahead of her, she heard a loud splash and a gasp. And almost immediately, her own forepaws sank into ice-cold water.

Storm cocked her head and held her breath, listening to the beautiful sound of running water. She plunged her muzzle into it and drank. Then she licked her jaws, closing her eyes in bliss; she hadn't realized how thirsty she was. "An underground stream," she breathed.

There was enough space for Lucky to turn his head; she could made out the glow of his eyes. "A stream," he croaked, his voice brimming with excitement. "Yes. And streams always find a way out."

Of course! Why didn't I—

"*Father-Dog.*" The faint call echoed along the tunnel.

Lucky said no more. He turned and bolted on along the course of the water, his paws sending up showers of droplets into Storm's eyes as she chased him. The pups' voices were high and excited now, and the air was full of their scent. There was even a sheen of pale light on the stream's surface, so that Storm could make out Lucky's shape as he skidded to a halt in a great fan of spray.

She drew up alongside him. A patch of black shadow to her left turned out to be a tiny natural alcove, receding deep into the tunnel wall; as they both crouched to peer hopefully into it, pallid light gleamed on a small, black, questing nose.

"Fluff!" Lucky's voice was hoarse with relief.

Gently he seized the pup by the scruff as she wiggled out, and he set her down at his paws. Storm began to lick warmth into her shivering body as Lucky reached forward again to retrieve Tumble.

"Father-Dog," whimpered Fluff. "We were so scared."

"I wasn't scared," whined Tumble, though his trembling body said otherwise.

Storm waited and watched, as though Nibble was going to appear out of the darkness any moment—even though she knew it was futile. Nibble wasn't there. . . .

She looked over the heads of Fluff and Tumble, having a silent discussion with Lucky. The golden-furred dog closed his eyes in despair, just for a moment, then looked down at the two pups they'd found. Storm got the message: *Let's not worry them anymore right now.*

They licked and nuzzled the two rescued pups, checking their soft hides for wounds and bites: Storm's heart turned over with relief when she found none.

Then her gut filled with a cold feeling as she imagined what the bad dog had planned for the litter. If they hadn't found the pups—if Nip and Scramble hadn't been around to dislodge the jammed stone—Fluff and Tumble could have starved, frozen, or been crushed to death as the cliff came down.

But that's not going to happen, Breeze, she vowed. *Your wicked plan has been thwarted.*

Not that they were entirely safe yet . . .

"We have to get out of here," she said in a low voice.

"Pups," asked Lucky urgently, "how did Breeze bring you to this place? Do you know the way out?"

"I don't, Father-Dog," said Fluff miserably. "It was so cold and we were so tired and we were scared and we were running. . . ."

"And we wanted to follow the stream back, but when we tried, we went the wrong way." Tumble's howl was plaintive. "We got lost. And Breeze told us there were monsters."

"Breeze and her vicious stories," snarled Storm.

"But she said they ate little dogs," Tumble went on, shivering, "so we thought it was better to hide in here and wait for you."

"Because we knew you'd come," whimpered Fluff.

"Of course we did," said Lucky, his voice choking. "I would never have left you here."

"We'll get you both out, pups." Storm's eyes met Lucky's. "And if there are monsters on the way, *they're* the ones who'll get eaten."

One monster in particular, she promised herself silently.

Even the stream branched at several points, trickling to puddles and then to nothing, but at least they had something to follow now. Quickly correcting any wrong turns, Storm and Lucky trotted though the darkness, ever downward, the pups walking between them. There was room to walk two abreast here, and Storm could feel Tumble's warm body pressed close to her legs; the pups seemed unwilling to lose any physical contact with their rescuers.

When the four dogs turned a final corner, and white light spilled through a low, ragged crack in the stone, Storm knew with a rush of relief that they'd made it.

Crawling on her belly, half dragging Tumble with her, she squirmed out into the daylight and relative warmth of the valley. Lucky followed through the gash in the rock, his jaws clamped gently in Fluff's fur to help her through.

Storm shook herself free of the dampness and cold and fear of the caverns. Even the nearby roar of loudcages couldn't disturb her: *The longpaws aren't the enemy here. Not right now.*

"You were right, Storm." Lucky was gazing up at the cliff. "We traveled a long way along the rock, many deer-chases—but we were inside the cliff the whole time. It's no wonder Daisy and the others didn't find this entrance; they weren't looking in the right place."

"And it's hardly visible anyway," remarked Storm, staring at the half-overgrown gash in the stone.

"Father-Dog, what are those?" Tumble was staring wide-eyed at the flashes of yellow loudcage-skin that were visible through the tree trunks.

"Never mind them just now." Lucky nuzzled his son. "They won't bother us. Storm and I will carry you back up the cliff now."

It's over, thought Storm, *but only for Fluff and Tumble.*

As if reading her mind, Lucky gave a sad and determined growl. "First we'll get you two to safety. Then we'll find your litter-sister Nibble. I promise."

Storm nodded. "At least you're safe," she told the two pups gently. "And you're going home."

CHAPTER THIRTEEN

The Sun-Dog had almost finished his run by the time the three Packs slouched back to camp, exhausted but hopeful. They had found two of the missing pups! Tumble and Fluff had had to be supported most of the way, but each of the adult dogs took turns to walk at their sides, providing a strong flank to lean on; Storm had offered to carry Nip and Scramble, but Arrow and Bella's pups were too excited to endure that. They were full of energy, bouncing and leaping alongside the older pups, calling out questions that Fluff and Tumble were too tired to answer.

"What happened down there in the caves?"

"*Were* there any monsters, Fluff? Were they real?"

"Now, my pups," said Bella gently, "leave Fluff and Tumble alone. They've had a terrible ordeal. They'll tell you all about it, but not just now."

Fluff and Tumble were bedraggled, and thin, and now and again they would shiver and whimper with fear as memories returned to them. But they were alive, thought Storm. *And they weren't meant to be. We've thwarted Breeze's plans—two of them, at least.*

What she did not like to contemplate was Breeze's reaction to thwarted plans. What would that bad dog do, when she discovered the pups had been rescued?

She still has Nibble. . . .

When Mickey and Snap set them down on the grass of the clearing, Fluff and Tumble sagged where they stood, their eyelids already drooping. But as their litter-sister Tiny came bounding from Sweet's den, they perked up, blinking.

Tiny looked well-rested, bright-eyed, and ecstatic to see her litter-siblings again. Sweet was running forward too, joy on her face, but Tiny reached the pups first.

"Fluff! Tumble!" Tiny skidded to a halt at the last moment, just before she could collide with her littermates.

Fluff and Tumble yapped happily, bundling the smallest pup to the ground. "You're alive, you're alive!" they barked.

They must have been so worried, Storm thought, her legs trembling at the thought of how close Tiny had come to dying.

Tiny was licking and butting her brother and sister so

frantically, Sweet had trouble reaching her pups to nuzzle and caress them.

"Where's Nibble?" Eagerly Tiny looked around and behind the two rescued pups.

"We don't know," said Tumble miserably.

Sweet sucked in an audible breath and gazed up sadly at Lucky; the atmosphere of celebration was abruptly dampened. Every other Pack Dog exchanged desperate glances.

This is a victory, thought Storm, *but none of us can be truly happy till Nibble's home, too.*

"But three pups are safe," she said aloud, and the other dogs turned to her, ears pricked. "We have to hold on to that. And we will get your sister back, we promise."

"There's nothing more certain," growled Lucky, nuzzling Tiny in greeting. "Another search party should go out now, investigate the area near that cliff—"

"I'll go," Moon spoke up. "I'm not too tired. Beetle, will you come?"

As Beetle nodded, Woody gave a growl. "I will, too. Lucky, you should stay with Sweet and your pups for now. We can handle this while you look after the little ones."

Lucky gave a tormented growl of agreement. "All right. But

keep an eye out for the longpaws while you search. They're not an immediate threat, I don't think—but we should still stay alert."

As the three dogs bounded into the forest, a bedraggled Sunshine padded forward, hobbling with tiredness. "We can talk to Fluff and Tumble tomorrow," she whined weakly, "but they need to rest now."

"Indeed they do." Sweet had gathered all three of her pups between her paws, clutching them close. "And so does every dog. Go on, all of you: sleep, you deserve it."

The dogs began to lope off to their dens, but Storm hesitated for a moment, gazing back at Lucky and Sweet and their still incomplete family.

Somehow she doubted Moon and Beetle and Woody would find Nibble near the cliff. Wouldn't the Pack have heard the pup while they were desperately digging for her siblings earlier? But every chance had to be seized, Storm thought grimly, and every clue had to be followed.

Because I can't help feeling that with Breeze still in control, our time is running out. . . .

The prey in the forest may have been dwindling, but there was more than enough the next day for the two starving pups. No

Packmate wanted to eat before they did—even Sweet seemed unable to swallow any prey before she'd made sure Fluff, Tumble, and Tiny had been given enough tender pieces of meat. Only when the pups were sprawled on the soft grass, their bellies pleasantly rounded and their eyelids drooping, did the other dogs take their share of the rations.

Gently Sweet nudged Tumble with her nose. "I know you're tired, little one."

"'M not tired," he assured her sleepily, "just really full."

Sweet laughed softly. "You're all going to get more sleep soon." Her eyes darkened as the Pack craned forward attentively. "But pups, we need to know your story. Tell us everything that happened."

At once, Fluff and Tumble blinked themselves alert, shifting so that they lay upright on their bellies. Tiny gazed up at them with misgiving. "Was it really awful?" she squeaked at them.

Fluff and Tumble looked at each other, and Tumble nodded. "All right, I'll tell it."

"First of all," said Lucky, licking the top of his head, "what did Breeze tell you about Tiny? After she'd taken her away?"

Tumble's eyes widened with horror at the memory. "We woke up in the hollow of the tree, me and Fluff and Nibble. Breeze told us Tiny had been bad, that she'd sent her back to camp in disgrace." He whimpered, distress shaking his little body. "We—we said we'd had enough adventure. Could we go back and be with Tiny?" He swallowed hard. "But Breeze said—she said—she said *No!* She barked at us, *so loud.* She was so angry. I thought she was going to bite us!"

Fluff nodded vigorously and said in a choked whisper, "She was *scary.* I'd never seen her like that. So we . . . we didn't argue anymore."

"I bet you didn't," growled Daisy. "And that was wise."

"What happened next? After Tiny went away?" Sweet lowered her head to gaze into Tumble's eyes.

The pup gulped. "Breeze t-told us one of her stories. Mother-Dog, I didn't *like* her stories anymore, and neither did Fluff, but she told us anyway! It was a *horrible* story . . . about pups who went down to—to visit the Earth-Dog and have an . . . an adventure."

"It was scary and awful," growled Fluff, "with dark tunnels and . . . and monsters. Breeze said the pups in the story weren't scared, and that was because they were *brave.*" She glanced at her brother. "But I thought the pups in the story were *stupid.*"

"Fluff *told* Breeze that," said Tumble, with a proud glance at his sister. "She said that right out, she said they were *stupid* story-pups!" Then his ears drooped. "But that just made Breeze yell at her again."

Fluff nodded, shivering. "And then she said we were all going on an adventure, just like the 'brave and not-at-all-stupid pups.' We were sick of adventures by then. But she *made* us go."

"She said—she said we were going to explore the *Earth-Dog's* den," said Tumble. His eyes widened so much, the whites showed, and he began to tremble again. "The Earth-Dog! We didn't *want* to go! But she made us, and we had to go deep, deep underground." A huge shudder ran through him. "That's where dogs go when they *die*, isn't it? It was a stupid, scary game!"

Storm stared at the two little pups. "But the two of you weren't stupid," she growled softly. "So don't ever think that. You knew it was a bad idea. You were braver than any story-pups."

Tumble's ears pricked up a little again. "Storm, it . . . it wasn't a game anyway. It *wasn't*. Once we were under the ground, Breeze turned *worse*." He gave a high, terrified howl that made Storm flinch. "She said horrible things. She—she . . . oh, Mother-Dog, she told us that she'd *killed* Whisper and Bruno and Ruff! And . . . and . . . Tiny wasn't back at camp at all, because she'd *killed Tiny*."

Fluff cowered on the ground beside her brother, whimpering in grief. "Breeze said . . . she said we were never going to see Tiny ever again . . . and that our parent-dogs were never going to see *us* ever again!"

"We were *so scared*. Her teeth in the dark, they glowed and gleamed." Tumble's eyes were glazed with the terror of the memory. "I th-thought she was going to kill us right there."

Sweet licked their heads gently, over and over. Her voice cracked as she reassured them. "You're safe with me. And that bad dog didn't kill your sister, little ones. Tiny is right here, it's all right. Everything's going to be all right."

"I know, but I keep thinking about it and—" Tumble shook his head violently. Then he cleared his throat and lifted his head a little. "So Fluff and I ran away. We ran and ran in the dark, but . . . Nibble . . . she didn't come with us." He whined in misery. "I th-think she was the most scared of all of us, and she couldn't move. But we didn't know she wasn't there with us, we just kept running. We didn't realize." He gave a grief-stricken howl. "We're so sorry, Mother-Dog!"

Sweet pulled him close again, licking his head again feverishly. "Don't ever regret what you did! You were very brave, Tumble, and there was nothing else you *could* have done. Two of you are safe because you ran. You're not to blame for Nibble not being here—*Breeze* is."

Tiny nodded firmly. "Breeze is the bad dog," she told her brother. "It's not our fault."

At least, thought Storm as she met Sunshine's eyes, that message already seemed to have gotten through to Tiny. *Soon Fluff and Tumble will believe it too.*

"And did she chase you?" asked Dart, her eyes dark with imagined horror.

"She d-did." Fluff nodded. "For *ages*. But she couldn't find us, because we paddled through the water to mess up our scent, and we hid in the dark and stayed so *quiet.*"

"That's when"—Tumble gulped hard—"that's w-when she barked at us. She said we could stay all alone in the d-d-dark till we *died*. She said our parent-dogs would never know what had happened to us, and your hearts would be so broken, you would die too, and it would be *our fault.*"

Mickey couldn't repress a furious snarl.

"And then," Tumble went on, "she said she was taking Nibble with her on the adventure. Because Nibble was the special one. Nibble had been too scared to run away and that made her the best pup. She was very, very special to the Fear-Dog because she was so frightened."

"That savage!" snarled Rake. "And Terror has yet more to answer for, too."

Chase growled in agreement.

"Terror has already answered for his crimes," said Storm darkly. An unbearable rage had risen in her as the traumatized pups told their story. "I made sure of that. But back then, I didn't know just how much he'd managed to twist one of his followers. *Breeze.*" She spat out the name.

"Tumble. Fluff." Lucky crouched down, his eyes intent but kind. "I know it's hard, but try to think carefully. Did Breeze say where she was taking Nibble?"

Miserably, both pups shook their heads. "Just . . . she said one thing, Father-Dog," whined Tumble. "That she was going to teach Nibble an . . . an 'important lesson.'"

"I remember what Breeze said, because it sounded crazy." Fluff scratched the ground dolefully. "She was taking her to 'where Storm insulted the Fear-Dog.' She was going to . . . going to give the Fear-Dog a 'gift,' when his time came. And that would make up for wh-what Storm did. And Breeze would get something back from the Fear-Dog because he *loves her.*"

What I *did?* Storm could only stare in bewilderment at the pups. Every eye in the Packs had turned to her, but she couldn't bear to look at any grown dog.

Where I insulted the Fear-Dog? What? When in the name of all the good Spirit Dogs did I do that?

Storm shook her head in confusion. But a creeping coldness filled her spine. She had an idea of what Breeze meant when she said she was going to give the Fear-Dog a gift.

Oh, Nibble. Where are you, little one?

"Is there anything else you remember?" urged Twitch, limping forward. "Anything at all, pups?"

Tumble and Fluff huddled closer together, shivering. "We heard Breeze p-pushing something," wailed Fluff. "There was a scraping sound."

"Like she was . . . pushing rocks?" whispered Tumble. "But we . . . we stayed still, *so still*. Till we were sure she was gone." His voice rose to a desolate howl once again. "It felt like *such a long time*."

Fluff shook her head as if she was trying to dislodge the memory. "And then we were so, so, *so* thirsty, so we crept back to where the water was."

"You were lucky that water was there," said Twitch gravely. "You wouldn't have survived without it."

Tumble sniffed and shook himself. He set his little jaws firmly.

"I think we maybe would," he growled.

Twitch lifted his ears in surprise.

"Yes, I think so." Fluff nodded. "Because of the other pup . . . the one who helped us."

"What?" Sweet jumped, pricking her ears, as Storm's blood ran cold.

"It was a little pup. She was very small. With a pale coat." Tumble gazed solemnly at his Mother-Dog. "When the Fear-Dog came for us, she kept him away."

Chills raced through Storm's hide. She couldn't speak.

"Did you get her out too?" Fluff turned suddenly to her Father-Dog, her ears rising in alarm. "Did you find her?"

"I don't think there was another pup there." Lucky flicked his tail in confusion. "I didn't see one. . . ." He glanced back at Storm with horror. "Did *you* hear another pup?"

She shook her head but said nothing. How could she possibly explain to Lucky that there had been another pup down there— but also, there had not?

Maybe when we've got Nibble back, she told herself, *and everything's calmed down.*

Sweet licked her jaws, perplexed. "Pups, I think perhaps the Earth-Dog sent a friend to help you? Oh, Lucky, I do hope there

199

wasn't another lost pup down there."

"She'll be all right," said a clear voice.

All the dogs turned in surprise to Nip. Arrow and Bella's little pup was panting happily. "You don't need to worry. Honestly. Because the pup, she isn't *lost*."

The grown dogs exchanged bewildered glances, but shoulders were hunched and heads shaken. It was only a pup-story, after all. Only Storm gazed fixedly at Nip, who was murmuring conspiratorially to Scramble. Both pups looked very contented.

So Tumble and Fluff, too, had been visited by their little ghost-cousin. Tufty had come to Tiny, and then she'd come to Tumble and Fluff. Storm's gut tingled with a sudden, happy optimism.

If they're not imagining it, if Tufty is still here, somehow . . . she's already helped save three pups. Maybe there's hope for Nibble, too.

"But what does it mean?" asked Woody. Storm's ears twitched and she almost responded, until she realized Woody was talking not about Tufty, but about Breeze's threats. "What *gift* is she giving the Fear-Dog?"

"Storm," said Lucky. "Are you *sure* you don't know where you insulted the Fear-Dog?"

"Hold on." Rake looked thoughtful, his brow creased. "According to Fluff, the gift is going to be given to the Fear-Dog *when his time comes.*" He glanced at his own Packmates, and at Twitch. "When we lived in Terror's Pack, that phrase meant something very special. Woody, Chase, do you remember? The Time of the Fear-Dog was when the night sky was darkest. When the Moon-Dog was as far away as she can ever be."

Woody nodded. "Of course. Yes."

"But . . ." Sweet rose to her paws, trembling. "The Moon-Dog's time is almost over. Last night she showed barely a whisker."

Lucky rose with a tormented growl. "We have, maybe, two journeys of the Sun-Dog at the most before Breeze carries out her promise." He rested his jaw comfortingly across Sweet's neck, but his eyes swiveled to stare fiercely at the gathered Packs.

"We don't have much time. *We have to stop her!*"

CHAPTER FOURTEEN

"Whisper?" murmured Storm. "Whisper, this isn't right, you should be resting with the Earth-Dog. . . ."

I can't rest, Storm. There'll be time to rest later. *His voice was clear, like light birdsong in her head, and she knew she was dreaming again.* Come with me, Storm.

Stretching, Storm rose to her paws. The camp was quiet, with not even the cry of a night bird to disturb the peaceful darkness. Whisper stood just a little way ahead, his ears pricked in her direction, his tail waving to beckon her. Storm walked after him, her paws surprisingly silent on the fallen leaves. Nothing rustled, and nothing cracked.

The place where she'd killed Terror seemed much closer than she'd remembered; they walked through a quiet, moon-silvered valley, then a cluster of white-barked birches, and suddenly they were there. Storm and Whisper stopped at the edge of the trees, still and focused as they watched the battle was fought in silence before them.

Where they stood, the air was quiet, but out there in the muddy clearing, a thunderstorm raged, and violent rain lashed the two dogs who struggled to the death in the sodden earth. Storm recognized herself, and it didn't seem at all strange to be watching her own life from the outside. She certainly recognized Terror: his glazed red eyes, his matted coat and burly, muscled body; the flopping, snarling jaws that tore at her younger self in a mad rage.

She'd been so much younger, Storm thought as she watched herself fight. This Storm was leaner and lighter, and there was an expression on her face that took the watching Storm aback: she looked so reckless and violent, and the light of righteous justice blazed in her eyes. This earlier Storm had known she was doing the right thing. At least, in this moment she'd known it.

Yet she'd been brutal. As Terror fell under her paws, dream-Storm lunged down to sink her fangs into his lower jaw. Pitilessly, she ripped it away and then stood there, watching blood soak into the drenched earth as Terror kicked and jerked in his final spasms. Dream-Storm trembled with triumph, raising her head to howl her victory.

The older Storm licked her jaws uneasily. At her side, Whisper said nothing, so she turned her head toward him.

"Is this the place, Whisper? Is this where I insulted the Fear-Dog?"

Still the little gray dog didn't reply. He turned away, his flank brushing hers, and she felt her hairs rise under his touch.

Then, in an instant, he was gone.

In the silvered glade of her dream, past and present, reality and memory seemed so confused. Yet that seemed odd, because it had grown so calm here. The torrential rain had stopped, and now the whole clearing was quiet and moonlit; the dead Terror lay on soft, fresh grass. And the younger Storm of her dream was gone, too, she realized; now the present-day Storm was alone with that haunting, terrible corpse.

Shivering, she looked up toward the Moon-Dog, full and brilliant. But as Storm stared, a black cloud drifted across her silver glow, blotting it out. As the great Spirit Dog was swallowed up, she, the glade, and the dead Terror were plunged into utter darkness.

The Fear-Dog. The Fear-Dog is on his way!

Storm jolted awake in the darkness of the hunters' den, her heart thrashing. Stretching out her forepaws, she half rose and opened her jaws to pant for breath.

She knew. *She knew.*

She stood, gave herself a violent shake, and squeezed out of the den to find Lucky and Sweet.

The Sun Dog had not yet risen, but the sky was just starting to grow lighter, as it did always just before he got up. The Alpha and

Beta were asleep, though lightly; the three pups were snuggled up in a tangle between them. Sweet's ears and paws twitched jerkily, and Lucky growled softly in a dream. As soon as Storm nudged them, they both woke quickly and completely, eyes snapping open.

"Storm?" grunted Lucky, lurching to his paws and glancing down at his three sleeping pups. "What's wrong?"

"I know what Breeze was talking about," growled Storm. "I know where I insulted the Fear-Dog. And I think I might know what she's planning."

"What? *Where?*" Lucky went tense, and Sweet's eyes widened with fear.

"The clearing where I killed Terror. That's the only place that makes sense. Breeze would consider that my most unforgivable crime, and she'd think of his death-site as sacred."

Sweet was shivering. "Yes . . . of course," she murmured. "And the *gift* . . ."

Lucky's growl was agonized. "We know what she wants to offer the Fear-Dog." Glancing down at the sleeping pups again, he lowered his voice to barely more than a rasp. "A death. She's going to kill Nibble for him."

Storm dipped her head. She didn't want to say the words out loud, but she thought Lucky was right. And from Sweet's terrified whimper, it was clear the Mother-Dog knew it too. It seemed so obvious now: Breeze would sacrifice Nibble to placate her dreadful Fear-Dog.

"There's no time to be lost, Sweet," she murmured. "We can still stop this. We *must.*"

"I agree," growled Lucky. "Wake the others."

The dogs of the Packs were easy to rouse, instantly alert and jumping to their paws. In a very short time they were gathered in the glade and ready for action; but to Storm, everything still felt sluggish, like another dream in which nothing and no dog could move fast enough. She was painfully aware of how little time they had; above the camp, the Moon-Dog held nothing like the full brilliant glow of Storm's dream. She had shrunk to a hairbreadth claw of silver.

The time of the Fear-Dog is coming.

Lucky was addressing the assembled dogs loudly and clearly, his bark sharp with urgency, but quivering with the dread he must be feeling for Nibble. "We need to go at once," he told them. "Breeze will be heading straight for the clearing where Storm killed Terror. We can't let her reach it before we do; I believe that once she's in that place, Breeze will act on her plan without hesitation."

Sweet choked back a whine of terror.

"Not all of us can run swiftly enough," Lucky went on, attempting a comforting glance at his mate, "so a group of the strongest, fastest dogs will go on ahead. We *have* to get there before it's too late."

"The fastest?" A small, scared whimper rose from Lucky and Sweet's den, and Fluff emerged, trembling. The pups must have woken up in the commotion, Storm realized, and they'd been listening.

Tumble squeezed out alongside his sister. "Mother-Dog? Are you leaving us?"

Tiny joined them both, wide-eyed. "Is it true, Mother-Dog?"

Sweet trotted over to meet them as they stumbled sleepily into the glade. "Oh, pups. I am a swift-dog and I was born to run. It's what I am, and I . . . I should go . . . I . . ."

"Mother-Dog," whimpered Fluff, pressing herself against Tumble. "We don't want you to leave us!"

"I think Fluff's right," said Lucky quietly. "They need you, Sweet."

Sweet turned to her mate, her expression tormented, her ears pinned tight to her head and her tail jerking. For long moments she didn't speak, as the pups whined beseechingly beneath her paws.

At last the Alpha gave a slow sigh. "Very well," she murmured. "I'll stay. These three pups need me. Please, my Beta, find our fourth. . . ."

He nodded, determinedly. "I will. I promise it, Sweet, by the Forest-Dog."

"And we will go with Lucky." Bella stepped forward, Arrow right behind her. "We'll do everything we can to get Nibble home. I can barely imagine how I'd feel if some evil dog took Nip and Scramble."

Lucky's throat convulsed with emotion as he inclined his head to his litter-sister and her mate. "Thank you, both of you."

Arrow nodded. "I hope we can leave our pups safely here with yours?"

"Of course," said Sweet. She paced forward and dipped her head humbly to the Fierce Dog. "Until you come home safe, I'll care for Nip and Scramble as if they were my own. I promise." Tentatively she butted Arrow's nose with hers, then turned and shyly licked Bella's muzzle. "After all that's happened between us, I appreciate your help more than I can say."

"Oh, Sweet," growled Bella softly. "Nibble is our kin. Of course we'll do everything we can. Nip, Scramble: Go with Tiny, Fluff, and Tumble for now."

Yelping, the two pups bounded over at once to their three new friends, and all five of them snuggled up together, a sleepy heap of scrabbling paws and licking tongues. They looked, thought Storm, like one big happy litter.

"I wish I could come," whined Daisy, padding forward. "but I don't think I'm fast enough."

"You're kind, Daisy, and brave." Lucky licked her head. "All of you are. But if it's just Storm, Arrow, Bella, and me, we'll move faster and get there sooner. Let's go."

They were turning to leave when Nip and Scramble suddenly extricated themselves from the tangled heap of pups and bounded over to Bella and Arrow.

"Mother-Dog," yelped Scramble, pawing at Bella's leg. "Wait!"

As Bella leaned down to them both, Nip jumped up and bumped his nose into hers. "We were listening. I know that's bad and we shouldn't, but we couldn't help it."

"You can't come with us, little ones, if that's what you're asking." Arrow rumbled a laugh.

"No, but—" Scramble licked his chops. "What you're going to do—it sounds really dangerous, Father-Dog."

"And it sounds scary," whimpered Nip, "and we don't want you to not come back."

"Oh, my beautiful pups." Bella crouched and pulled them toward her with her forepaws. "I'm not going to lie to you. It *is* going to be dangerous, and we *will* be scared. But we're doing this for Sweet and her pups. They're your kin, too!"

"Be good for Sweet while we're gone," murmured Arrow, bending his head to lick them.

"We will," the two pups chorused, a little mournfully.

"Yes," said Bella. "I know you will. And when your Father-Dog and I return, we'll bring you another new pup-friend to play with."

"*Promise* you'll come back," whined Nip.

"We promise," said Bella gently. "Nothing could keep your Father-Dog and me away from you, my pups, not while we're alive."

For a moment the two pups hung their heads, tails tucked between their hind legs. They stayed there, quiet and subdued, until first Nip's ear twitched, and then Scramble's. Their heads came up and they glanced to the same side, both of them staring very intently at a spot to their left.

Storm's fur rose, and chills rippled through her blood. She was getting used to the sensation, and she almost expected what came next.

"It's all right," barked Nip, suddenly cheerful again. "We're not worried anymore!"

"No, we're not," said Scramble, his tongue lolling happily. "Because Tufty says we'll see you again."

CHAPTER FIFTEEN

It felt strangely right, thought Storm, to pad through the forest with Lucky, Bella, and Arrow at her side. They had walked all day; sometimes exchanging quiet, brief words, sometimes silent, but the silences were not uncomfortable ones. Golden sunlight slanted through the trees, and insects danced in the beams; the trek would have been idyllic if they were not so haunted by their fear for Nibble. There was a sense of shared urgency, of quiet understanding and determination. The four of them had such an odd, fractured history, but they were bound by kinship, and by old Pack loyalties.

Their mission might be dangerous and desperate, thought Storm, but this was how things were meant to be. *We're supposed to be a Pack, even if only for this moment.*

"Bella," said Lucky, clearing his throat as they padded on.

"Bella, there's something I want to ask you. When all this is over, when Nibble is safe"—he drew another awkward breath—"will you and Arrow and Storm stay with us?"

Bella cocked up her ears in surprise, and Arrow, beside her, tilted his head.

"We were wrong," Lucky went on. "Our Pack was wrong and stupid to drive you away, and there's nothing we'd like more than to welcome you back. We would swear to treat you as true Pack-mates, with as much trust and loyalty as you have always given us."

"I . . . this is very sudden, Lucky," Bella murmured, taken aback.

"I know. But I want our pups to grow up together. They are kin, just as we are. We share memories, Bella, and so should they."

Uncertainly, Bella turned her head toward Arrow, then blinked at Storm. Arrow was expressionless; Storm licked her jaws, unnerved.

Bella was right, she thought: Lucky's offer *was* sudden, and very unexpected. For all her confidence in this rescue party, and this mission, Storm couldn't help remembering the bad feeling that had lingered in the Wild Pack: the hostility that had driven away first Bella and Arrow, and then Storm herself. Not knowing what to say out loud, she glanced over Lucky's back and gave Bella the tiniest shake of her head.

Bella gave a gentle growl: "We have our own Pack now, brother, and our own territory. We've made a life for ourselves, and it's a good one."

Lucky sighed sadly. "I understand," he said. "But will you at least think about it? All three of you?"

Bella hesitated. She shared apprehensive looks once again with Arrow and Storm, then nodded slowly.

"Yes, Lucky. That I can promise you. We *will* consider the idea."

He nodded. "That's as much as I could have hoped for right now." He picked up his pace, trotting ahead, as Bella, Arrow, and Storm met one another's eyes, wordless.

Then, abruptly, Arrow halted, one paw raised. His nose jerked up, and his nostrils twitched.

"Rabbits," he growled.

"They're just beyond that rise," murmured Bella.

Storm paused, her belly rumbling. They hadn't eaten since they'd come across that nest of mice just beyond the meadow, and prey would help the journey ahead to no end. Preoccupied and impatient they might be—especially Lucky— but fighting the bad dog on empty stomachs would not be a good idea.

"Lucky," she called softly. "Wait!"

He was striding on, seeming deliberately oblivious. His tail flicked slightly to indicate that he'd heard her, but he didn't stop.

"Lucky!" She picked up her pace, taking a few trotting steps, then halted in indecision. They were perfectly placed right now to stalk those rabbits! If they ran after Lucky now, they'd lose their advantages of quietness and surprise.

It made sense that he was so obsessive about finding the pup, but it was clear to Storm that he wasn't thinking straight—in fact, he wasn't thinking about anything other than Nibble. And dogs who didn't think things through tended to be the dogs who ran into trouble, who got themselves hurt. *If anything happens to Lucky,* she thought, *we'll never find Nibble. And the Pack would have lost its Beta— and Sweet her mate, and Tiny, Fluff, and Tumble their Father-Dog.*

Clenching her jaws, she coiled her muscles to bound after him, but to her surprise Bella leaped in front of her.

"No." Firmly Bella shook her head. "Storm, I'll go."

Without another word, the golden dog turned and loped swiftly and quietly after her litter-brother, bringing him to a halt. As he turned his head, Storm noticed the irritated look he gave Bella.

The two littermates stood some way ahead, in a misty beam

of late sunlight, talking quietly. Storm and Arrow waited, watching. The two golden dogs were so alike, thought Storm, with their glowing coats and dark, intelligent eyes—no dog could mistake them for anything other than litter-siblings.

Storm's heart was in her throat, but after a long conversation she couldn't hear, Lucky nodded once. Then he and Bella turned and padded back toward Storm and Arrow.

"Very well," Lucky growled quietly. "Let's hunt."

"I've never seen this land before." Bella stopped as Lucky turned impatiently.

"I don't remember it either," Storm said. "I'm sure it didn't look like this when we came this way before."

She could still taste the sweetness of rabbit in her mouth, and she licked her jaws. They'd caught two, but after their long trek, it had barely seemed enough to fill her belly. All the same, she didn't dare ask Lucky if they should hunt again. His brown eyes were so hard and fierce—focused, determined, and *desperate*.

Lucky looked from one dog to the other, then turned to face the sweep of grassland again. It formed a long, low, smooth slope, all yellowing grass with barely a hint of a late wildflower.

"I smell no dogs," said Arrow gruffly. "This must be unclaimed territory."

"There's not much scent of prey, either," remarked Bella, narrowing her eyes. "Perhaps no dog *wants* to claim it."

She made a good point, thought Storm. A constant, unnerving rumbling filled the air, making the earth tremble beneath her paws. There was something oddly unnatural about the evenness of the hill, and the strongest scent was one of loudcages. And there was that other tang she'd smelled before, though not often: a sharpness that caught the back of her throat. *Like the scent of the black path to the Light House.*

"Let's go on over that rise," she suggested, nodding to where the land rose slightly. "But carefully, and we should stay low."

Reluctantly Lucky nodded, and lowering his belly, he crept forward, leading his companions down the shallow slope, and then up to the crest of that strangely even ridge.

Storm crawled up beside him, with Bella and Arrow behind her, and peered over. She inhaled sharply. *Yes.* Before them, stretching as far as she could see in both directions, lay one of the flat black paths of the longpaws. Along it thundered loudcage after loudcage, an incessant stream of them, roaring and rumbling as they raced toward and past one another.

As if they're charging in for a fight, then dodging it at the last moment. Storm wrinkled her muzzle in fearful bewilderment.

The sharp black path scent rose powerfully to her nostrils. Beside her, Lucky had narrowed his eyes, glaring in frustration at the racing loudcages.

On her other side, Bella growled. "How will we get over the hardstone?"

"I don't—" Storm flinched back, gasping. Two more loudcages had appeared, racing past the bigger ones. No, not cages; their longpaws sat on top of them, not inside. The roaring beasts were smaller, but faster, and they only had two paws; the longpaws that rode them were covered in black skin, even their heads. *Faceless longpaws, like the one who nearly took Mickey away on the shore of the Endless Lake. . . .*

"This is hopeless." Arrow was staring at the streaming loudcages, his eyes wide.

"We'll get across," growled Lucky. His fangs were clenched in determination. Suddenly he threw back his head, giving a howl of fury. "We *have* to!"

He was almost drowned out by the screams of more small loud-beasts, racing and dodging through the loudcages. Their riders crouched forward, urging them on. Storm flattened her ears against her head, her heart pounding with terror.

As the loud-beasts vanished, the noise faded a little, and Lucky turned to Storm with fiery eyes.

"Nibble is depending on us. We can do this!"

"Look." Arrow had half risen, his forelegs stiff and shaking. "They're gone!"

The other three dogs turned to gaze at the wide black path. Arrow was right. Its hardstone surface was entirely free of loud-cages, though their distant thunder still echoed in the cold air, and the choking stench of their breath lingered. Storm pricked an ear.

"You're right. The herd has passed!"

"Slowly, now," growled Lucky, rising to his paws and slinking down the slope toward the path. "Careful . . ."

He paused at the edge of the path, sniffing the wind. Bella turned her head this way and that, craning her ears for the sounds of approaching loudcages.

"Let's go," murmured Arrow.

All together, the four dogs moved onto the path. One step, two, and then another; the faraway rumble did not grow louder.

Yet something raised the hackles on Storm's neck. She glanced down. Beneath her paws, the hardstone was trembling.

"Wait," she breathed. "Something is moving. . . ."

They paused and looked at her, taut with apprehension.

"It can't be Earth-Dog growling again," she muttered. "Can it . . . ?"

The rumbling became a crash of deafening thunder. Around the curve of the path hurtled the biggest loudcage Storm had ever seen: a massive, square-faced monster belching thick black smoke.

For a fleeting instant, she found herself frozen with shock. Then she yelped in terror.

"Back!"

All four dogs whipped around and sprang for the grass. A mighty wind slammed into them, sending Storm tumbling forward and rolling. *It touched my tail!* She spun, flinching, as the huge brute thundered past, making the ground shake. All four of them pressed their bodies to the ground, and Storm shut her eyes tight, feeling the gale of the creature's passing pin her ears back against her head.

Sky-Dogs, she thought, as her heart convulsed in terror. *It nearly had me!*

CHAPTER SIXTEEN

It seemed to take forever for the ground to stop shaking. Storm cowered with the others, her tail tucked against her rump, her paws trembling.

"Is everyone all right?" asked Bella hoarsely.

Storm nodded slowly, glancing at Lucky and Arrow. Their eyes were so wide, the white rims showed.

"Is the path clear?" Arrow's voice shook.

Lucky nodded slowly. With gritted teeth, he rose to a crouch and edged forward once again. "We'll get across it," he muttered, "*this time.*"

But yet again, the thunder rolled, and another loudcage came rumbling around the curve. It was smaller, its skin yellow, and this time the dogs were ready, crouching low as it passed. But Storm knew no dog could have run across its path and lived. It was slower than the last, and stocky, its blunt face broad and toothed, its paws gigantic as it trundled heedlessly past them. That gaping lower jaw could scoop them all up without it even noticing.

The brute took far longer to vanish around the far bend, but as soon as it did, Lucky was on his paws. "Now!"

But before he had the chance to move forward, another two-pawed loud-beast came racing along the path, its faceless longpaw rider goading it ever faster. Behind that one came another, and then another. The pause after that seemed longer, but as soon as the dogs rose, a red loudcage came from the opposite direction, roaring toward and past them.

Storm gave a high bark of frustration. The pattern was becoming clear now: every time the dogs set a paw on the hard-stone path, the loudcages would appear, scaring them back into the grass, leaving nothing but a stench of smoke and a mocking echo of thunder.

In the stillness after yet another monstrous yellow beast had passed, Lucky shook himself.

"We're going to have to risk it," he said in a hard voice.

"I don't think it's possible," warned Arrow. "We'll have to find a way around it."

"There *is* no way around!" barked Lucky. "I've seen these paths before, when I was a City Dog. They go on forever, but we can do this if we're quick!"

"However quick we are," protested Storm, "those things are faster."

"Then move between them," growled Lucky. "I promise you it's possible. These are faster than the ones I used to dodge, but if we take it in turns, and dart forward between them one at a time, we can get to the other side, I know it."

"Lucky, I know you're desperate to cross this," said Bella quietly. "But I remember when I was a Leashed Dog and my longpaws would take me for walks alongside these paths. The loudcages run in all directions, without warning. They confuse you with their noise and smell, and you can never tell how long the gap between them will be."

"I know." Seeming to gather all his patience, Lucky took a deep breath and touched his nose to hers. "But Bella, we're doing this for Nibble. We can't let the Pack down now. It's our instincts that tell us we can't do this, and I'm not bowing to some ancient *feeling*. If we use our thoughts and our wiles instead, we can make it. We have no choice; Nibble *needs* us to get across."

Bella stared into his eyes for a long moment. Then, slowly, she nodded.

"I'll go first." Arrow stepped forward, his eyes glittering with fierce determination. "I'm fast. You can watch me, see my mistakes—and how I succeed."

Bella hesitated, then nodded and pressed her cheek to his. "Very well. Run fast, my mate. Please . . . please don't come to any harm." She closed her eyes. "And don't stop for any loudcage, no matter how they roar."

"If you hear one coming," said Lucky, "ignore it. You hear them long before they arrive. Don't stop to look. You can do this, Arrow."

The Fierce Dog took a long, deep breath, tensing his muscles. As the path rumbled and trembled, he hesitated, waiting as a blue loudcage raced around the corner and past the dogs. Then, as the sound faded, he and Storm exchanged a glance, and then he looked at Bella. The ground was no long vibrating. Without another word Arrow clenched his teeth and bolted forward.

No loudcage appeared from nowhere to pursue him. He was a blurred shape fleeing toward the far side of the path, his paws barely touching the surface. It was only a matter of moments till he bounded to the safety of the far grass, skidding to a halt and turning to face them. He was wide-eyed and panting, but he'd made it. Storm's heart soared.

"Yes!" barked Bella, relieved.

Arrow reared back on his hind legs and barked his joy, spinning in a circle. "Now you, Bella!"

Lucky nodded to his litter-sister. "Yes. You go next, Bella. Paws on the path."

The three remaining dogs once more placed their sensitive paws on the black surface, concentrating hard. Lucky cocked one ear, then the other.

"I don't hear anything," he murmured.

"If that's the case . . ." Bella hesitated. "When it's safe, we should all cross at once. Arrow made it, didn't he?"

Storm and Lucky exchanged a glance.

"It would be faster," said Storm.

"I don't like it." Lucky shook his head. "If a loudcage *does* come, then all three of us could be killed, and then who could help Nibble? And three dogs will panic more—we'll want to help each other, and then we could freeze. We'll do this separately."

"All right." Storm gave a reluctant nod.

"Bella. Get ready." Lucky tensed again, listening.

The path was still. A distant hum was all they could make out of the loudcage voices. Lucky gave Bella a sharp nod. "Go now."

Sucking in a gasp of air, Bella sprang forward. She was not

as fast as her mate, but all the same, Storm had never seen her move so quickly. Her tail lashed frantically as she hurtled across the hard black surface, and when she plunged down into the grass, Arrow fell on her, licking her face and yapping in delighted relief.

Lucky barked in congratulation and turned solemnly to Storm. "Now you."

"No." Storm shook her head. "You go next, Lucky, while it's quiet. It's your pup who's lost—Nibble needs *you*. You have to stay safe, just in case . . ."

"No, Storm." Lucky laid back his ears and stared at her intently. "I was a City Dog, a Lone Dog. I'm *used* to these things, so I'm the least likely to panic. I'll go last, when you're all safe."

About to argue more, Storm caught the look in his eyes and sighed. She gave a single, resigned nod and turned back to the path.

Placing her paw pads on the hardstone, she concentrated hard, half closing her eyes. Her ears lifted from her skull, she craned to hear the faintest noise.

Nothing. The path was still, the air quiet.

She extended a forepaw and placed it cautiously on the path. No vibration rattled up through her bones, and she took another step.

"Go," murmured Lucky behind her.

A few anxious, trotting steps, and then she was running, her claws rasping on the hardstone. The far side was closer now, and she could see Arrow and Bella, their faces urgent and anxious. She was in the middle of the path. *Not far now. A few more paces—*

Her paw pads tingled. Her bones shook. The hum of a distant monster became a droning growl.

Something's coming!

Storm jolted to a stop, her heart hammering. Her legs were so stiff, the muscles so tense, they felt as if they'd never move again.

Back. I need to go back to Lucky.

No. Forward!

She swiveled her head frantically. In one direction, Bella and Arrow and safety. Behind her, Lucky. And safety.

I'm going to choose wrong!

"Move, Storm!" Lucky's howl split the air. She could hear Bella and Arrow barking dementedly.

Bella and Arrow? Or Lucky? I don't know. . . .

I don't know!

There was a buzzing in her ears, a shimmering tension in her limbs. *If I move, I'll make it worse.* Her paws itched horribly. *That way. No! This way!*

"Storm! *Storm!*"

The loudcage was coming, she could see it. It loomed, faster and faster, bigger and bigger.

Stay here, stay right here. It will run past—

It didn't want to hurt her. Did it? It would swerve, dodge, surely. But if she moved, it would hit her.

Stay!

Move!

Go!

She couldn't think. The thunder filled her head. So loud, she couldn't hear the desperate barking howls anymore. *Stay. Run.*

And with a monstrous blaring howl, the loudcage roared toward her. All Storm could do was squeeze her eyes tight shut.

It slammed into her flank, flinging her into the air—

No. What hit her was not cold and hard and deadly; it was a warm furred body. Panicking, legs flailing uselessly, she crashed into the hardstone and tumbled and rolled.

And there, in the spot where she'd frozen, sprawled Lucky, scrabbling with his paws as the gigantic loudcage bore down on him. Rigid, Storm panted in terror as he dragged himself across the hardstone, kicking frantically and rolling clear as the round black paws of the loudcage crashed over the place where he'd lain.

Storm could not look away; she saw the wind of the monster's passing raise every hair on Lucky's body.

Lucky lay absolutely still for long, horrible moments, his eyes wide and white-edged. His flanks heaved.

He's alive. Oh, Sky-Dogs, he's alive.

Shaking so hard he could barely move his paws, Lucky hauled himself up. He staggered to Storm as she stood up, shaking violently.

"You—you—you pushed me—"

He was still pushing now, shouldering her across the remaining hardstone till her paws touched the soft grass of the slope. They stumbled onto it and stood together for long moments, propping each other up as Bella and Arrow yapped and cried and licked them comfortingly.

"Thank you, Lucky," rasped Storm. "I panicked . . . I couldn't move . . . thank you . . ."

"We made it." His voice was a hoarse rasp. "We all made it. That's all that matters—" He gave himself a hard shake.

"Now let's go and save my pup."

CHAPTER SEVENTEEN

They had been almost faint with relief to leave the hardstone and its loudcages behind; they had run without pausing to the dark line of trees beyond the second longpaw-formed strip of grass. It had been such a dizzying relief to flee into the shadows of a new forest. The pines were enormous, ancient, and seemed to stretch on forever. Storm was certain they were going in more or less the right direction, but who knew what other changes the longpaws might have made to the landscape? She'd suggested the four dogs spread out and scent all around as they walked, searching for any sign of Breeze or Nibble.

But now, the dogs had been trekking through the trees for so long, the exhaustion and terror were catching up with them. Her legs felt weak, and though Lucky forged on, intent and determined, she could see the tremor in his tail that betrayed his delayed shock.

"Lucky, don't run!" yapped Bella, not for the first time. "We could miss the scent."

Lucky glanced briefly back over his shoulder, then frowned. But he slowed to a brisk walk, sniffing more carefully at each tree trunk. Storm knew it was hard for him, that his impatience to find his pup must have been almost unbearable, but she also knew Bella was right—if they couldn't find the spot where Terror had died, and soon, they might never find Breeze and Nibble.

She felt impatient too. *If I get my teeth into Breeze's tail, even the Sky-Dogs won't save her.*

Storm paused to shake out her fur. Once, it had unnerved her to feel this kind of implacable fury—it had made her fear becoming the kind of Fierce Dog that the rest of the Pack was afraid of. But now her rage didn't bother her so much. All she wanted was to save Nibble and make sure that Breeze had hurt and betrayed the Wild Pack for the very last time.

The forest was peaceful—almost too calm. The searching dogs were all jumpy and on edge, Storm knew, and it worried her to her bones that they hadn't yet caught up with Breeze. *She's had the pup for too long. She could have done anything to her!*

"Here!" Lucky's yelp came from up ahead.

Storm, Bella, and Arrow scrambled to his side. He snuffled at a patch of bramble, raking it with a forepaw.

"This scent—it's definitely Breeze and Nibble," he growled. "And it's fairly fresh. They had to have come this way!"

Before any of them could react, Lucky had sprung into a swift run, his tongue lolling. His haunches veered between tree trunks, and Storm saw his shoulder bump painfully into a tree; he rebounded instantly and kept running as the other three loped after him.

"Lucky!" yelped Bella. "Calm down!"

He wasn't listening. Storm could hear his crashing progress through the undergrowth as his pounding pawsteps drew farther away. She could even hear his high, excited pants and intermittent gasping whines of anticipation.

Squirrels darted up trees in a panic as he pounded on, oblivious. A flock of starlings burst from the treetops, cackling in alarm.

Bella gave a panting snarl of frustration as she ran after her littermate. "If Breeze is anywhere near, she'll hear Lucky coming from a forest away!"

"She might change her plans to throw us off," barked Storm,

agitated. "Or worse—she could play it safe and just kill Nibble now."

"She could escape faster without a pup," agreed Arrow in a deep growl. "She's coldhearted enough to make that kind of choice."

With a soft gasp, Bella put on a burst of speed, bounding through the undergrowth after Lucky. Storm, at Arrow's side not far behind her, saw her strive to come abreast of him. As Lucky slowed to veer around a thick broken pine stump, Bella leaped to slap a paw onto his back.

Lucky staggered sideways and slumped against a tangle of thick undergrowth. Bella pounced to straddle him, placing her jaws softly at his throat.

"Stop," she murmured through his fur, as Storm and Arrow caught up. "Stop, Lucky!"

He almost sprang back to his paws, but Bella sank her jaws deeper into his throat fur and growled softly as she pinned him down harder. Storm and Arrow exchanged a look of misgiving. Lucky was kicking and struggling now, his eyes rolling back as he snarled at his litter-sister, but she held firm.

"Lucky, calm down. You *must*, for Nibble's sake!"

That seemed to get through to him. His eyes darkened and

his muscles went limp as he stopped fighting. Carefully, slowly, Bella drew back, her chest heaving. "Lucky, if Breeze is close, she'll hear you. We can't afford to alert her. Not now." She gazed at him, her eyes pleading.

Lucky's flanks rose and fell with his desperate, panting breaths. He spoke through gritted teeth. "I can't slow down, Bella. I've tried to make myself, but I can't do it! Not now, not when we have the scent!"

"You have to." Her voice was level and low. "You're playing into Breeze's paws if you dash in without thinking. This is our one chance to catch her, Lucky, and if we fail today, we won't get to grow old together watching our pups." She crouched lower beside him. "Imagine it, Lucky, and focus on that—your pups and mine, playing together, swimming in the pond, learning to hunt and fight. I want that for them. I want them to grow up together the way that you and I never got to—as kin. Don't you want that, too? Don't throw away our chance by rushing in without thinking."

Lucky panted, his eyes creased; it must have been a huge effort for him to control his instinct to run to his pups. Storm's heart ached for him, but she knew Bella was right. "Yes," he whispered at last. "That's what I want too, Bella. And yes, I have to stay calm. You're right."

"Of course I am." A smile crept into Bella's voice. "I'm *always* right, litter-brother."

With aching slowness, Lucky clambered to his paws. His head hanging low, he blinked up at Bella.

"What you said." He licked his jaws. "Does it mean you're considering it, Bella? Rejoining the Pack with Arrow and your pups?"

Bella stared off into the woods. Then she tilted her head. "Maybe. *Maybe*, Lucky. I can't deny it would be good to see the pups grow up together."

"Then," he said, giving himself a thorough shake, "let's go and find my lost one."

The four dogs set off once more, keeping this time to a steady and determined pace. Storm could tell that Lucky was making all the effort he could to control his impulses. She could see the tension in his jaw, the stiffness of his limbs, but he walked with a brisk rhythmic stride.

Storm glanced up through the branches. The Sun-Dog was beginning to glow orange as he loped toward his western den, and his beams dappled the forest floor with dark golden light. Insects danced in his last rays, and the sky had taken on a lilac tinge.

"We must be close. I'm sure these were the woods on Terror's territory." Lucky had his nose lifted, scenting the air.

"Look," murmured Arrow. He stopped, eyeing a broad, empty space beyond the trees. Between him and the clearing, a tall metal fence barred their way. "Is that a clearing?"

"A new one, by the look of it," said Lucky. "One made by long-paws."

The dogs stood in the tree shadows and stared. Lucky was right, thought Storm: This was no natural glade. It was *vast*. Huge numbers of trees had been cut down, and a few of their stumps remained at the edges of the clearing. Each of them was severed as if by an enormous, single fang; the flat wounds of their stumps were still raw, glowing deep orange-gold in the late light. The whole expanse of the forest floor was littered with pale shavings and splinters of wood, soft to the touch of paw pads—though it wasn't the forest floor, not really; this was an open meadow now. *If you could call it a meadow,* thought Storm, *when nothing grows anymore.* Over the devastation hung clouds of insects, attracted by the sap and the fresh, sharp scent of resin.

This must be the work of longpaws, Storm realized; no ani-mal of the forest could sever a tree in a single bite and uproot their gigantic stumps. The great trunks themselves had vanished, though Storm could not imagine even longpaws carrying away such huge lengths of timber. Perhaps the loudcages had dragged them off to be devoured? There were plenty of those: Ranks of the sleeping yellow monsters crouched on the other side of the clearing, backed against the far fence. From the torn ground rose new longpaw dens: those tall, straight, unnatural stone creations. Their eyes were blank and empty, though, and there was no sign of longpaws within them.

Arrow ventured toward the fence, paw by careful paw. Even on this side of it, the forest had been ravaged. The others followed him, gazing around in awe at the destruction.

"Look." The Fierce Dog nodded. "Huge holes over there, where the loudcages have dug up more trees. The longpaws have clawed at the earth, too. They've hurt everything."

It was true—a vast expanse of soil had been turned over and exposed, and gouged into it were the brutal claw marks of the loudcages.

Storm pinned her ears back, her heart fluttering. "They're harming the Earth-Dog and the Forest-Dog at the same time," she whispered. "Are the longpaws *trying* to provoke the spirits?"

"I hope the Spirit Dogs aren't angry enough to make another Growl." Bella shuddered.

As they stood there in the fading sunset, a bright white light suddenly flooded the whole clearing before them. Storm jumped and gave a yelp of shock. Lucky, his hackles raised, crouched and stared up.

But there were no longpaws in sight. Storm and the others followed Lucky's gaze to the huge metal trees within the fence. Their tops were too bright to look at for long, a white glare as intense as the flash of the Lightning Dog. It spilled out beyond the fence, touching their paws with its cold glow. Though the forest behind the dogs was already dusky and darkening, the vast glade was as bright as daylight.

"Let's keep going. We should be getting close to the spot where Terror died, and this feels like a bad place," said Bella. She was shivering beneath her fur.

"Not just because of the longpaw damage," murmured Storm, feeling a chill creep along her spine. "There's something else. Can it be . . . ?"

Storm clenched her jaws, trying to think. Even with her eyes tight shut, she could still see those great loudcages on the clearing's far side, their yellow skins livid in the unnatural white light. They slumbered silent, motionless, so why did she imagine that they were moving?

No, it was something moving between them—a hulking, brutal figure that stalked in their shadow, his malevolent yellow eyes reflecting their lurid hides.

Storm's eyes snapped open and she gave a strangled whine. "It is!"

"What do you mean?" Lucky turned to her, alarmed, and Arrow and Bella cocked their ears.

Her throat felt tight, and her blood thrummed hot beneath her pelt.

"The place where the mad dog Terror died isn't beyond all this—this *is* the place. We found it. This is where Breeze was heading."

She stood on trembling paws, gazing around. Lucky, Arrow, and Bella were silent too, their hackles as high as her own. And no wonder, Storm thought; this place buzzed with menace. It hung there in the air like the insect-clouds. She swallowed hard. "This is where I insulted the Fear-Dog."

"And it'll be where Breeze brought Nibble," Lucky growled.

"We have to get through that fence." Arrow flicked his ears toward it.

"I don't like those lights," murmured Bella, but she followed as they stepped cautiously across the devastated border.

The oddness of the soft, pulverized wood beneath her paws sent shivers through Storm's hide, but she walked on, trying to be silent. The glare of the white light was oppressive, and she felt as if she was exposed to every hostile eye in the forest. Ahead of her, Arrow reached the barrier of the fence; he shied away at first, blinking in the glare, then pawed tentatively at the wire.

The prickling fear became more of a distraction with every step, so that when a strange scent drifted to Storm's nostrils, it took long moments for it to coalesce into a threat.

But belatedly she halted, tensing. "What's that?" she growled.

"I smell it too." Lucky's tail trembled.

"Dogs," said Storm in a low voice, "but like no dogs I've smelled before."

"I have." Arrow backed away a pace from the fence, his muzzle peeled back to show his teeth. "I think . . . those are Rough Dogs."

"I know the scent too." Bella's nostrils flared. "I'm almost sure it's Rough Dogs." A shiver rippled through her.

Storm pricked an ear. "I've never heard of those."

"I have." Lucky's eyes widened. "I remember now. Long, long ago, I had a run-in with a pair of them. I was a Lone Dog then. I remember running. *Hard*."

"I don't know—" Storm glanced around at her companions, bewildered, but at that moment, barks rang out across the ravaged clearing.

They were deep, sonorous, resonant hollers that shook the ground, and they seemed filled with the threat of savagery. Three shapes broke out of the shadows between the loudcages and loped toward them in bounding, thudding paces.

Storm froze, staring, her shoulders tensed. Under the fierce white light, the dogs were soon clearly visible. They were not unlike Fierce Dogs, their glossy coats black and tan, their fangs white. But there the resemblance ended. They were not long-legged and lean; they were colossal, stocky brutes with square heads and thickly muscled necks. There wasn't a suggestion of fear or hesitation in their blunt, snarling faces. The fence lay between the two groups, but staring in disbelief at the hulking attackers, Storm wouldn't be surprised if the Rough Dogs crashed straight through it.

At Storm's flanks, Lucky, Arrow, and Bella had dug their forepaws into the flattened earth; they stood tall and stiff, hackles bristling and fangs bared. For a horrible moment, Storm quailed with panic. *But Arrow, Bella, and Lucky have met dogs like these before. They know what to do.* And her three companions stood there, stalwart and implacable, facing down the oncoming challenge. Storm bared her fangs and did the same.

They'd done the right thing, she realized with a flood of relief.

Not a rabbit-chase ahead, just beyond the fence, the three power-ful strangers jolted to a halt and snarled, hackles high.

"Intruders!" barked their leader.

"Away with you," snarled the dog on his left.

"Go," grunted the third. "Go or die!"

At Storm's side, she sensed Bella's shiver of fear, and Storm knew that her resolve was splintering. At any moment, she might turn and flee. Yet their first instinct had been the right one, the Fierce Dog within Storm knew it: They must not show weakness, or they were lost. The only way to win this standoff was to go on the attack.

With a deep growl, Storm bounded forward a pace. "*You* go! Leave here!"

That sent the three Rough Dogs into a frenzy of disbeliev-ing fury. Their barks and howls deepened, battering Storm's ears, their sheer volume almost throwing her off-balance. But she dug in her paws grimly and snarled in their faces. At her side, Lucky and Arrow did the same.

With an abruptness that was almost as shocking as the attack, the Rough Dogs fell silent. Together they stared at Storm and her companions, their fangs still showing at the corners of their sla-vering lips.

"We know who you are, strangers," growled the leader. "Be gone from here."

Storm glanced quizzically at Lucky. "You know—"

"We've been expecting you, and there's no way we'll let you through." The second Rough Dog shook his brutal head, sending slaver flying.

"How do you—" began Bella. But she was cut off by the leader.

"We were warned," he barked, and Bella took a shocked pace back. "Warned by the good dog."

"Yes, the good dog and her pup. Friendly, she was." The third of the Rough Dogs licked her jaws. "Told us, she did, that a Pack of liars would come through after her. That you are not to be trusted. None of you!"

A low snarl rose from Lucky's throat, and Storm knew he was about to howl with rage. She bounded hurriedly forward to block his furious lunge. "Wait!" she barked at him, before turning to the brutes on the other side of the fence. "Did this *good dog* tell you the pup was hers?"

"The pup was hers," barked the leader. He hesitated for a moment and glanced at each of his friends. Then he nodded. "She said so!"

Storm took a breath, gathering her patience. "Think about it," she growled. "What did this good dog look like?"

"Brown!" barked the second Rough Dog.

"What did the pup look like?" Storm asked quickly.

The second dog's ears flickered with a moment's unease. "Uh . . . golden?"

"That means nothing," said his leader confidently. "Lots of brown dogs have gold pups."

"More gold dogs have gold pups, though," said Storm. "Aren't I right?" She wrinkled her brow, as if suddenly confused herself.

"More. Yes," snapped the leader.

Storm nodded at Lucky behind her. That rumbling snarl was still growing in his throat.

"The pup looked nothing like that older dog, that *good dog.* Did she? Here, smell my leader. He is that pup's true father. I swear it by the Forest-Dog."

The three Rough Dogs stared at Lucky with interest.

Lucky's growl grew muffled, and he stepped forward, his muscles still trembling with suppressed fury. As he pressed close to the fence, the three Rough Dogs gathered to snuffle at him. Storm could see the Beta dog clenching his jaw to keep from snarling—or worse—at these guards.

In only moments, the huge leader sprang back, snarling with

offended annoyance. "She tricked us, brothers!"

"The good dog was a bad dog, Brick," said the second, his eyes wide. "The good dog was a liar!"

"From now on she is the *bad dog*," declared the leader, shaking his head violently.

"We don't like to be tricked, do we, Brick?" growled the third. "How dare she trick us? We are not stupid dogs!"

"Indeed you're not," barked Storm, trotting forward. "You are not stupid, you're clever dogs. We are clever dogs too, and the bad dog tricked *us*. She's deceptive and a liar, and any good dog can be tricked by her."

"Any good dog," echoed Brick, the leader, looking flattered.

"Yes. A good dog like you: a clever dog." Storm took a breath, and her voice grew hard and dark. It was easy to persuade these strangers when she spoke the truth. "No dog—*no* dog could imagine another dog being as wicked as the liar. She isn't just a bad dog, my friends, she's *evil*. Any dog can be fooled by her if they don't know her."

The three Rough Dogs exchanged knowing looks, and then Brick nodded to Storm again. "She isn't far," he told her angrily. "She's on the other side of this here camp, and she passed through not long ago. I'll show you the way in. Feel free to hunt down that bad dog. My Pack won't stop you."

"Thank you." Weak with relief, Storm bowed her head.

"Here." Gruffly Brick padded along the fence. "This is where the bad dog came through." He tugged at the wire with his teeth, and with a few jerks of his powerful neck, it gave way. The mesh bowed inward, leaving a gap beneath it that was promisingly wide. "If you just wriggle a bit, you—"

He stopped, jerking his head up, and every dog fell silent and still.

The howl that rose from the far side of the clearing was eerie, an ululating wail that held madness and evil and horror. Every hair on Storm's pelt prickled and rose, and coldness gripped her gut.

"Come to me! Come to me! I bring you my gift!"

"Sky-Dogs," breathed Arrow, shuddering.

"That's Breeze," howled Lucky. "And she's *calling to the Fear-Dog.*"

CHAPTER EIGHTEEN

"Hurry!" barked Bella. "Get through the fence!"

Lucky plunged down into the gap, kicking and scrabbling as if his life depended on it. *It's more important than that,* Storm realized. *Nibble's life depends on it.* She gripped the wire in her teeth and yanked hard to widen the gap so that the others could wriggle through more easily.

"Nibble! Nibble!" Lucky gave sharp yelping howls in the deepening twilight.

Storm cocked an ear, growling in frustration. If she could only tell him to keep calm—but the most important thing right now was to get herself and Bella and Arrow through.

"Thank you," gasped Bella, shaking soil from her coat on the other side of the fence.

"Good, you can go find your pup," growled Brick.

"We will," rumbled Arrow as he squeezed through. "We—"

That awful howl split the air again, echoing across the waste-land.

"Reward me, Great One, for my perfect gift to you!"

"Nibble, I'm coming," barked Lucky hoarsely.

Bella was already bounding to block his way. "Hush! You can't let her know how close we are! I *promise*, we'll save your pup, but we still need to be stealthy."

Storm pressed herself flat to the ground, tasting earth in her teeth as she wriggled under the fence. With no dog holding the fence for her, the wire scraped her back and ribs, and the soil itched in her fur, but at last she was through and free. She shook herself hard.

"Follow me," growled Brick. He turned and trotted in heavy, loping paces into the heart of the longpaw camp, his comrades loping over to join him. "That howl, it sounded like it was coming from up there—see? There, high up in that broken den."

Storm paused, one paw lifted. Now that she was right in the center of the camp, she could see the new longpaw dens properly, and it was unnerving. These were not quite like any she'd seen: so tall and straight, yet somehow unfinished. They looked as if they were meant to rise higher, but their tops had been snapped off: as if another Big Growl had struck here, but without leaving debris or broken walls. The stones simply rose and rose, straight and true, till they . . . stopped. There was no roof or covering. It was very strange. *Perhaps they only want to rise farther.*

How did the longpaws manage to build so high? wondered Storm. She hated to admit it, but she was impressed, although she couldn't see why they would bother to make such huge dens for themselves and their packs.

From high in one of those unfinished dens, feverish howls rose. There were so many spaces and gaps in the walls, the sound echoed and rebounded across the camp; just as with the tunnel in the cliff, it was impossible to tell exactly where the sound came from. Storm turned, uncertain and frustrated, twitching her ears this way and that. The other dogs milled around her, pacing impatiently in the loose soil. Lucky looked frantic.

A mocking bark drifted down from somewhere up in the high dens. "Isn't this a terrible place?"

Storm froze, and she bit back angry barks. *Breeze knows we're here.*

"Oh, such a place to get lost . . . !" Her voice trailed off as she began panting with excitement. She wanted the Pack Dogs to know how much she was looking forward to what she was going to do. "So many sharp and dangerous things. Small spaces, high drops. A dog can't run or jump, because a dog might slip and fall. An awful place!"

A low, dreadful growl was rumbling from Lucky's throat. Storm moved close to him, pressing her warm shoulder to his for reassurance. "Careful, Lucky," she murmured. "We can't put a paw wrong now."

"Don't you dare hurt Nibble, Breeze, you—" Lucky howled, then stopped, as if he couldn't think of a bad enough insult. He snarled in torment once again.

"A dog could get lost forever in here," came Breeze's singsong voice. "Especially a little one."

Lucky was shaking; his legs trembled with the longing to rush forward, and his nostrils were flared wide in his desperate search for Nibble's scent. Storm licked his ear rhythmically, trying to calm and console him. Arrow and Bella stared up at the unfinished dens, their faces taut with anger.

The dens looked even more ominous now; dark clouds were rolling across the dusky sky, turning twilight almost instantly to night. Spots of cold rain hit Storm's fur, and a shiver rippled through her.

When Breeze spoke again, the mockery was tinged with rage.

"How arrogant your Pack is! Always thinking you know best, that your way is the only noble way for a dog. You had to kill my dear leader, Terror, to prove it, didn't you? But *why* should you kill him, if you were so right and good? Were you so afraid that he'd prove you wrong? Were you so frightened of his better way?" She gave a coughing, sneering laugh. "You think the world belongs to you and your Wild Pack. Your arrogance! You killed my Terror in cold blood!"

Lucky jammed his forepaws into the earth as the rain began to fall harder. "No dog murdered Terror!" he howled. "He died in combat. Fair, honorable combat!"

Breeze chuckled again. The echoing sound was eerie enough to raise Storm's fur all over her body. "What do you know of honor? You are bad dogs! Worse than bad! The Fear-Dog will *make all of you pay!*"

Brick grunted, bemused. "May I just say," he said, "she sounds a little insane."

Lucky tore himself away from the others, brushing Bella and plunging through fresh puddles of rain toward the high longpaw dens. Frightened for him, Storm raced in pursuit, ignoring the awful prickling of rage in her gut. *I can't let my Fierce side out—not even here.*

But if it came down to saving Nibble from that mad creature Breeze, she knew she'd release the Fierce Dog and would not feel the least bit bad about it. *Even if I tear her apart, I won't feel the slightest bit of guilt.* Clenching her fangs, Storm flew after Lucky. He darted into the dark mouth of the first longpaw den he came to, and Storm followed with a deep unease. It wasn't clear which, if any, of these places Breeze was howling from. Any one of them could be a trap!

Inside, surrounded by unfamiliar shadows, she halted, her flanks heaving. There in the middle of the floor stood Lucky, a gleaming gold, trembling shape of fury. His fur was raised so much, he looked huge.

"They're not here," he rasped without looking around.

Tentatively, Storm padded forward to his side. "This place is so strange, with odd spaces and tunnels," she murmured. "Breeze's voice could be coming from anywhere."

"And she knows it," snarled Lucky. "She's taunting us."

Storm nodded and padded cautiously to the nearest passageway, sniffing at the darkness within. This place was so cold, colder than any dog's forest den, and a mist of rain fell straight in through the open roof. The fine white dust beneath her paws was growing sticky, clogging her paw pads. She could hear the patter and rattle of rain on the walls, and the distant grumble of thunder. But there was no scent or sound of Breeze or Nibble.

"I don't care how clever she is," snarled Lucky. "I am taking my pup back from her tonight." Turning, he stalked back outside.

Storm followed, giving the den a last look of misgiving. Arrow, Bella, Brick, and his comrades were waiting in the now-steady downpour, and they all turned in silence and began to pad through the camp, sniffing methodically at every cranny and gap.

"Brick," asked Bella in a low voice, "do you have any idea where she might have taken Nibble?"

He shook his heavy jowls. "Us Rough Dogs aren't allowed inside these dens, so we don't know them well. Our job is to stop strange longpaws getting into the camp and make sure no one steals from our longpaws. I'm sorry."

"Don't worry," growled Lucky from up ahead. "We'll find the bad dog anyway."

Storm shook water from her coat; the rain was falling hard now, drenching every part of the dogs' fur. Lucky's coat had turned from gold to a bedraggled brown, and every one of them was streaked with mud.

"Here," said Lucky brusquely, slinking through an entrance into another tall den.

Storm flinched. Just inside, the passageway was blocked by a strange, pale barrel propped up on metal bars; it stank of stale, earthy wetness, and its open mouth was splattered with dried white mud. Something about the thing made her hackles rise.

"Maybe we should try to get in another way," she suggested.

"No. I think Breeze has taken Nibble in here; I can smell her, even past that white mud. We don't have time to waste." Lucky dropped onto his belly and crawled beneath the thing. Halfway through, he stopped, nudging at the door beyond with his muzzle.

"Lucky . . . ," began Bella.

With a yap of anger, Lucky's haunches tensed and swung with effort. His rump bashed against the mud-barrel, and it began to topple, with a slow inevitability that made Storm yelp and scurry back. She bumped into Arrow, who almost tumbled into Brick. Writhing backward, they all shot back out into the open yard, with Lucky reversing last.

The barrel finally passed the angle of no return. It fell suddenly, crashing into the hard floor. The white mud inside was liquid; it splashed and poured out, a thick river of sticky sludge. Panting with panic, the dogs dodged, trying to avoid the creeping mud.

"Oh, my stubby tail." Brick gave a heavy sigh. "We're going to get in so much trouble for that. Right, Brunt?"

"Yup," said Brunt. "You think we can lick it up?"

"Ugh, no," said Brick. "It sticks to your tongue. Remember, Stub had to go to the vet when she drank it?"

Brunt shrugged in resignation.

The Wild Pack dogs were shaking themselves, trying to claw and lick away the white mud where it had caught in their fur. It tasted vile; Storm shuddered and spat. Brick was right: it stuck to a dog's teeth.

"Could've been worse," pointed out Brick. "But you'd all better roll in a puddle or something. It turns hard as rock if you leave it."

"You'll never get it out of your fur," nodded Brunt. "Show 'em, Nail."

Looking embarrassed, the third Rough Dog turned around and presented her rump. Storm gasped. It was missing great patches of fur, with bare skin exposed, and it looked both painful and utterly humiliating.

"See," rumbled Brunt, "that's where the longpaws had to shave off Nail's fur to get the mud out. Go roll in a puddle."

"I'm hoping it'll grow back," said Nail brightly.

"Yeah, sure it will." Brick sounded unconvinced.

Storm and the others needed no further coaxing. They bounded over to the spreading, rain-pocked puddles and rolled thoroughly, over and over, checking one another for any last scraps of white mud.

"I think you're all done, Bella," said Arrow, examining her chest. "Yes it's all gone. How about me?"

"You're fine," Bella told him, peering close. "Lucky, have you—" She stopped, raising her head and peering around.

"Lucky?" Storm tensed.

"He's gone back into one of the dens," growled Arrow, the stump of his tail quivering as he glared at the doorway.

"No!" gasped Bella.

"Breeze will hear him coming," barked Storm. "She'll get away!"

"That impulsive . . . litter-brother of mine." Growling, Bella shook her head. "Arrow, you go after Lucky. Storm and I will find another way inside, and we'll cut Breeze off if she tries to leave. Go!"

Arrow sprinted off through the rain, lean and fast and determined, his nimble paws dodging the spilled sludge as he vanished inside the den. Springing forward, Bella barked to summon Brick, Nail, and Brunt, and the Rough Dogs joined her and Storm in running around the side of the structure.

The glaring white light didn't pierce between the dens, and Storm's heart thrashed inside her chest as they trotted through the black shadow between the tall walls. Now that they were so close, terror for Nibble seemed to fill every part of her, burning in her blood and throbbing in her head. It was impossible to hear any of Breeze's movements through the hammering of the rain, and even Storm's sense of smell seemed hopelessly confused. There was too much to sort out: the smell of longpaws, the stench of loudcage-fuel, the musty scent of that white mud. Rain filled her nostrils and her mouth. And layered over everything was the awful tang of panic.

This was hopeless. She was going to be useless to Nibble. *Get a grip, Storm!*

As they emerged from the shadows into the white glow of a broad yard, the oppressive air was split by a high yelp of terror. Every dog froze.

"Nibble?" Storm backed onto her haunches, staring up with the others at one of the dens.

Above them, the torrential rain was illuminated by the glare of the white lights, so that the sky seemed pierced by countless silver claws lashing down. It was so hard to see through the downpour, but the silhouette above them was clear enough: a tiny dog stood on a wooden platform supported by metal bars. She stood rigid, trembling, her paws jutting over the edge.

And she was *so high up*.

Beside the pup stood the ominous shape of Breeze, and in the lights her eyes were visible: glowing wild with triumphant glee. The rain drove down onto them both, but though the pup shivered and whimpered, Breeze did not seem to feel it at all.

Storm bounded forward and gave a furious bark of challenge. "Come down and fight me, you evil coward!"

Breeze tilted her head, almost as if she was considering it.

"Go on!" yelled Storm. "If you really want to avenge Terror, surely you want to fight the dog who killed him? Come and take your honorable victory, Breeze!"

Breeze tipped back her head and gave a delighted howl that sent teeth of fear along Storm's spine. "I don't fall for the Wild Pack's tricks. Not anymore! If I come down there to fight you, Storm, the others will leap in and kill me! I know that's how you work, don't I?" Her voice took on that horrible, mocking singsong quality again. "'Work together, work together, we all work together. All for one, and every dog for all the rest. No dog stands by while another is in trouble!'"

Storm clenched her fangs. Breeze might be a coward, she might know perfectly well that she had no chance of outfighting Storm—but she had a point. If any one of them was in danger, or if it looked as if Breeze might win and Nibble would be lost forever, the other Pack Dogs would leap in to protect or avenge.

That's what makes us Packmates.

"Ah, Storm. Good try, but you won't tempt me down to my own death, oh no!" Breeze's fangs glowed white in the rain-drenched glare. "I have work to do and a *gift* to give! Now your Pack will know pain and grief! Grief like a fang biting into all your filthy hearts. The wound will never stop bleeding! It will bleed forever, like the wound to my heart when you murdered Terror. How will you bear it? You are not as strong as me! This pup, so small and adorable—look at her! Try to remember her like this! Because soon, she'll be broken into pieces—countless pieces!"

Storm drew back her lips from her teeth, snarling with helpless rage. So Breeze meant to push Nibble to her death? Beneath her paw pads she could feel the hard, cold ground. *No!* Nibble would break on the stones of the longpaws. High above Storm and her friends, the pup stood rigid, shaking with terror. *And there is nothing we can do!*

"Keep her busy." Storm heard Bella's hard murmur at her ear.

"I'll try to find a way up to the top. Don't let her push the pup, Storm! Keep her distracted!"

Storm turned to protest—what could Bella do, with the pup perched so precariously up there?—but the golden dog had already spun and raced off, vanishing into the shadows behind the den.

Yet maybe Bella was right. *It's worth a try,* Storm thought dully. *There's nothing else we can do. Maybe it's a risk we have to take.*

Distract her: That was what Bella had said to do. Her blood hot with fury, Storm sent a volley of barks toward the sneering bad dog.

"Hey, Breeze. Let me tell you something before you do anything rash."

Breeze cocked her head sweetly. "Talk all you like, Storm. It will change nothing."

At Storm's side, Brick snarled, low in his throat. The other Rough Dogs glared up, looking at Breeze with disgusted horror. Storm took another pace forward.

"Remember when I killed Terror?" she barked, her jaws feeling heavy—like her mouth was refusing to speak. For the first time in her life, she was hoping a dog would believe that she had a Fierce nature. "Of course you do, Breeze. That's what drove you mad, right?" Storm peeled back her muzzle, hoping her fangs would flash as sinister and white as her enemy's. "But I never told you—never told any dog—something very important. I killed Terror . . . and I liked it. Oh, I *enjoyed* it, Breeze. I remember it, dream of it, almost every night. How pathetic he was! Such a pitiful dog, pleading for his life in his last moments, like some frightened rabbit. Terror? Hah! He didn't deserve the name. He should have called himself *Trembler*, because that's all he did when I fought him—he trembled in fear, like a coward!"

Breeze tensed, then began to pace madly back and forth on that high wooden platform. She kept her wild eyes fixed on Storm, and in the white glare Storm could see slaver dribbling from her jaws. Then, horribly, Breeze stopped. She crouched back on her haunches and raised a paw behind Nibble.

Brick gasped in horror. Nail and Brunt made appalled growls of protest. Storm let out an earsplitting howl of hate, chilling enough to make Breeze flinch and hesitate.

"Listen to me, Breeze! Listen, and I'll tell you a secret. I'll tell you something I've never told *any* dog."

Breeze angled her head and looked down again, coldly interested.

"Let me tell you, Breeze: I wish Terror was still alive, too!" *So that I could kill him again,* Storm thought, but she managed not to say it. She fought to soften her voice. "I know it sounds strange for me to say that, but I do. Lately I've been thinking that he maybe wasn't a mad dog, not really. He had a hard life. He struggled in the world after the Big Growl, maybe more than any of us. Maybe he just figured out that a dog has to be ruthless to survive! Maybe our Packs would have found a way to coexist, if we had listened to him. After all, Terror was a clever dog, wasn't he? I think I could have learned a lot from him."

Desperately Storm craned her head up, peering through the driving rain. Breeze had gone very still. Slowly she nodded.

"We could have been one Pack. Perhaps, if Terror had—"

Breeze stiffened again, rising stiffly to her paws. "Stop!"

For a moment, Storm thought it was the faraway thunder she was hearing. Then she realized it was the low, insane growl in Breeze's throat.

"Trying to trick me, Storm? Again?"

"No! Breeze, listen." Storm breathed hard. "You of all dogs know what I'm capable of. You used my own nature against me, to drive me out of the Pack. You *spoke* kindly of me, but you always believed I was an irredeemable savage. Didn't you?"

"Oh, yes." Breeze's soft growl drifted down through the rain.

"And I was right! And your beloved Pack believed it too, so very easily!"

Storm clenched her jaws together. Even though she was talking to a vicious, cruel bad dog, it was still like a claw in her belly fur to know how easily others believed her to be as vicious as the dogs of Blade's Pack. "So surely," she murmured, "you can believe me now. I tell you, I can see the value in learning from a dog like Terror! I *do* wish he hadn't died."

Above, despite the hammering downpour, there was stillness and silence for an achingly long moment. *I've gotten through to her,* thought Storm with a surge of hope. *She listened!*

Something was moving behind Breeze: a pale, furred shape, its shoulders hunched low and threatening as it prowled closer.

Bella? No—

A sound must have alerted Breeze, a claw on wood perhaps. She spun around, backing toward Nibble, and howled like the Fear-Dog itself.

"Get back! Get back, you trickster! A paw closer, and I'll smash this pup on the stones!"

CHAPTER NINETEEN

Storm flung herself left and right, indecisive, staring up as the rain lashed and stung her eyes. Beside her, the Rough Dogs hollered and barked in futile protest. Above them, Bella snarled, halting as Breeze edged tauntingly closer to the pup.

"Breeze! Don't you dare!" barked Storm, as the others howled in fury. She had never felt so utterly helpless. A huge mound of soil was piled to her left, heaped against the wall, and it was just possibly big enough to let her climb up there. But there was no way she would manage it in time. Breeze would see her coming from far away and push Nibble to her death.

She could hear more barks and yelps, faint and distant and distorted by echoes, and she recognized the voices of Lucky and Arrow. *But they won't get there in time, either.* It was clear from the panicked note of their howls that the two of them were some-where inside that building, lost and disoriented by the many walls and passageways. Bella's route through the back must have taken her straight to the top...

At least Breeze did not have any cohorts who could go after Lucky and Arrow and fight them off, but there was no telling what might happen to the two dogs in the darkness—they could easily fall from some unfinished wall, or through a gaping hole in the ground.

"Brick." Storm spun and faced the big Rough Dog. "Would you and Nail and Brunt go find my friends? The ones who were with us earlier? I think they're going to need help, and you all know these buildings better than any dog."

"Hunh," grunted Brick, glowering up at the platform. "I want to take care of Breeze myself. No dog tricks me and gets away with it! And *no* dog should ever hurt an innocent pup!"

"Please, Brick? This is how you can help—by finding Lucky and Arrow. If you don't, the pup might die. Please!"

She had only just met these dogs, but the desperation in her eyes must have been vivid. Glancing at his friends, Brick nodded gruffly.

"All right. Anything to thwart that liar." He jerked his head, and his two companions bounded after him into the half-built den.

Panting, Storm eyed the mound of earth. No, it wasn't possible to climb it, not in time.

Not if Breeze is watching me . . .

Staring up at the platform again, she met Bella's eyes. Holding the golden dog's gaze for a moment, she glanced sideways at the earth mound, then back at Bella.

Bella hesitated, then gave her a single, barely perceptible nod. Without giving a hint of warning, she sprang at Breeze, taking her by surprise and tumbling her onto the wooden slats of the platform. Breeze rolled a little distance from Nibble, thrashing and snarling as she fought Bella off.

They could both fall to their deaths, thought Storm, whining in anxiety. But she couldn't afford to watch, or Bella's maneuver would have been in vain. Dashing to the earth mound, she bounded onto its flank and scrabbled up a few paces.

The soil was sodden and crumbly, and she could barely get purchase. Digging her claws in, she snarled with effort. Earth clogged her paw pads, making it even harder to climb, but Storm struggled on up, shoving with her haunches.

Oh, Sky-Dogs! Why does this have to be so hard?

A chunk of soil broke loose beneath her forepaws, and she skidded back again, but she plunged forward to brake her slide. Grimly she dug in again, reaching out with one forepaw at a time to drag herself higher. Rivulets of rain were pouring down the mound now, forming channels that washed the soil away. There was water in her nostrils and mouth, and Storm had to choke back a sneeze that would have alerted Breeze above her.

Losing her grip again, she collapsed onto her belly in what was now practically a mud hill. Panting, she lashed out with a forepaw again, sinking her claws into the earth. *Up. And again. Higher.*

As she struggled on, the sounds of fighting reached her through the drumming of the downpour. Snarls and whines erupted above her, and an agonized yelp as teeth met flesh. But she couldn't tell who had cried out. Storm's blood thundered in her ears, and her lungs burned with the effort as she dragged herself up on her belly.

Hold on, Bella!

She wasn't anywhere near the top, Storm realized with an indrawn breath. The fighting was closer now, and she could make out the rake of claws on wood and the rasping, snarling breaths of battling dogs—but the crest of the mound seemed farther away than ever. *I'm not going to make it.* Staggering to stand upright, she found her balance and sank her paws into the sodden, sloping earth. Straining her ears, she blinked through the rain, desperate to see.

Breeze was so *fast.* She darted and dodged like a rabbit, ducking away easily from Bella's snapping jaws. Bella's lunge almost took her hurtling over the edge of the platform, but she scrabbled to a halt just in time. As the golden dog fought for balance, Breeze sprang in to bite down hard on her shoulder, drawing more blood that washed away instantly in the rain. There were bites and vicious scratches on Bella's neck and throat, too, and a gash on her haunch that Storm could see when she turned to attack Breeze again.

Enraged, Bella was lunging at the brown dog, but Breeze evaded her, then snapped at her leg. Bella yelped in fury and tried again; but yet again, Breeze was too quick. This time she seized hold of the golden dog's neck before Bella shook her violently away.

Bella's flanks were heaving, her tongue lolling with exhaustion. *Breeze is wearing her down,* thought Storm with a lurch of fear. *Retreat, Bella!* she wanted to bark. *Catch your breath!*

Clearly, Bella had already come to that decision. She was backing off, still snarling, as Breeze prowled forward once again.

Storm couldn't watch—not just because of her terror for Bella; she had to focus on Nibble. *That's why Bella is doing this, after all. I can't fail her!*

"Nibble," she growled. "Nibble!"

The little pup trembled at the edge of the platform, her eyes riveted on the battle before her.

"Nibble!" rasped Storm more urgently.

The little golden head turned, fearfully, and Nibble peered down through the rain.

"Listen to me," growled Storm. "You have to get away. Do you understand? You have to climb down this mound."

"I . . . can't." The pup's whimper was almost inaudible.

"You must!"

"It's so high." Nibble's whole body shook.

"You won't fall, Nibble, I swear it. Jump onto the top of the mound, *now*."

Nibble crouched down, her ears flat, staring at Storm. She edged her forepaws over the platform. Then she jerked back. *"I can't."*

Storm's heart pounded with tormented fear, but she managed to keep her voice low and level. "I promise you, Nibble, I will *not let you fall*. Jump, and climb down to me. It isn't far."

"It looks so slippery. And steep. And *high*."

"It's not as bad as it looks," lied Storm. "I'll catch you."

The pup stared in silence, her eyes wide with terror.

The torrent was growing worse, Storm realized, the downpour almost solid. Rain stung her back and shoulders so hard, she was breathless. The hill of earth would only get more dangerous, not less. The rivulets that streamed down its flanks were growing to rushing streams, and the soil was sliding and crumbling, loosening with every moment.

Sky-Dogs, can't you at least help? Don't you want us to save Nibble?

Somehow Storm managed not to let her panic show. Meeting Nibble's eyes, she gazed at her steadily.

"I know I let you down before, Nibble. I understand why you're afraid. I sleepwalked once, and I took you to the Endless Lake and put you in danger, but I *swear* I did not mean to hurt you. I would *never* deliberately harm you! What I did is never going to happen again, I promise. I'm going to take you home, and you'll sleep safe and warm tonight, curled up with your Mother-Dog and your Father-Dog and your brother and sisters. Tiny and Fluff and Tumble are all safe, and they're waiting for you. I *promise you*, Nibble."

Nibble swayed on the platform's edge and blinked hesitantly.

"I'm s-scared," she whispered, glancing fearfully over her shoulder at the snarling, fighting dogs.

"I know you are," Storm told her firmly. "But I'm going to keep you safe. Trust me. Nibble, *trust me*."

The pup turned back to face her. She opened her jaws and took a deep breath. Then she set her small teeth and leaped.

It was only a fraction of an instant till she collided with the top of the earth mound, but still Storm's heart leaped to her throat, almost choking her. Blood pounded in her ears as she gazed at the pup, flopped there on the crest of wet earth. Nibble was gaping at her, eyes huge and white-rimmed.

"Now," murmured Storm. "You have to come down to me. Come, Nibble. I'm here and I can't climb higher, but you *must* come to me, and I *will* catch you."

The pup visibly gulped, but she rose to a shaky crouch and set a forepaw down the slope. Water streamed over her legs, covering her paws with loose soil, but she took another step. And another. Her little shoulders were tense and trembling, but one by one she put a paw after the other, each one sliding a little as it touched the muddy surface.

"Yes. That's it. You can do this, Nibble." Storm tried to keep the tremor from her voice.

One paw went out from under the pup, and she gave a grunt of fright as her chest hit the ground. She straightened herself hurriedly but stopped, giving high-pitched pants.

The poor thing, thought Storm. *She's half-drenched in mud. Of course she's terrified!* But she was close now, only a dog-length above Storm.

"You're almost there, Nibble," Storm coaxed her gently. "Just get to me. That's all you have to do, and I'll take you the rest of the way."

An anxious growl came from beneath Storm, and she twisted to peer down. Lucky was pacing frantically back and forth as Arrow stood still, staring up. *Brick and his friends found them. That's something. Now I need to get him his pup.*

As she turned back to Nibble, Storm realized the pup had spotted her father, too. Her eyes brightened, and she gave a half yelp, half gasp of delight. The pup stiffened eagerly and set a confident paw down on the wet slope. One step, two steps, faster now—

A great clump of soil detached itself from the slope beneath the pup's paws. Nibble jolted sideways and tumbled onto her flank. But the soil was still sliding with the flood, and it gave way beneath her; she rolled helplessly down the slope away from Storm.

Ignoring Lucky's howl of distress, Storm threw caution to the Wind-Dogs. She sprang up, took three precarious, leaping bounds across the mound's flank, and pounced, grabbing Nibble's scruff in her jaws. She swung the pup up into the air, focusing on keeping her grip even as the ground slid away beneath her paws. Her legs seemed to be working independently now, flailing and striking wildly for balance on the shifting earth as she hung grimly on to Nibble.

At last the hill stopped moving for a moment, and Storm sagged where she stood, panting. Hearing a gasping sound above her, she twisted her head and looked up.

Bella stood on the platform's edge, staring anxiously down at Storm and the pup.

"Storm!" she barked. "Are you all right? Is Nibble?"

Storm felt her own eyes widening. A dark, stocky shape moved behind the distracted Bella. She wanted to bark a warning, but she couldn't—to do that, she would have to drop Nibble—

A tormented, muffled howl escaped her throat. Bella's eyes widened with realization, and she began to spin back toward her enemy—

And Breeze cannoned into her haunches and shoved her hard.

For a moment that felt to Storm like forever, Bella seemed to turn in the air, scrabbling with her claws for a safety that was already lost.

Then she plummeted to the ground far below.

The sound of her body hitting the stone was the ugliest Storm had ever heard: a dull, wet crunch that echoed even over the lashing rain. All the sound around them seemed to fall to utter silence, as if the Sky-Dogs had just . . . vanished.

Then Arrow gave a howl that seemed to break the world.

Once again, the rain was loud and unrelenting, drowning every sound. Storm could only watch, and grip Nibble tightly, as Arrow fled across the yard to where his mate lay motionless.

"Bella, no! Stand up! Please, Bella, stand up! *Please!*"

Lucky stood frozen, his jaws loose, his ears the only part of him that twitched frenetically. It was as if, thought Storm, he was caught between his sister and his pup, unable to run toward either. Storm herself could not move. Her paws were sunk in the sodden soil as if she would be rooted here forever, like a tree. Her dream flashed through her mind's eye, over and over again.

A golden-furred dog, falling to its death.

Falling.

It wasn't Lucky . . . It was Bella.

Falling.

Cold swept through her like an icy river. She could not hold the pup for another moment. Setting Nibble gently down on the earth between her forepaws, Storm tilted back her head and gave a tortured howl of grief.

"*No! No, no, no, no—*"

Nibble gazed up at her, subdued and sad. "Storm?"

That jolted her from her unbearable grief. Shaking herself as well as she could without losing balance, Storm lowered her head to the pup.

"Nibble," she said hoarsely. "Nibble, I need to go back up there. I need to find Breeze, because she must pay for what she's done. I need to fight the evil dog, little one, but I will help you down first."

Solemnly Nibble gazed into her eyes and nodded. "I know you have to go after Breeze," she said. "You don't have to wait."

"I have to help you—"

"No, you don't. It's all right." To Storm's wordless astonishment, the pup rose confidently to her paws. She glanced down at the remaining slope, glittering with the streaming rain in the

275

white glare. "I'll be fine. Tufty's going to show me the way."

With a flick of her tail, Nibble set off down the slope, every paw sure and steady. Not once did she hesitate, or waver, or slip, although she would occasionally stop and wait, her head slowly moving like she was . . . *like she's watching another dog show her where to step.* Storm gaped in disbelief as the pup reached the flat stony ground and was enveloped in her Father-Dog's waiting embrace.

Crouching, Lucky held her between his paws, licking and licking at her head and body. It was the moment they'd all longed for, yet Storm could only stare in silence as the hairs rose across her pelt.

Nibble's never heard us talking about Tufty. So if she only imagined a pup, and that gave her the courage she needed to get down the hill . . . why would she pick that name?

The fear, the eeriness, the relief, the anger: All of them were kindling inside Storm's chest to a raging, irresistible need. Turning away from the reunion, she stared up into the pelting rain once again, seeking out Breeze at the edge of the platform.

The bad dog was gazing down, looking no more than mildly interested at the havoc and grief she had caused. Storm clenched her jaws hard. A growl came from somewhere: a murderous, furious promise. Storm realized it was emanating from her own throat.

Breeze's eyes met hers. Her tail was wagging, her eyes bright and smug.

Storm planted a forepaw in the drenched earth of the mound and began to climb.

CHAPTER TWENTY

This time, her steps did not falter. Storm took no notice of the shifting ground, or the torrents of water: She simply stalked up the slope, sure-footed and defiant. Even the rain in her eyes did not slow her down. Driven by a cold intent, and a righteous fury, she dug her paws stretch by stretch to the crest of the earth hill.

Breeze's face was barely visible through the driving rain, but Storm could see the dark shape of her well enough. She stood immobile and disbelieving as Storm clambered to the summit of the earth mound. Then, as Storm reached the top and snarled at her, she turned tail and hurtled into the shadows of the den.

With a great bound, Storm landed on the wooden platform, feeling it shudder beneath her paws. She sprang off it and into the building, racing after Breeze. Her determination surged as her enemy fled; clearly, Breeze knew that this was a fight she could not win. All Storm had to do was catch her. *She's scared of me, very scared. And she's right to be.*

The pounding of paws and the skitter of claws echoed oddly in the bare walls. Breeze's panicked flight took her down a flight of stone steps and along a narrow passageway; she darted sideways into a dark opening. Storm skidded after her, scrabbling to a halt as she realized Breeze had vanished.

The bad dog couldn't go far. Breeze might know this unfinished den better than Storm did, but there was no muffling her high and panicked breaths, or the click of her claws on bare stone.

She's close.

Storm hunched her shoulders and prowled forward. Beyond a second doorway, eyes glowed in the dark; she sprang, bolting in pursuit. But she'd taken only three paces when pain jolted through her paw and into her leg. Storm stumbled, yelping.

Something sharp pierced another paw pad. Clenching her jaws, Storm halted, watching Breeze dodge around a corner and vanish up ahead. The floor was littered with longpaw rubbish, shards of broken clear-stone, and discarded metal spikes. Breeze, realized Storm, had been here long enough to know where to put her paws.

It was an advantage. But not one that was going to do Breeze any good.

Curling her lip in a snarl, Storm padded more cautiously forward, placing her paws lightly and flinching quickly when they touched something sharp. In the next room, the floor was clearer, and nothing glittered in the white light that leaked in from the yard. Storm bounded forward again, following the thudding paws and panting breaths of Breeze some way ahead.

She had to catch up. Breeze could not be allowed to get away with this!

Storm broke into a sprint along another passageway and burst into a wide, dark space. There, ahead of her, Breeze cowered against a wall. Did she think if she looked pitiful enough, Storm would spare her? Growling, Storm sprang. . . .

But Breeze was *fast*. The frightened, shivering dog suddenly dodged, her eyes turning hard and spiteful, and twisted into a run. Storm cannoned into the wall where she'd been, knocking the breath from her own lungs.

She shook herself hard, furious, and peered into the shadows. "I forgot you could act so well," she howled.

"It's easy when your enemies are stupid," spat Breeze. "Easy when the Fear-Dog is at your side!"

Storm lunged toward the voice, but again Breeze was already gone, spinning and racing away. Storm crashed hard into a pile of stone blocks, feeling her skull crack against a jagged edge, and she fell hard onto her flank.

She staggered to her paws, her head spinning, snarling with frustration. From the shadows in the passageway came Breeze's malevolent chuckle.

Storm's ribs hurt, she was dizzy with pain, and she could feel a trickle of blood in her fur. That wound wasn't painful so much as irritating. Hauling herself upright, she prowled once more toward the source of that mocking laughter. Peeling her muzzle back from her fangs, she gave a howl of anger and flung herself at the slinking dog-shape, but yet again Breeze dodged, rolling. This time, she snapped her jaws as Storm tumbled past her, and Storm felt the cruel bite of fangs in her underbelly.

She tore herself away, panting and growling. Breeze was pacing, her muscles tense, waiting to see which way she would pounce this time.

"Oh, I see the Fierce Dog," taunted Breeze. "Not hidden inside you anymore, though. She's on show! Is this how you're going to earn your way back into the Wild Pack, Storm? By unleashing your monstrous self again?"

"I'm not the monster here," barked Storm.

"We'll see about that." Breeze gave a throaty giggle. "Bad dogs always lose, and the good dogs win. Isn't that what you've learned? So whoever prevails today must be the good dog, right?"

Storm glared into those vicious glowing eyes, her flanks heaving. Something moved behind Breeze, and Storm's ears pulled back suddenly in shock.

No! Had Breeze brought her own allies? Because there *were* two huge dogs behind her: shadowy, menacing shapes that seemed to shift and change as Storm watched. Storm sucked in a breath of fear.

But the two huge beasts did not seem to be challenging Storm. They faced each other: Storm could see their glowing stares, locked together. One pair of glowing red eyes; one pair of icy shimmering blue. Black hackles rose on the dogs' silhouetted necks.

She glanced back at Breeze, unnerved. But Breeze took no notice whatever of the two mysterious dogs behind her. It was almost as if—

She doesn't know they're there.

Storm's hide prickled. Breeze was completely oblivious to the showdown at her tail. She couldn't see the massive dogs.

So why can I see them?

She'd hit her head harder than she thought: That was the only explanation. She was seeing things in the shadows, things that weren't there. Storm shook herself violently again. She lunged at Breeze, snapping her jaws, but her legs felt weak and she staggered, missing the bad dog completely. Breeze chuckled and feinted sideways, and Storm felt the sharp sting of her teeth in her flank once again.

She's using the same strategy she did with Bella. She's so fast, and she wants to tire me out.

Storm shook her head, clenching her teeth. She was not going to end up being another of Breeze's victims. But shaking herself wasn't helping the pain—maybe it was making it worse. Her head swam, and the room seemed to spin around her. Those two huge shadow-dogs still faced off behind Breeze, locked in their own private battle, and for a moment Storm thought another dog had joined them. A small, thin dog, as insubstantial as the huge ones; a pale, shimmering shape—

"Whisper?" she rasped.

He gazed fondly into her eyes. *I'm not imagining him. It's Whisper. From my dream.*

But I'm wide awake . . . aren't I?

Whisper glanced down at a small shape beside him. The pup was so very small, far smaller than Nibble. She was littler even than Nip and Scramble, though she looked a bit like both of them.

Storm's mouth dried. She could feel her heartbeat in her throat. She didn't know this pup. Yet she *had* met her, just once. The poor little thing had been nothing but a bundle of damp fur, a scrap of lost life. She, Arrow, and Peaceful the she-wolf had buried this pup before she'd had a chance even to breathe the world's air.

"*Tufty?*" she tried to say, but no sound came out.

Tufty was gazing at her, very seriously.

Of course . . . She never learned to speak, thought Storm.

The little pup's dark eyes looked pleading, as if she wanted so badly to tell Storm something. Tufty tilted her head.

You're telling me something, but I don't know what it is, Tufty. I don't know!

Something real and hard struck Storm's shoulder and she rolled with the blow.

Your life is at stake. . . . Stop dreaming, Storm!

Shaking her head clear, she saw Breeze shooting away again, her sneaky attack done for now. Dragging herself up, Storm hobbled after the bad dog through a large gap in the wall. Her fur was immediately drenched again as rain pelted her; she was outside the longpaw den. Storm stopped, finding her bearings. She was glad of the cold torrent: It cleared her head and banished the fuzziness.

Now Breeze stood facing her, her shoulders low in challenge.

Off to her side, Storm caught sight of Lucky, Arrow, and the Rough Dogs, huddled over Bella's motionless body. Nibble leaned against her Father-Dog's leg as if afraid to lose contact. *They haven't seen us.*

Storm curled her lip. "It's just you and me, Breeze. Fight me like you have courage in your dark heart!"

Breeze barked with laughter, and Storm saw Brick, Nail, and Brunt jerk their heads up. The three Rough Dogs twisted and came bounding toward them, but Storm crouched back on her haunches and gave a sharp howl of command.

"No! Stay back! This is my fight, my justice. I'll defeat her fairly!"

The three Rough Dogs hesitated and scrabbled to a halt on the slick wet ground. Beyond them, Lucky and Arrow had turned, their ears high, their eyes wide and alarmed.

"You hear me? I'll deal with this traitor!" barked Storm.

Arrow took one step forward, then halted. Slowly he nodded, letting his head hang in grief. Lucky's eyes were agonized, but he too dipped his head.

Storm turned back to Breeze. The rain was easing now, turning to a misty drizzle, and she could clearly see the vicious cold light in the bad dog's eyes. Breeze darted one way, then the other;

she made a quick lunge forward, then drew back.

No. You won't disorient me again. I'm ready for you.

Hunching her shoulders, lowering her head, Storm stalked forward, never taking her eyes off her enemy. Breeze was backing away now, and uncertainty and fear crept into her expression. Storm followed her, implacable, as Breeze reversed into the broad, light-flooded yard. Storm showed her fangs and felt her hackles rise. Pace by pace, she drew closer to the retreating dog—

And her forepaw sank in mud.

She tugged it out, the paw feeling sticky and heavy. Her heart jolting, Storm looked down as she lifted her other forepaw; it too was clogged with sludge. . . .

The spilled white mud. Breeze has lured me into a trap!

Storm snapped her head up, her heart thrashing in sudden panic. If she got stuck here, Breeze could bide her time and finish her off at her leisure. Sure enough, Breeze was not backing off anymore; the fake fear was gone from her eyes, which glittered with menace as she crept closer to Storm.

I'm not going to avenge Bella, Storm thought, her flanks heaving with the panicked breaths that felt like they might tear her flesh off her bones. *I'm going to die here.*

The very thought brought a fierce, cold clarity back to her

mind. *No.* She could not let that happen! Not only for herself, but for Bella, for Whisper, for Bruno: for every dog who had died at this malicious creature's paws.

Breeze was close now, her grinning snarl white in the glare. She reared back very suddenly, her jaws wide, and slashed with her paws.

Storm was ready. Ducking, she swerved out of the path of those savage claws, and as Breeze stumbled, she yanked her own paws free of the sludge and spun swiftly. The bad dog was off-balance, swaying as she tried to avoid the white mud.

With one blow of her clogged forepaw, she struck Breeze across the head so hard, the dog toppled sideways. White mud splashed up onto Storm's legs, but she ignored it, slamming her forepaws onto Breeze's heaving flank. The mud was soaking into the bad dog's brown fur, almost as if it was sucking her down; Breeze struggled and kicked, but she couldn't rise.

"You have to die!" she was howling beneath Storm's paws. "The Fear-Dog demands it! You deserve it! You cannot kill me! You have to—"

Storm lunged for her neck. She felt her fangs sink into the soft flesh of Breeze's throat, felt them pierce the skin, and her mouth filled with warm, bitter blood. Breeze was still yelping and howling in rage, her lips foam-flecked, but her struggles grew weaker as Storm bit down harder.

"You have to d—"

The voice was abruptly cut off. Beneath Breeze, the wet white mud mingled with dark red as blood pooled under her throat. Her flanks still heaved, her breath still rasped, her eyes stayed wide and white-edged. . . .

And then she was still.

Beneath Storm's mud-caked paws, the warm flanks didn't stir. Breeze's eyes were wide open, but her tongue lolled stiffly from the corner of her mouth.

The pool of blood spread farther, as if it would flood the whole wide yard.

Storm didn't move. She stood above Breeze's body, her flanks heaving. *I'm still breathing. Breeze is not.* Triumph and savage revenge thrilled inside her.

Breeze was gone at last, and with her the last vestiges of Terror's reign. As if even the Sky-Dogs approved, the rain had stopped. The yard was silent but for Storm's own heaving breaths.

A movement caught her eye, and Storm glanced to the side. Whisper and Tufty gazed at her, their eyes full of pride and certainty. Together, they dipped their heads once. Then, exchanging happy looks, the little gray dog and the tiny pup turned away. Side by side, they leaped into a run and bounded away.

Her heart aching, Storm stared after them, longing to call them back. But it was already too late. Whisper and Tufty had not run two rabbit-chases when their bodies faded like mist. Storm blinked hard, but however hard she peered against the white long-paw-light, it was no use. Whisper and Tufty had vanished.

They were here only long enough to help me, Storm thought, her heart clenching with gratitude and grief. *And now they've gone together to the Forests Beyond.*

Dragging her paws free of the muck, she shook them hard, and gouts of half-dried mud flew onto Breeze's corpse. Storm backed hurriedly away from the mud and the dead dog. Suddenly she needed to be out of sight of the corpse, and she urgently needed to be with friends. Turning on her heel, she loped to where Lucky, Nibble, and the Rough Dogs stood guard over Bella's body. They drew apart as she approached.

Arrow had lain down beside his mate, curled around her, and pressed against her body as if the two of them were only sleeping.

Storm halted. Her heart felt as if it were tearing in half, like it was a piece of prey being fought over by a pair of hungry dogs.

The Watch-Dog and the Fear-Dog. It was them I saw behind Breeze in the longpaw den, I know it.

And they both won today.

Crouching back on her haunches, Storm tilted her head to the sky and uttered a wailing, drawn-out howl of grief. It was too much to bear; her heart could not hold this much sadness. Bella was dead: Bella, who had taken her in when no other dog would. Bella, who had trusted a Fierce Dog with her pups. Bella, who had helped a confused, unhappy Fierce Dog believe in herself, believe that she truly was a good dog. Because Bella was good.

The vengeance she had wreaked on Breeze should have eased Storm's misery, but it seemed at that moment that nothing ever would. Her howl filled the night, and Storm hoped that Bella might even hear it as she ran among the stars in the Forests Beyond.

At last the howl in her throat died as she sagged with weariness. Every muscle in her body seemed to ache, but she made herself stand up straight.

Lucky looked as if his whole world had shattered around him. He stared down at Bella and Arrow, his whole body shivering beneath his golden fur.

"I'd only just found her again," he growled in a broken voice.

"We were going to raise our pups together. We would all be kin once more. Family. A strong, happy Pack, safe for all our pups . . ."

Silent, Storm watched him. *He's falling apart. And I can't blame him.* Turning her gaze to Arrow, she saw that he hadn't moved at all; he lay with tight-shut eyes, still coiled around the broken, sodden body of his mate. Nibble, shivering between Lucky's forepaws, gave a low, incessant whimper of confusion and unhappiness.

It's up to me. Some dog has to keep it together. The grief cannot break us.

Swallowing hard, Storm walked over to where the Rough Dogs stood, respectfully somber but looking a little uneasy.

"Brick, Nail, Brunt . . ." She cleared her throat. "Will you help me take Bella into the forest? She can't be buried here, in this longpaw place."

Brick nodded slowly. He glanced at his comrades, who looked as confused as he did. But they all gave subdued growls of assent.

"We don't know what your traditions are," began Nail softly.

"No," said Brick, turning to Storm. "But whatever form they take, I reckon this brave dog deserves honor. Of course we'll help you."

The rain had cleared altogether, and daylight had brought an almost cloudless sky that seemed fresh and brand-new. The air was cold, the leaves and grass touched by silver beads of dew that was almost frost. But Ice Wind's teeth had not yet bitten into the land, and they had managed to dig a hole for Bella in the dark, crumbling soil. The exposed earth smelled rich and sweet.

Perhaps there's no better place for Bella to lie, thought Storm. *The soil will hold her softly as she waits for Earth-Dog to claim her.*

She and the Rough Dogs had dug deep, and Storm's muscles trembled with exhaustion, but at least it had been a job to focus on, something to distract her from the horror of her friend's death. Brick and his friends stood back, looking almost as tired from the exertion as she was.

Bella lay sprawled on the wet grass beside the grave, her eyes peacefully closed. Arrow hunched over her, motionless.

"We should give her to the Earth-Dog now," said Storm gently.

Arrow did not protest as she thought he might. Without a word, he stood straight and began to push Bella gently with his muzzle toward the hole. As Storm moved to help, he shook his head, and she stepped back. Pawstep by pawstep, he nudged his mate to the edge of the hollow and gently rolled her into her resting place. As she tumbled abruptly down, he gave a gasp of misery, then a sharp whine of grief, before growing quiet again.

Storm glanced from him to Lucky. "Who will speak?" she asked softly.

"I will." Lucky nuzzled Nibble, then stepped to the edge of the grave and stared down at his litter-sister. "Oh, my brave, bold litter-sister. Bella and I were born together, raised together by our Mother-Dog. How could I almost forget her?" He took a shaking breath. "But I did. We were separated, and I forgot. All I had were dreams: dreams of a dog who looked just like me, who played with me and fought with me and slept by my side. I thought it was only an echo in my heart, reminding me of the littermate I lost." Falling quiet, he licked his jaws. Then he said, "But now I think the Spirit Dogs kept her memory alive in me for a purpose. I believe we were always meant to be together—that we were always fated to find each other." His voice cracked. "And I am so glad and grateful that we did. . . ."

He ducked his head, and Storm saw his throat convulse. Nibble crept between his forepaws again, and tilted her small head up to lick gently at his muzzle.

"Don't be sad, Father-Dog," she whined. "It'll be all right. You'll feel better soon. . . ."

Storm stepped to Lucky's side. "Arrow," she said quietly, "you don't have to say anything."

"But I do." The Fierce Dog rose to his paws, his legs shaking a little. He walked to the edge of the grave and gazed down.

For a long, silent moment, he simply looked at his mate's body. Then he lifted his head and let out a howl of intolerable pain that made Storm flinch with pity.

"Sun-Dog!" he barked wildly. "You run free up there. You lope along the sky without a care. Not a care for anything, not even the dogs below! How do you play like that when there's such pain down here? What use are you, throwing your light when all it shows me is misery and grief?" His eyes were tight shut, and Storm had the feeling he wasn't raging only at the Sun-Dog, but at the whole world and all the Spirit Dogs in it. "I'm alone now! I'm alone! How can I raise our pups on my own? *How?*"

Storm padded to his heaving side and nuzzled his shoulder gently. "You are not alone, Arrow," she murmured. "You're not. You are with the Wild Pack. You're one of them. You saved the pups of their Alpha and Beta, Arrow. Every dog will welcome you, they'll accept you without a qualm. They'll give you nothing but love and support, and they'll help raise your pups as if they were their own. *I know it.*"

"Yes." Lucky walked to Arrow's other side. "Nothing will change the fact that we drove you and Bella away. I'll spend the rest of my life regretting what we did, Arrow. But I promise you, on my life and the lives of every Packmate: We will spend every day making up for our mistake. You will never have to fear exile again, not ever. That's how we will honor Bella's memory. Your pups will grow up safe and strong and loved, Arrow. You have my word."

Arrow stood silent, staring down at Bella, his eyes still ravaged by grief. For a long time, there was no sound but the subdued song of birds, and the light whisper of the forest leaves.

"Thank you," he said at last. "Thank you, Lucky. I'm glad to accept that promise."

"Then let's say farewell to Bella," murmured Storm. "We'll send her to the Earth-Dog knowing that her mate and her pups will be safe."

Arrow nodded once. He moved to the heap of excavated earth, and led the way as they raked it back into place.

Clod by clod, under a clear blue sky and with birdsong chorusing around them, Bella's golden-furred body vanished, joining with the Earth-Dog.

CHAPTER TWENTY-ONE

The journey back to camp passed in silence, each dog wrapped in thoughts and memories. They took turns carrying the exhausted Nibble, and supported her between them when they grew too tired to bear her little body any longer. Cold sunlight pierced the branches above them, and a brisk breeze stirred their fur, but Storm could not revel in the beauty of the day. She felt shocked and numb, as if an invisible barrier separated her from the surrounding landscape.

"You know, I wasn't thinking clearly before." Lucky's voice breached the silence just as they entered the camp's familiar borders. "We should have asked Brick and the others to join the Pack. Don't you think? That was silly of me. They might have joined us. They're big, strong dogs. Good hunters, I imagine. I really should have thought of it before they left."

Storm gave him a sidelong look. His eyes still looked a little glazed; Lucky was talking for the sake of talking. However incongruous his words, she felt a wave of sympathy for him. It was obvious: He could not bear thinking about his lost litter-sister.

"They'd have been useful Pack Dogs," she agreed gently. "And I'm sure they'd have fitted in well. But they were loyal to their longpaws, Lucky. They only helped us out of kindness. Not every dog belongs in a Pack."

"Yes, but—" Lucky jerked his head up as a noise erupted from the direction of the camp. It was an urgent, high howl of anxiety.

Storm stiffened, her hackles bristling.

"Lucky, what's that?" She took a pace forward. "How can they be in danger? Breeze is dead!"

Lucky's tail lashed in agitation. "Let's get back there now!"

He broke into a run. Despite her worry for the Pack, as she raced behind him Storm felt a tingle of relief. At least for now, as he bounded over logs and pushed through tangled undergrowth, he was like the old Lucky again: bold and determined and focused.

The wolf Pack? thought Storm with a surge of alarm as she ran. Could they have decided to hunt down the dogs? They could have followed Bella and Arrow when they came to find Storm; they could have decided that they wanted no dogs encroaching on their land. . . . *No. They only wanted to protect what was theirs.* They'd had no interest in expanding their territory, especially not so far away. But if it wasn't the wolves, and Breeze was dead, who could possibly want to attack Sweet and her Pack? No other member of Terror's former Pack had gone mad like Breeze, *surely.* . . .

Yet the yipping howls continued, scared and frantic. Storm's heart thundered as the clearing came in sight.

She burst through the border of thick scrub, Lucky right behind her, and skidded to a halt on the edge of the glade. Sweet stood stiff-legged in the center, her head tilted back as she bayed and barked. Every other Pack Dog surrounded her, their tails lashing in distress.

"Every dog must be ready to leave here at a moment's notice," cried Sweet. "We do not move till my pup is found, but when Nibble is safe—"

"But what if she isn't?" yapped Chase. "I know you don't want to think it, Alpha, but—"

"Tumble! Fluff! Tiny!" A squeaking bark erupted behind Storm, and Nibble bounded past her, hurtling unsteadily into the clearing. She ran to her litter-siblings and was enveloped in licks and hugs.

Sweet gave a high, whining gasp and leaped down to barge

through her Pack. She fell on Nibble, licking and nuzzling her, drawing her close with her forepaws.

"My pup. My pup! You're safe!"

Whatever the Pack had been discussing so anxiously, it was momentarily forgotten as all the dogs crowded around Nibble, barking in joy. Sunshine spun with excitement, her plume of a tail thrashing so fast it was a blur.

"You found her! You found her!"

"Oh, my pups," Sweet was yelping. "My pups. I will never let anyone take you again. Lucky?" She turned, bright-eyed.

"Sweet!" Lucky trotted to her side and pressed his face to hers, growling softly. "Yes, we found her. She's safe at last. But—what's going on here? Why did you assemble the Pack?"

"I'll explain." Sweet glanced past him in surprise as Arrow padded into the clearing, slower than the other two, his head sagging. "Is Arrow hurt? Where's Bella?"

A silence fell over the Pack. The dogs twitched their ears and shared glances, apprehensive.

"Bella . . ." Lucky cleared his throat. "Bella died saving Nibble. My litter-sister is gone."

Sunshine gasped and cried out. Moon gave a howl of distress. The other dogs whined in grief, their ears and tails drooping.

"Oh, Lucky, *no*." Mickey sounded hoarse. He glanced with pity at Arrow.

"She was . . . she was so brave," croaked Lucky. "We couldn't have rescued Nibble without her."

"Arrow, Lucky," growled Sweet softly. "I am so, so sorry."

Lucky jerked his head up. His tail quivered and his fur rippled with a shiver of grief. "We will mourn her," he said. "But tell us, Sweet. What happened while we were gone?"

Sweet seemed to gather herself, and her eyes grew serious and intent. "The longpaws came."

"They came *here*?" Lucky gasped.

Mickey nodded and gestured with his muzzle. "They stood right there, not a rabbit-chase from the edge of the camp. We watched them from the bushes."

"Lots of them," whined Sunshine. "So many. They came in loudcages, and then they growled and barked at each other for such a long time. Pointing and gesturing and nodding and . . ." She shivered. "I didn't like it."

"They seemed to have a plan," growled Beetle. "And it won't be good."

"I think," said Sweet grimly, "they were planning to set up their own camp. It was the way they pointed at the trees."

Lucky shook his head slowly. "Where we found Nibble . . . that was a longpaw camp, and it was new. The longpaws had flattened a part of the forest, torn down trees, cleared away all the undergrowth. They were building huge dens. Permanent ones."

In the silence, the dogs stared at one another. Storm felt her heart lurch with a heavy foreboding.

"They're going to take our territory," whimpered Moon.

"Yes." Lucky nodded and closed his eyes briefly. "Yes, I think they are."

"And there's nothing we can do to stop them." Sweet's head drooped.

"We'll have to leave," whined Chase, and the Pack suddenly erupted with protests and arguments and complaints.

"But it's perfect here!"

"It took us so long to find this place. . . ."

"How can they do this? How can they just take over our camp? It's not fair!"

Two small shapes were padding through the milling dogs, their tails tucked under their rumps. The dogs near them fell silent as they watched the pups with sympathy. Nip and Scramble slunk to their Father-Dog and nestled against his legs, wordless.

Arrow bent his head to nuzzle them gently. He opened his

jaws to say something, then closed them again, his face racked by grief.

"Father-Dog," mumbled Nip, "I hope Mother-Dog can look after Tufty now."

Seeing Arrow's tormented expression, hearing his choked whimper of helplessness, Storm stepped forward.

"I'm sure she will, Nip," she murmured. "And Tufty will look after Bella, too."

"What are we going to do?" whined Nip. "What are we going to do without her?"

"I didn't want her to go with Tufty," whimpered Scramble.

Arrow coughed to clear his throat. "I didn't either, Scramble," he rasped. "And she didn't want to leave you, but she had to. Don't worry, my little ones. I'll look after you as best I can."

"And so will I." Her heart wrenching, Storm nuzzled the pups' heads.

"I know you are grieving," said Sweet softly, taking a few paces toward Arrow. "But we must keep all the pups safe now. We must leave here. Tonight."

Sunshine yelped with horror. "Tonight?" She twisted her head to stare up at the clouds that roiled across the darkening sky. "You can't mean right now, Alpha? We'd be traveling in the dark!"

"And Thorn can barely walk yet," protested Moon.

Sweet shook her head sadly. "I'm sorry, my Pack, but I'm serious. Longpaws are unpredictable, and when they decide to do something, they act *fast*. They could start tearing down these trees at dawn. Either they won't care what dogs they hurt—or they'll start rounding us up before they even touch the forest. They'd take us away in cages, Sunshine, and put us in Trap Houses. You don't want that, do you?"

Sunshine whimpered and bowed her head.

"We'll help Thorn walk," Sweet assured Moon. "And we can travel in short bursts. But we *must* leave, and leave now." She turned to Rake. "My friend, you and your Packmates would be welcome to join us—perhaps for good, or perhaps just for now. I won't forget how you stayed to help us search for my pups."

Rake glanced at his small Pack, and Woody nodded his big head. "Thank you, Sweet. We should all stay together, at least for now."

"The world is going back to the way it was, my friends," said Sweet. "Even a Big Growl doesn't stop the advance of the longpaws. They're going to put the world back the way they want it; they will rule it once again, and no dog can stop that. If we want to preserve our life as a Wild Pack, we must leave this place. All we can do is decide where to go."

No dog protested. Dart gave a soft whimper, and Mickey gave a dejected shake of his head, but every dog knew that Sweet spoke the truth.

"I believe I can help with that last problem." The voice was Arrow's, strained but clear, and every dog turned in surprise to listen to him.

"Go on, Arrow," said Sweet gently.

"I can lead you to territory in the north. That's where Bella"—Arrow faltered slightly—"where Bella and I made our camp after we were exiled. It's a good place. It may not be our forever camp, but it's safe, for now at least. Longpaws won't come so far into the hills. We can start again there."

Sweet bowed her head in respectful gratitude. "Thank you, Arrow. We will follow you."

"Of course we will," Sunshine yapped. "And we trust you, Arrow."

"Then," said Lucky, giving a last yearning look around the camp, "we should go."

Arrow nodded. Gently nudging his pups, he turned and paced out of the camp, across the scrub border and into the forest. One by one, the Wild Pack followed him, subdued but determined, their heads and tails low. One or two of them gave longing looks back at the place where they'd made their home, through Ice Wind, New Leaf, and Long Light; but no dog's paws hesitated or lingered. They dutifully followed Arrow as he led them north toward a new home.

Storm waited till all of them had crossed the camp's border, then fell in behind Sunshine the Omega. She wanted to protect the rear of the party and watch for threats that might come from behind them, but it was more than that. She also wanted to take in the sight of the combined Packs as they all followed Arrow's lead, trusting in him absolutely. These were the dogs who had been suspicious of the Fierce Dog for so long, whose hostility had eventually driven him from the Wild Pack. Yet now they padded after him, unquestioning, knowing they were safe to travel under his leadership.

Storm gazed at them, her heart clenching with pride and sorrow.

If only Bella could have been here to see it.

"To me, my Pack, and listen well!"

Two journeys of the Moon-Dog after they had left their old camp by the Endless Lake, Sweet sat tall and proud on a ledge of rock above their temporary camp, overlooking the semicircle of wind-cropped grass where the Pack was eagerly gathering. A chill breeze swept across the stunted plants of the mountainside and rustled the branches of the pines; drifts of early snow dusted the pine tops and powdered the exposed crags above them. Up here, the air tasted fresh and sharp, and it was clear to Storm that Ice Wind was close.

Storm sat back on her haunches, gazing expectantly at Sweet. She had wondered how it would feel to have the swift-dog as her Alpha once again, but she needn't have worried. It felt right, and comfortable, and entirely apt. After the long journey through the foothills and up into the mountains, Storm knew Sweet had learned the same lesson as the rest of the Pack: that Fierce Dogs were trusted allies, guides, and friends. No dog would ever again flick Arrow those hostile, frightened looks; no dog would ever flinch as Storm turned a little too quickly.

We belong in this Pack at last. Wherever our journey takes us, we are home now.

As the Pack settled and quieted, Sweet's clear voice interrupted Storm's thoughts.

"Come forward, young ones."

Slightly overawed, Lucky and Sweet's four pups padded

forward hesitantly. Then, as they gained confidence, they broke into an eager trot and stopped below their Mother-Dog.

"You are here to choose your grown names," she said, gazing fondly down at them. "This is how you become full members of our Pack." She lifted her eyes to the semicircle of grown dogs. "Once, we would have demanded a dead prey-creature for this ceremony: a pure white rabbit. It was a fine tradition, and well-suited to our old lives in the low lands. But much has changed for all of us. We have learned and grown in the last moons, all of us. We know now that change is not to be feared, but to be welcomed as a challenge. As a sign that we can adapt and thrive, I say that from this day, a pup's word will be enough. Storm once chose her name with no white rabbit to swear on; did that matter? No. She chose well, and wisely, and became one of the finest Packmates we'll ever know. She needed no symbol."

Storm's heart warmed, and her throat felt choked as she gazed at her leader.

"That's how it will be for all of us now," Sweet went on. "We will trust our pups to see inside themselves, and know their true natures, and live up to the names they choose. They need no dead thing to swear on." Her eyes shone. "So: Nibble, Fluff, Tumble, and Tiny, we welcome you to this gathering and to this Pack. Tell us what names you will be known by from this day."

The pups glanced at one another and nodded. Fluff stepped forward.

"I choose the name Earth," she declared. Her voice had deepened a little; she still sounded so young, but the squeakiness of puphood was gone.

Nibble advanced to her sister's side, her fur bristling with excitement. "I am Forest."

They both nodded to Tumble. He took a proud pace forward. "I am River."

The three of them turned to watch Tiny come forward. She quivered a little, but her eyes shone with pride. "I am Sky."

There were indrawn breaths and gasps around the Pack, but every dog was nodding, their tongues lolling with approval. Storm's skin prickled beneath her fur, and she felt a rush of happy pride. *These are important names, big names. They suit them.*

"You have chosen well, my pups," growled Sweet, her eyes glowing. "Those names are a lot to live up to—but I know that you will."

"The whole Pack knows it," agreed Lucky, gazing around at the dogs' enthusiastic faces. "It's ambitious to take the names of Spirit Dogs. But it might also earn a dog their watchful eye . . .

their protection and guidance."

The Pack erupted in approving barks and howls as Earth, Forest, River, and Sky drew back among them. They were showered in licks and nuzzles of congratulation, until even the bold River began to look shy and overwhelmed.

Storm chuckled softly as she watched them. Sky looked so pleased and proud, her still-small chest puffed out with happiness. She was going to be a strong, confident dog, Storm knew. *Not the runt anymore, Tiny!*

Something at the edge of the pines caught Storm's eye. She half rose and jerked her head around, ears pricked, instantly alert. She sucked in a breath. *Dogs! Dogs in the camp!*

But they were dogs she knew. Her heart thudded, and a chill rippled along her spine.

They stood very still, their ears and tails held high, and their eyes glowed with quiet delight. A golden dog who looked just like Lucky stood proudly beside a tiny pup; Storm blinked in startled happiness. *Bella . . . You found Tufty.*

But a whole Pack stood around them, and Storm recognized them all: there was burly Bruno, and the fast hunt-dog Spring, who Storm had last seen limp and drowned in the Endless Lake. Now her glossy coat gleamed, and her eyes were as bright as Storm remembered. Storm's own littermate Wiggle, killed by Blade when he was still a pup, stood beside her, safe and content. There was Fiery, steady and calm as ever, and little black Ruff beside him with her floppy ears. Martha stood next to Fiery, strong and gentle; a small dog Storm didn't know sat happily at her paws, and Storm guessed this must be Alfie, who had left the longpaw city with Bella, Daisy, and Mickey all those moons ago. It was surprising, yet at the same time oddly comforting, to see their former half-wolf Alpha there, a little apart from the others, his expression wry and amused.

Before them all stood Whisper. He nodded once to Storm, his thin tail wagging happily. Then, only a little reluctantly, he turned away, and the others followed his lead. They broke into a sudden joyful run, and just as she'd seen Whisper and Tufty do before, they vanished into the air like wisps of mist.

Now her old friends had all truly gone, Storm realized. Her heart tightened inside her, and she felt an odd lurch of longing, but the sharp fang of grief had loosened and subsided. *One day I'll see you all again, in the Forests Beyond.*

But not now. Now it's still my time to run and hunt with the Pack . . .

Where I belong.

EPILOGUE

Leaves drifted from the birches in a gentle golden rain, flashing and sparkling as they turned in the dying rays of the sun. Already there was a covering of them on the rough grass of the mountainside glade where Storm basked in the day's last warmth. A leaf landed on her nose, and she puffed it away.

Was that Ice Wind she could feel in the touch of the breeze? It seemed so sudden; Long Light's warmth had lingered this year, lulling the Pack into thinking that it might last forever. Yet now it had sped away like a running deer, and with it their first full year in this new home: a year of peace and contentment for the Pack, without so much as a sniff of an enemy Pack, or a giantfur, or an angry longpaw.

Storm was glad they had traveled this far north, and so high up the mountain's slopes. Prey had been plentiful in the days of

Long Light, and she was cautiously optimistic for their prospects in the coming Ice Wind. Last year, their first Ice Wind on the mountain's slopes, had been a swift and hard lesson, but they had learned it. Hunger had pinched their bellies, but never so much as to threaten their survival. This time, they knew the places to find prey and shelter and fresh water that didn't freeze. The Pack would be fine, Storm knew.

The decision to move had been the right one. Now and again the dogs had risked forays down into the foothills, and they had seen the longpaws' work at a distance: the dens that rose from the ground with breathtaking swiftness, the growling, roaring loudcages, the hardstone tracks laid across what had once been forest and meadow. The longpaws were indeed reclaiming their world—but their world was not up here on the mountain. This place belonged to the dogs and to the wolves.

The dogs had even come to an agreement with the wolf Pack, each keeping watch and warning the other of any approaching threats. Not that there had been many of those: a distant walking longpaw couple, maybe, or a loudbird rattling far overhead.

Behind Storm, the wispy grass rustled, and she turned her head. Earth, Forest, and Tough appeared over the rise, white-patched hares clutched in their jaws. Storm nodded a greeting.

"Hello, you three. Good hunting?"

"Really good." Earth shook her shaggy brown fur with satisfaction. "Well done, Tough. I didn't think you were going to catch that last one."

Tough grunted with pleasure and flopped down beside her. "That hare was doomed from the start," he joked. "No prey gets away from me and Forest, not once we have a plan."

Storm parted her jaws and panted with amusement. It was hard to believe little Nip—the scrap she'd seen emerge from his Mother-Dog—had grown into such a strong young dog already. And it touched her that he'd chosen the name *Tough* in homage to his lost sister Tufty, while paying respect to the Fierceness of his heritage. It was the perfect name—and so was Golden's. Scramble's fur had only ever had small sandy patches, he was mostly dark brown and black like his Father-Dog, but he had chosen the name in tribute to his Mother-Dog, Bella. His eyes, gentle like hers, were certainly touched with golden light.

The Pack will never forget Bella or Tufty, not while these two are always with us.

"Are you going to let Alpha and Beta know you're back?" she asked the three young dogs.

"They already know." Forest gave a short yip of greeting, and

Storm turned her head to see Lucky and Sweet, watching from the entrance of their den. Lucky nodded fondly, his eyes full of pride and delight.

With his attention all on his pups and Tough, Storm took a moment to study her foster-father. She narrowed her eyes. Were those flecks of gray on the Beta's muzzle? It was possible. How old *was* Lucky? No dog had ever asked. Storm wasn't sure even Lucky knew. Out here in the wild, it was hard to keep track of how long a dog had lived.

Across the clearing toward the low rock outcrop, Arrow was stretching out his forelegs, clawing the ground lazily. Rising to her paws, Storm trotted over to him.

She would never stop being happy and relieved that the Fierce Dog had chosen to stay with the Wild Pack. He still missed Bella every day, Storm knew that—but he had a home, and a family who had done everything they could to help him raise his pups.

"Tough had a good hunt," she greeted Arrow as he stood up straight and shook himself. "And Golden will be going out later with Mickey and Dart. You've got fine, strong pups, Arrow. Bella would be so proud. She *is* proud."

Arrow's eyes grew longing and distant. "I think so too, Storm."

"Let's go and talk to Alpha and Beta. Look, the pups—I mean, the youngsters—are showing off their prey to them."

Arrow padded at her side toward Alpha and Beta, who greeted them with soft, happy barks. "Are you enjoying the sunshine, you two?" asked Sweet. "The hunting is still good. Earth, Forest, and Tough have brought back hares."

"I saw," said Storm, touching her nose to Lucky's. Yes, there were definitely gray hairs sprinkled there in the golden fur.

"It's good territory," he murmured.

"It is." Sweet nodded. "Thank you again, Arrow, for leading us here. I expect it to be our Pack's territory even when I'm no longer Alpha." She turned her head to Storm, and the look in her dark eyes was so intent, Storm jumped and flicked her ears back. Their gazes locked for a long, solemn moment, and Storm felt a tremor pass through her.

She's waiting for me to agree. No, not agree . . . approve.

"That's a pleasant thought," added the swift-dog, stretching contentedly as if she hadn't just gazed straight into Storm's soul. "Shall we plan the next Great Howl? The Moon-Dog is due to show herself fully in a few days. . . ."

As the other three talked, Storm fell quiet, thinking. That meaningful stare of Sweet's had been so frank, so clear, yet Storm couldn't quite believe the message it had held.

Was she really implying I will be Alpha one day?

It seemed such a distant, fantastical prospect, but for the very first time, Storm wondered what it would be like. With a stir of nerves in her belly, she turned to watch the rest of the Pack go about their daily evening routines: little Sunshine, the Omega, cheerfully carrying bedding; Beetle chatting contentedly to his mother, Moon; Daisy, Mickey, and Chase sprawled in a last patch of sunlight. Thorn and Twitch, the two three-legged dogs, raced each other for fun around the camp's perimeter.

Her anxiety faded, and Storm felt something else creep through her blood: a warm sense of hopeful confidence. If she *was* destined to be Alpha one day, she would do everything in her power to be the best one that she could be.

The Wild Pack had faced so many dangers and tests, had suffered so much sadness and tragedy. Storm was sure they would have their troubles to face in the future, too; the easy happiness of this last year could not last forever. That was the nature of life in the wild, after all.

But their lives had been so much more than struggle and discord and the fight for survival. They had been friendship, and family; good hunts, and heart-stirring Great Howls, and the joy of watching pups grow and thrive.

I can lead them, if I'm called to do it. I'll lead them well.

The future lay before the Pack like the sweeping valleys of the mountains: full of struggle and conflict and companionship and joy. And if her friends needed her to lead them through it, Storm would lead them with gladness and courage.

It was life in the wilderness, life as a free dog, life with dogs who knew no longpaw master, dogs who protected and sheltered one another.

It was the life of the Wild Pack.

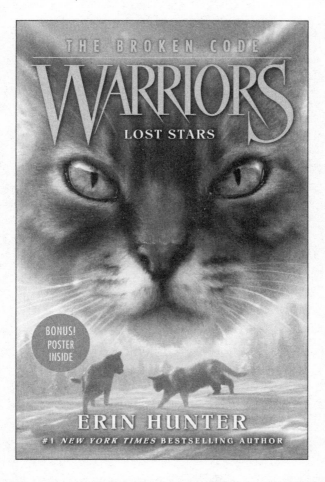

WARRIORS

How many have you read?

Dawn of the Clans
- ○ #1: The Sun Trail
- ○ #2: Thunder Rising
- ○ #3: The First Battle
- ○ #4: The Blazing Star
- ○ #5: A Forest Divided
- ○ #6: Path of Stars

Power of Three
- ○ #1: The Sight
- ○ #2: Dark River
- ○ #3: Outcast
- ○ #4: Eclipse
- ○ #5: Long Shadows
- ○ #6: Sunrise

The Prophecies Begin
- ○ #1: Into the Wild
- ○ #2: Fire and Ice
- ○ #3: Forest of Secrets
- ○ #4: Rising Storm
- ○ #5: A Dangerous Path
- ○ #6: The Darkest Hour

Omen of the Stars
- ○ #1: The Fourth Apprentice
- ○ #2: Fading Echoes
- ○ #3: Night Whispers
- ○ #4: Sign of the Moon
- ○ #5: The Forgotten Warrior
- ○ #6: The Last Hope

The New Prophecy
- ○ #1: Midnight
- ○ #2: Moonrise
- ○ #3: Dawn
- ○ #4: Starlight
- ○ #5: Twilight
- ○ #6: Sunset

A Vision of Shadows
- ○ #1: The Apprentice's Quest
- ○ #2: Thunder and Shadow
- ○ #3: Shattered Sky
- ○ #4: Darkest Night
- ○ #5: River of Fire
- ○ #6: The Raging Storm

Select titles also available as audiobooks!

HARPER
An Imprint of HarperCollinsPublishers

www.warriorcats.com • www.shelfstuff.com

SUPER EDITIONS

- ○ Firestar's Quest
- ○ Bluestar's Prophecy
- ○ SkyClan's Destiny
- ○ Crookedstar's Promise
- ○ Yellowfang's Secret
- ○ Tallstar's Revenge

- ○ Bramblestar's Storm
- ○ Moth Flight's Vision
- ○ Hawkwing's Journey
- ○ Tigerheart's Shadow
- ○ Crowfeather's Trial

GUIDES

- ○ Secrets of the Clans
- ○ Cats of the Clans
- ○ Code of the Clans
- ○ Battles of the Clans
- ○ Enter the Clans
- ○ The Ultimate Guide

FULL-COLOR MANGA

- ○ Graystripe's Adventure
- ○ Ravenpaw's Path
- ○ SkyClan and the Stranger

Coming soon!

EBOOKS AND NOVELLAS

The Untold Stories
- ○ Hollyleaf's Story
- ○ Mistystar's Omen
- ○ Cloudstar's Journey

Tales from the Clans
- ○ Tigerclaw's Fury
- ○ Leafpool's Wish
- ○ Dovewing's Silence

Shadows of the Clans
- ○ Mapleshade's Vengeance
- ○ Goosefeather's Curse
- ○ Ravenpaw's Farewell

Legends of the Clans
- ○ Spottedleaf's Heart
- ○ Pinestar's Choice
- ○ Thunderstar's Echo

HARPER
An Imprint of HarperCollinsPublishers

www.warriorcats.com • www.shelfstuff.com